THE
LOWBORN

THE
LOWBORN

TOLA AKINBORO

To order additional copies of this book, contact:
Xlibris
1-888-795-4274
www.Xlibris.com
Orders@Xlibris.com
739636

Acknowledgments

My thanks goes to The Lord Jesus Christ, my righteousness and inspiration, without whom this book would not have been completed.

I thank my family for the inexorable support they gave.

I also appreciate Kunle Ogundele who has been helpful in every sense all the way.

Kunle Olabode and Jordan Dobrowski, thank you for your contributions.
In advance, I thank my numerous readers.

CHAPTER ONE

He leaned forward then backward again. No posture seemed comfortable. As he sat in the lobby of the hospital, he pondered in his heart. He had been sitting there for about half an hour completely lost in thought. He placed his jaws in his two hands as his two elbows rested on each knee. His eyes were wide open but blank; not even the flow of people in the lobby provided an attraction. New patients arriving, visitors coming in to see patients, and the continuous perambulation of the nurses with their shoe heels making tapping sounds on the tiled floor. None of these had enough potency to distract the retired soldier from the issues that shrouded his mind.

He was supposed to come to the hospital as early as 7:00 a.m. to take over from his wife, who had slept by their son's bedside over the night. The couple had decided to take turns staying with their son as advised by the doctor, but he had come in late. He arrived at eight o'clock just after the doctor had completed his routine check on the patients. The doctor had left a message with his wife to see him as soon as he arrived. The wife had earlier inquired from the doctor if it had to do with their son's health status, and she had received no response from the doctor. As soon as the retired soldier came in, his wife reiterated the doctor's message and said to her husband, "I will go with you."

"No," Usman replied. "If he intended to talk with both of us, he would have told you. Go home, take care of yourself, and prepare for the afternoon. When you return, I will let you know whatever the doctor says, that is if it concerns you."

At that moment, his wife broke into his wandering mind. "No, I will wait here. He wants to talk to you about my son, and I want to know whatever it is. Go, I'll wait here for you," she insisted. Usman gave her a long hard look, and she left the lobby for the ward room where their child was sleeping. A while later, a slim and fair-complexioned female nurse appeared in the lobby. She signaled to him to go in and see the doctor. "Doctor is ready to see me?" he inquired.

"Yes, sir, he is waiting for you," she replied. As he walked along the corridor, he realized he had been so caught up by the message that he had not bothered to look at the boy on the bed. As he walked to the doctor's office, he silently prayed it would not be bad.

"Come in, Mr. Usman," the doctor said when he saw him put his head through the small opening of the door.

"WO2 Usman, retired," he corrected, shutting the door behind him.

"Oh, I see. I'm sorry about that. Good morning." The doctor stretched across his desk with a simple smile, and they shook hands. "Please have your seat." He continued, "Mr. Us . . ." He hung on his word with his tongue in his cheek, and with his mouth forming an O shape like a child who had just been naughty, he cast his eyes at his desk and said, "Sorry, again. Is it okay if I call you Officer?"

"Retired Officer," Mr. Usman replied.

"Yeah, but calling you Officer is okay by me, if you don't mind. Adding 'Retired' is rather long," said the doctor, smiling. But when he noticed Usman's emotionless face, who was only interested in his primary issue there, the doctor proceeded with the discussion.

"I asked you to see me concerning the latest development on your son's health. I must tell you it is not very encouraging. I have written a report on it this morning," he said as he rummaged through his desk, in search of something. "Okay, this is it." He handed a piece of paper over to Usman. Usman ignored the paper and, looking straight into the doctor's eyes, said "What is wrong with my boy?"

"All right, I should save you all the medical jargons. Your son, Mr. . . . hm, hm, Officer, just developed what is simply called a weak heart. This requires an urgent operation which cannot be done here in Kogi. He will have to be taken to the University College Hospital at Ibadan. None of that is really the problem, but, ah, ah, hm, you see, the operation is a very expensive one," the doctor said, casting his eyes on his desk again.

"How much, Doctor?"

"Ah-ahmm, mh, like a million naira, I suppose."

"Thank you, Doctor," Usman said, rose, and left.

"Officer Usman, I understand the financial condition of your family, and I'm sorry about your son's health . . .," the doctor said, but Usman was gone. In the corridor, on his way back to his son's ward, he looked up to the ceiling. His lips parted, as if to say something, then he kept quiet and continued walking to the ward. When he got to the ward, he paused at the door, was in deep thought for a brief moment, then suddenly grabbed the door handle, turned it, and went in. As soon as Usman's wife saw him, she got up from beside her son and came to him with probing eyes that pierced his. She kept searching for the most minuscule expression on his face to confirm her fear. "What did he say?" Her eyes did not leave her husband's eyes. He moved to the side of the bed his son was stretched out on and rubbed his leg. He noticed the boy was breathing heavily but still fast asleep. He looked at him all over carefully, his visage void of his feelings.

"What did the doctor say about my son?" she asked again as she moved closer to him, her eyes moving from his eyes to the boy on the bed.

"Nothing . . . He only said we needed to get more drugs."

"More drugs? Why? Is he getting worse?" She brought her two hands to her chest. "Are you sure that was what he told you?" she asked suspiciously.

"Of course, why would I lie to you?"

"Okay, if it were just drugs, why didn't he tell me? Why did he wait for you to come to him, alone? Eh, eh?"

"They are expensive drugs, and he thought telling you might embarrass you since he's aware of our financial troubles. Now that is enough. Take your things, go home, and get some sleep." He carried her bag and gave it to her, all the while not looking her way. He held her by the shoulder and rubbed it. He did not say anything. He opened the door for her, and she left. He took the only chair in the room, carried it to the side of the bed, and dropped his buttocks into it. He took his son's hand, kissed it, and put it to his head. The boy was pale and lean. At twelve, he was quite tall already. He had the semblance of his mother. His legs, long, thin, and bony, though emaciated, seemed strong still. He wore faded old pajamas. Usman made a real effort to fight back the tears. The door flung open, and a nurse walked in briskly.

"Sir, you have to excuse me now. I need to administer food and drugs to the patient, and that would take about one hour. You have to wait in the lobby." She took the small aluminum tray she was carrying to the small cupboard beside the bed. "Do you have his food here, sir?"

"Yes!"

"Thank you, sir. I'll take over from here," she said with an assuring smile that could be interpreted as "Don't worry, I'll make him well just now." Usman then left the ward. "Hello, honey, good morning. It's time for breakfast," the nurse said, trying to wake the boy for his meal.

Usman had been oblivious of everything around him since he had been waiting in the lobby. He didn't know where to start, and all of a sudden he almost didn't know what his problem was anymore. He didn't know the beginning or the end of it; he could not pinpoint exactly what he wanted, what his problem was, the solution to his problems. Everything eluded him. Money? He thought, *Will money solve my problems? How much will be enough to cater for my family for the rest of our lives, and where would I get it? Would I go and work again after about thirty years of service? Do I still have the strength?*

Abruptly, he remembered he did not warn his wife about the landlord, who had threatened that morning to throw their things out of the house if by the end of the day they did not pay him the eighth-month rent they owed. Even that did not move Usman. *After all, it's not any worse than the latest of my predicaments. And my son, of course, I can't get the money from anywhere, but even if I do, can it save my son's life? Besides, I don't even know the probability of success of the operation.* He straightened up on his chair and kept his focus on the floor, then he looked up and left the hospital. Outside the hospital, Usman cried. He sobbed as a child would; covering his face with his hands, he moved away from the busy entrance of the emergency building to where an oak tree cast its shadow on the fence surrounding the hospital. There he poured out tears, his bitterness. When his weeping abated, he looked up into the sky with wet eyes.

"I don't know who you are, and I don't think anybody does, at least completely. I don't know what names you really go by, as different sects and people call you different names. As a matter of fact, I may not know who or what I serve. At this point, I despise every religion, and I don't know the meaning of life. I don't know how we all got here and what we are supposed to be doing here, but one thing I know, we didn't just get here. Somebody put us all here, a deity, and I call you God. If you put me on earth to enjoy it and you gave me my son as a blessing, then don't make the earth bitter for me and do not curse me by the death of my son. Let him live!" He brought out his handkerchief, wiped his tears, and went back into the hospital.

He sat at the same lobby he had just left earlier, rested his elbows on his knees, crossed his forearm over his knees, and rested his head on them. He slept off.

After a while, the nurse who excused him out of his son's ward passed by, saw him, and woke him up.

"Sir, I've been through with your son since. You can now go in to see him," she said. "He has eaten and would be sleepy again soon. It's the medications." Usman gave her a long look, as if he was trying to remember who she was.

"All right, thank you," he replied and returned to his sleeping position; a minute later, he rose and went into the ward. His son was asleep. He sat on the chair he had put beside the bed before he went out and rested his head on the edge of the bed. He slept again and did not wake up until his wife brought his lunch.

"How is he?" she asked as she came through the door. She went to the small drawer where she put the big bag containing the food warmer. She then moved to the side of the bed.

"He's fine. I've not seen him awake today."

"Why?" the wife asked, looking at him.

"I had to go out for a while after you left. When the nurse came in to attend to our son, before I came back, he was asleep again."

"Wake him then," she said and moved to do so.

"No, leave him alone. He needs all the rest he can get now." He paused. "I think I need to go and look for money," he continued as his wife turned to look at him inquisitively. "Yes, that means I will be traveling to Lagos to see my friend."

"What do we need money for?" she asked, her eyes searching through her husband's.

4

"What do you mean what do we need money for? Don't we need money? If for nothing, won't we feed?"

"For feeding I can manage," the wife affirmed.

"You can't keep managing. You have been trying to kill yourself for this family, and I can't let that happen. I have to do something, and if I can't get a job yet, then I have to get help from wherever I can get it," Usman lamented.

"Is there anything you are still not telling me about this child?" But Usman only hissed and did not answer. "And this your traveling, when do you want to do it?" She was looking at him from the side of her eyes.

"Today, I want to go today. We need money, whatever we can get as soon as we can," he swiftly said, motioning with his hand as he spoke.

"And what makes you think your friend is any better than you are, since you both are retired?" she asked again, more reluctantly, still looking at him from the side of her eyes.

"I don't know, but I think we should try. Whatever he can afford is better than nothing. If he doesn't have it, he could borrow for me," he defended.

"You mean you won't be coming back today?" she asked, facing him.

"Of course, I can't come back today. What if he doesn't have it and has to run around to get it for me, which will most likely be the case, as you have rightly said. I don't know how long that would take him. Besides, today is almost gone, and I have not even left yet."

"The remaining of the loan I got from the cooperative is in the breast pocket of your uniform in the wardrobe, and *please don't set my eyes on the road*," she pleaded.

"I won't. I don't think I should stay longer than two days. How is Fatima?"

"She's fine. She's still with Mama Joy, our neighbor. Check her there when you go home, but don't tell her you're traveling, or else she would cry to go with you."

"That's okay." He was quiet for a moment and stood up. "Let me go home to prepare," he said. He touched his son on the leg, looked into his eyes, sighed, then moved close to his wife and patted her on the shoulder. His wife moved to the chair he got up from. "Take care of our kids and yourself," he said as he left.

His wife watched him close the door behind him and kept staring at the door as if he was still there. She knew he was keeping something from her, and it had to do with what the doctor had told him. *If not, why would he decide to travel all of a sudden to get some money to buy drugs?* she thought. She knew he was more troubled than he showed, more because he could not bear to see their only son lying on the hospital bed, the same way he watched their first son lie dead on the hospital bed after he was hit by a car. But Usman had forbidden her to ever allude to him anymore, not even in prayer, and he himself had never made mention of his name since. He loved him dearly.

"But whatever the doctor said to my husband, he must say to me," she said to herself as she stormed out of the ward to the doctor's office. She opened the door without knocking.

"Doctor, what did you tell my husband?" she demanded, standing in the doorway, hands akimbo. The doctor swallowed heavily and motioned to the chair before his desk. "Please sit down."

She looked on for a while before she made up her mind.

"I thought he might not want you to know. That was why I didn't tell you. I guess I am right because obviously, he has not told you himself."

When Usman got home, he went straight to the neighbor's house to see his daughter. He didn't want her to see him while he was leaving. She was seven, and she looked so much like her father's mother, so he called her his mother.

"Mother, how are you?" he asked her as he carried her.

"Daddy-y-y," she mumbled.

"Have you eaten?" he asked her. She answered in the affirmative. He then gave her and his neighbor's daughter five naira notes each. The girl's parents were out. He left his daughter there, went home, picked some money and a change of clothes, and set out. The farther he got from home, the more relieved he felt. He got to the bus terminal and boarded one going to Lagos. Through the course of his journey from Kogi to Ibadan, he felt as if the breeze blowing into his face was blowing away the pain in his mind. But the moment he passed through the town, he rested his head on the back of the seat in front of him and slept as if he's been waiting to get to that point.

On getting to Lagos, at the Ojota motor park, rubbing his eyes and yawning with his bag in hand, he walked for a few minutes toward Maryland then faced the main road to cross to the other side. He looked to his right and left and ran across to the middle, unconsciously and completely distracted; forgetting that the road was a dual carriageway, he walked leisurely onto the next carriage. Out of the blue, for a moment, he thought he saw his first son and looked back. He only heard the impact on himself, not feeling it so much. .

CHAPTER TWO

"Mr. Benson Kingsley?"

"Yes!"

"Would you come in, please?"

Ben rose and followed the manager into his office, closing the door after himself.

"Have your seat, please." The manager motioned to the chair in front of his desk.

"Mr. Kingsley, you graduated eight years ago."

"Yes, sir. Yes, sir." He shifted uncomfortably in his chair. "From the University of Nigeria, sir."

The manager looked into the papers he was holding and back at Ben.

"Mr. Kingsley, I must confess you have impressive credentials here. With a second-class upper degree in mathematics, I believe you have great chances. But if I may suggest, why don't you go for your master's degree? It's really going to add a lot of value to your CV, if you know what I mean?"

"I understand you, sir, but you see, it wasn't easy for me in my undergraduate days. I'm left alone with my mom, who is quite old. She tried her best selling her little farm produce to raise money for me, and I had to work part-time too before I could manage to scale through the university. Now I live on my own, and my mom is very old in the village. I need to take care of her. If I can get this job, then I would start my master's degree on part-time. Please, sir, I need the job."

"Mr. Kingsley," the manager responded soberly, "I'm sorry about your circumstances. You see, we all pass through such a phase in our lives. But I have to tell you this. Just yesterday our general manager filled in the last vacancy with a cousin of his, so I'm afraid we have no place for you. You may check back some other time."

Ben bowed his head and looked into his open palms, then it quickly occurred to him that he was in an office. He looked up, making efforts to hold back the tears that were now at the corner of his eyes.

"I will do anything, sir, anything. I can be your errand boy."

"I know how you feel, Mr. Kingsley, and I'm very sorry. I promise I'll keep you posted and in mind."

"Please, sir, please help me," Ben said, almost sobbing.

"I'm sorry, Mr. Kingsley, I'm sorry."

They looked at each other for a moment, and when the manager bowed his head, Ben knew he was powerless about his case. He rose and left the office.

Back on the road, he had been walking for about two hours now, deliberately, looking at both sides of the road as if looking for something lost; but he was actually looking for any sign of vacancy in any establishment no matter how small or demeaning. He had lost hope in newspapers now. *White-collar jobs are meant for people with godfathers and connections,* he thought.

He had just gotten a message from home that his mom was sick again. The last two times he was called, he had ignored the calls and prayed she got well, and he guessed she probably did because he wasn't called back until now. This time he knew he had to send some money for her upkeep, albeit little. He had to.

If there was anything Ben hated most about himself, it was his appetite. Whenever he was hungry, it seemed like the only thing that mattered in the whole world to him at that particular time. He dipped his hand in his left pocket and brought out the fifty naira note left of the hundred naira he had borrowed from his neighbor before he left home in the morning.

Why has God given me this kind of appetite? The rich should have this because they have the money to feed themselves! I don't. I need this fifty naira to get home, but this is two o'clock, and I've not eaten anything today, and of course, there is nothing to eat anymore today once I get home. Why don't I just eat now and walk home looking for vacancy while I go? After all, it won't kill me, and of course, when there is life, there is hope.

He walked into the next canteen he saw and sat down, close to the door. He watched around him for a moment, looking into the people's faces and into the plates in front of them. His eyes eventually rested on a very young man sitting adjacent to him; and when his eyes lowered to his plate, he blinked rapidly, opening his eyes wide to stare at the man's food. He wondered how much the food will cost looking so sumptuous from afar. Then something blocked his view, right in front of him. He began to raise his head slowly, and then he locked eyes with one of the waitresses. He quickly pulled in his tongue that had been hanging loose out of his widely opened mouth and jammed his mouth closed.

"What do you want?"

"Car!" He was silent. *"Abi,* what does it look like I want? Stupid question," he answered sarcastically. Still looking expressionlessly at him, the waitress asked, "What will you like to eat?"

"What did you cook?" he jabbed at her offensively. And just before the girl started saying anything, he added, "Don't even bother. Just give me good food, everything to a total of fifty naira." He looked away.

"Good food?" the waitress mimicked as she walked away.

He resumed his initial point of focus. By now the young man was almost through. He then examined the rather slovenly dressed man and concluded, *He must be a mechanic, an apprentice of some sort. A mechanic, a mechanic, for god's sake! Why should a mechanic eat this kind of food and I, a degree holder, suffer this kind of fate? I should have studied good mechanical engineering for those four years, not in the university. No! At a local workshop of course, a roadside one. At least I would have been guaranteed of some reasonable meals.*

His view was blocked again as well as his thought, as his plate of food was let down in front of him.

"Weeeeew," he whistled. "What?" He was lifting one side of the plate so it tilted. "What is this?" he asked, looking up at the girl.

"Food," she answered vacuously.

"No, I thought it is shit. I didn't know it is food, you this ram head. I asked for a fifty-naira worth of food, not ten naira," he said, still tilting the plate at one side with a finger.

An elderly woman walked up to him and asked in pidgin English.

"*Oga*, wetin be the problem?"

"I asked this your zombie here for forty-naira food, and here is what she gave me."

"Oga," the woman said, "is me serve your food, and that is fifty-naira food. Shee make I carry am carry your money give you back?"

He looked around slowly from the corner of his eyes, and when his eyes rested on his food again, he glared at it for a moment, and he quickly thought, *I may not get a fifty-naira food this much at some other place.* He shook his head slowly, paid, and waved the two women in front of him off.

In five minutes, he was through. He grabbed the jug of water in front of him and poured a cup full, gulped it, and poured out another cup. He was downing the third one when a man walked by in front of him and stopped.

"Please, allow me pay for your food," said the man adorned in a *buba* and *sokoto*.

He almost spilled the water but quickly covered his mouth full of water with his hand and motioned with the other hand till he had swallowed the water.

"What did you say, sir?"

"I asked if I could pay for your food."

"Oh nooo, that won't be necessary. Oh, is it because I argued with them? Oh no, I was just trying to make them realize that they seem to be cheating people without knowing it. You see, you see, it's not as if I don't have money. Of course, I have money," he said, grinning and trying to smile.

"But I insist."

"Ah, don't bother at all," he said, grinning again. And the man straightened up to proceed.

"But as you have insisted, I guess I have no choice." Ben said

"Thank you," the man said, brought out a hundred naira note, and placed it on the table and started walking away.

"You are welcome—thank you" was the response.

"I recognize that kind of folder when I see one because I carried one for about five years myself before I realized we all won't knot tie to work, and besides, most of us are more gifted than we think," the man remarked, glancing back at the overwhelmed graduate, smiling.

"Thank you," Ben said quietly the second time. Then he quickly grabbed the money, as if it could get blown away by the wind. He gulped three more cups of water and rose,

Should I take a bus home now? he asked himself on the road. *No, it's not a good idea. Who knows what will come up tomorrow? As a matter of fact, I must keep every kobo I get now for feeding, lest I die. I can always walk. After all, that's what the legs are meant for. Even if I walk the whole of Lagos, as long as I'm eating, all is well. It is said, "Food for the belly, belly for the food, both shall perish one day,"* he concluded as he walked on.

In fact, I still need to keep walking, just in case I see a vacancy. I need to know what time it is fast, he thought as he looked around for the closest person with a wristwatch.

"Excuse me," he said to a woman just walking past him. "What time is it, madam?"

"Four thirty," she said after consulting her watch and moved on briskly.

"Thank you," he said, smiling. *That man must have gone in there to eat at four o'clock. He most likely takes his lunch there. He is a good man. I must see him again. He's my friend now, so we should see and be together again whenever we have the opportunity.*

After walking for sometime, he touched his right pocket again to feel the money, checking if it's still there.

Had I known that man would be paying for me, I would have ordered more. Now I've been walking out the whole food I ate. I must have been walking for about an hour and a half or so now, and I'm almost beginning to feel hungry again. Thank god, that's the last turn home. Just then it dawned on him. *My god, my landlord.* He came to a standstill.

I promised him today, so he must be waiting by my room now. Ahm-ahm-ahm, what do I do now? Okay, I guess I have to stay out late, till he has gone to bed, then I'll sneak in and be out again before dawn. He walked into a bar close by and sat down at a corner table.

"What can I do for you, sir?" a bar girl asked him.

"I don't want anything. I just want to while away time. I will be leaving very soon."

"But you can't sit down here if you are not taking anything," the girl lamented.

"Why can't you just—," he shouted and cut himself short. "Okay, okay, I'll order something, but not now. I'll let you know when I'm ready, okay?" The girl looked him over with disdain and left him to attend to someone else. Then he drifted away into his world of thoughts again and remembered his ordeal with his landlord just a week before. He had come back from his daily routine of job hunting that evening and found two heavy planks of wood hammered across his door to prevent entry. He immediately knew what the problem was but pretended not to have any idea, then he walked to the adjacent door and knocked on it.

"Yes, come in," a voice from inside the room commanded.

Ben opened the door and stepped in halfway, holding the door handle.

"Sorry, my dear brother," he said, taking a good look around the room; and when his eyes eventually rested on the occupants, on the three-by-seven bed, he was stunned. He stood there petrified, eyes and mouth wide open at a large but rather short man with a girl, both desolately naked. He was still looking, breathing heavily, when the voice startled him again.

"What's your problem, you fool?" said the man on the bed.

"What?" he replied, suddenly waking up from his shock. "Ah, sorry, I made a mistake." He was looking as if he was going to cry and laugh at the same time. "I-I-I made a mistake." He then turned around all at once to bolt out of the room and ran his head onto the door frame.

He shrieked, quickly slammed the door shut, and started cursing, holding his forehead. On getting to his door, his landlord was waiting.

"Where is my money?" he yelled. "Where is my money? You promised you'll pay up in a week. That was two weeks ago, and you haven't paid up till now. Haven't I tried? Give me my money now or you won't sleep in this house tonight, and in the morning, I'll throw your things out."

He took his hands off his forehead and was still patting it lightly when the landlord saw it.

"What happened to you there?" He pointed to his head, and Ben pointed to the room he had come out from, grimacing.

"When I saw my door blocked," he started to explain, "I went next door to find out what was happening, then-then, I-I-I hit my head on the door frame."

"Which door?" asked the landlord. Ben pointed to the door adjacent his.

"Ha ha ha" the landlord burst in laughter. "That door? Are you that stupid? Have you ever seen anybody else in this whole house knock on that door?" Then he laughed some more. "Don't bother telling me what you saw. It's okay. Just because of that, you can stay, but make sure you get me my money. I'm giving you another week." And with just two pulls, he extracted the wooden planks from the door. He walked away laughing, again. Between his bursts of laughter, he looked back and asked Ben, "I hope you didn't break my door frame?"

Ben brought out his keys from his pocket and unlocked the door, locked it after himself, and fell on the bed. Recalling how he got there, six months earlier, after he was ejected from his former house for owing six months' rent. He thought further and realized that he had been ejected from every house he had lived in, six months after he got in, for not paying at all. He looked around his scanty room that lacked furniture, only his father's old mattress on the floor, two shirts, one jacket, one tie, one singlet, one pair of pants, a pair of boots, and a few very clean kitchen utensils. Of course, he hardly had any visitors, so he never thought of putting the room in order. *After all, there is nothing to put in order,* he thought to justify himself.

The next morning, he was out of the house before the door adjacent his was opened, and so he did every day since then.

"Excuse me," the bar girl interrupted his thought again. "What can I do for you?" she asked Ben. "Have you made up your mind now what you want to take, because you've been here for two hours?"

Then Ben quickly looked unto the wall for the clock.

"How time flies!" he exclaimed. "Eight o'clock? That's good." Then he realized the girl was still staring at him.

"Okay, can I have some water?"

"Forty naira," the girl said bluntly.

"What, what, water to drink, why?"

"Sir, we sell bottled water. This is a bar, not a canteen."

He calmed down and said, "Okay, you see, my sister, I really don't want anything. I just wanted to while away time a little. Please, please, okay, just let me be. I won't make any trouble please. Just bear with me for a little while more."

The girl then walked away saying nothing. Some moments later, she was walking toward Ben. He thought she was coming to drive him out of the bar, and then he realized she was holding a cup and a jug of water. On getting to him, she left both on his table, turned, and walked away.

"My god!" he said slowly and quietly. "This girl is completely different from that reckless girl at the canteen. She is well mannered, disciplined, and beautiful," he said, grinning to himself while pouring the water.

"No wonder the ugly girls work at the canteens and the beautiful ones at the bars," he told himself as he drank.

CHAPTER THREE

"Thank god, thank god, thank god, I can smell life again!" he shouted as the main gate of the prison that had confined him for the past three months was shut behind him.

"I don't hope to ever see inside you again, hell. Man, I hate it in there," he said, looking back at the massive premises that had an inscription on the wall—LOS ANGELES STATE PRISON—bold but blurred from accumulated dirt of many years.

"Mr. Charles Oggbu?"

Startled, Charles turned to the direction of the voice and hesitated, looking suspiciously at the two white men, who apparently had been waiting for him.

"Mr. Charles Oggbu?" one of them asked again.

"Who wants to know?" Charles inquired, making efforts to sound relaxed.

"The LA Police Department," the same man answered. He was the taller one. He flashed his ID.

"I'm under arrested?"

"Nobody said that yet," the same man replied. "We'll just like you to come with us for some questioning, that's all."

"Questioning, my ass! What for? What have I done again?"

"You'll be wise to make this easy on yourself, sir. Just come with us." Charles thought for a moment. Refusal of this invitation may lead to arrest on the spot. "You know what, I've been in there for three months, and I just wanna get home to my family. They must miss me terribly by now, so I hope you won't waste my time at your office?"

The two officers kept mute.

When he couldn't get any reply from the tall one, he slowly looked into the eyes of the other officer. "Shall we go then?" he said nervously.

The two officers then positioned themselves on his two sides and held him by his hands as they led him to the waiting car.

"I thought you said this is not an arrest?" he asked, almost panicking.

"Nobody said that, mister," the tall officer said as the other officer opened the back door, pushed him in, and slammed the door shut.

The other officer took his position behind the wheels and his colleague beside him.

"Did your family come to visit you at all, Mr. Oggbu?" the stocky officer asked, talking for the first time.

Charles looked up into the mirror to see his eyes. "My name is Ogbu and not that shit you pronounced." Then he hesitated, and when the silence became unbearable, he said, "No, why do you ask?"

"I just wonder how greatly they must miss you." The tall officer chuckled.

Annoyed at the officer's insinuation, Charles remembered what took him to prison.

Elina had always been a very easygoing woman, but she and Charles knew that she could be mean if she wanted to. Being angry, she had once promised Charly, as she fondly called him, that she would set all his clothes on fire if she ever saw lipstick stains on them again; and Charly had not taken her seriously. A week later, he did not only come home with lipstick stains but also forgot a lady's underwear in his pocket because he was drunk. By the time he woke up the following morning, all his clothes were a heap of ashes in the yard. Another time, Charly was talking to a woman he called an agent who was assisting him to look for a job since he didn't have his work papers yet, and it was Elina alone who catered for the family. She didn't believe him but kept quiet. An hour later, Charly was still talking to this agent of his, very quietly. When Elina could not bear it anymore, she yelled at him to hang up because she knew he was talking to one of his girlfriends and that he was incurring another bill for her to pay. When he did not heed her yellings, she threatened to throw the TV he had brought home from nowhere out of the window, and he still didn't hang up. She threw it out without a second warning. As the TV went out of the window, the phone dropped from Charly's grasp as he shouted, "Noooooo!" running to the window. He watched the TV he had just finished paying the previous week land on the ground and crash with a big bang. Elina turned and stormed into her room without any remorse. As Charly cursed and wailed, he followed her into the room ferociously; red eyed, she was sitting on the bed. He grabbed her by the neck and pulled her to her feet. He raised his hand to hit her in the face. Then just between her clenched teeth, Elina found the breath to say to him, "If you try that, if you ever lay your hands on me, if you beat me, I'll ruin you in America." He hesitated and slowly lowered his hand. He believed her; by now he had learned to believe every word she spoke in anger. Yet Elina was easygoing and peaceful.

Sometime later, Charles started being friends with a guy named Tony. Elina didn't like it. "I don't want you to have anything to do with him," she had lamented.

She felt Tony was very dubious and was always loaded with money that she knew Charly wanted to be a part of.

"You're going to be stealing very soon because this Tony you are now friends with is a thief," Elina yelled at him one day as he went off with Tony in his new Mercedes-Benz. Then he stopped coming home when he got hooked on alcohol. Elina would go looking for him all around town, in bars and clubhouses, to no avail. Then he would come home after some time and give her some money. Elina would beg him to stay, rejecting the money, but Charly would always leave the money on the table for her and leave. By then he was always dressed expensively. He would at times come home in one of Tony's cars. When Elina got pregnant with their baby, he came home more often.

"I'm doing all for us, babe, for you and the baby," he would say just to pacify his wife, who still believed strongly that Tony would get him in trouble someday. The day he brought Elina home from the hospital, he had arrived at the hospital in a new car, and Elina had refused to enter it.

"Charly, I want to go home in my car and not in a stolen car," she said.

"It's not stolen, honey. I just bought it," he explained.

"Where did you get the money? You can't afford this."

"All right, honey, we can talk about this when we get home. Please, just come in now, and let's go home. You're embarrassing me," he said quietly in her ears.

While driving home, he looked at his wife from the corner of his eyes and, seeing that she was still frowning, tried teasing her.

"So what name are you giving her?" he asked.

"You shouldn't just be asking me that. An Italian would've had a name ready for his child since conception, or at least before birth, and that is the first thing he would say when carrying her."

"I thought you didn't want me to be like a Sicilian?" he derisively said.

"Yeah!"

"Why then are you asking me now to act like one?" he asked, looking at her with his head turned completely sideways, looking off the road.

"Face the road, Charly," she said, but he didn't listen to her,. She repeated herself, intensifying the tone of her voice.

A truck emerged from the sloppy bend ahead. Charles was looking at her expressionlessly. She looked into his eyes, wondering why he was looking at her way so seriously, unmindful of the road. Now the truck was fast approaching, and Charles had left his own lane to face it. She first saw the reflection in his eyes.

"Charlyyyy!" Elina shouted, reaching to grab the steering wheel with her free hand, still holding the baby with the other one. Charly turned off the road with a swift whirling of the steering wheel.

"Ah ah ah," he laughed loudly and uncontrollably.

Elina, still holding the baby with one hand, pressed the palm of her other hand to her forehead, trying to breathe steadily.

"Oh, sorry, honey, did I get to you that badly? I was only trying to express my joy." He tried to touch her; she pushed his hand away.

"By killing us?" she protested quietly but gravely.

As he was about to apologize again, she held out her palm to his face to stop him from talking. She closed her eyes and rested her head on the headrest. Charly didn't try to break the silence till they got home.

Charly pulled over in front of the house, got out of the car, and ran to Elina's side to help her out. He opened the door and tried to take the baby from her. She hesitated and got down from the car.

"You can as well go burn that car or keep it to yourself because that's the last time you'll ever see me in it, and if I ever see it around here again, I'll do the burning for you." Charles drove that car away and never brought it home again.

He came home that night in a cab. For two days, Elina did not talk to him; and for another one week, she did not let him touch his baby.

"That's my child as well," he would say.

"I don't think so," Elina replied. "If she's your child, you wouldn't be trying to murder her and plan to make it look like an accident."

"Is that the way you see it?" Charly yelled in surprise, jaws dropping. And he almost cried.

"I'm sorry, honey, please, I really am," he soberly apologized.

Four days later, they were seated together in the garden, as Charly seldom went out anymore because of the incident. Elina had warned him not to try to forcefully take the child from her, or she would tell what he did to the authorities. So she was sitting opposite him holding the baby to her chest as if some arm was going to befall the child if she let go. She could feel Charles's eyes all over her.

"Honey, so what name should we give her?" he asked remorsefully.

"No! That's your duty as the father."

"No! I want you to give her the name."

"Really? Oh, thanks, honey!" She beamed a smile. "I'm so grateful. I've been planning to name her after my mom, but I was afraid you would not approve of it."

"Christiana?"

"Yeah," she said, looking pleadingly.

"Fine, fine by me!" Charles said. Then she went to him, kissed him, and put the baby gently in his lap.

Charles could not believe it. Beaming with smile he lifted her up high as if showing her to God. Elina looked at him and knew that he loved their baby. She went in and got a bottle of wine and two glass cups. She was making an effort to open it because Charles was holding the baby.

"So, if I may ask, why Christiana? I mean after your mom."

"She's a good woman, gentle spirited and very peaceful."

"I thought you said Sicilians are very terrible people? Is your mom excluded?"

"Yeah! I should think so. Somehow she's an exception with a few others," she said, making a face as if to remember.

"And you?"

"Yeah!"

"Yeeeah what, if I may ask?" he asked, making a face and shaking his head.

"I mean yeah, I'm one of the few good ones that are peaceful and gentle spirited," she said, walking into the house.

"Really," said Charles, looking as if something just hit him. Elina was coming out to join him and the baby. A car honk blared from outside; they looked into each other's eyes, and Charles looked away guiltily and held out the baby to her.

"You won't even stay home to play with your child?" she said with clenched teeth, in her Italian accent, obviously livid.

"I'll soon be back, honey," he said and leaned toward her to kiss her, but she looked away. He looked at her closely and walked away.

"I hope she grows to know her father," she said. He walked on.

That night, Tony and Charles drove out of town to a nightclub where drugs were sold at the bar and nude women walked around to entertain. Tony was greeted by lots of people whom Charles was seeing for the first time. As they pulled their chairs to sit down at a corner table, a guy in a leather jacket tapped Tony on the shoulder.

"The boss will like to see you."

"All right," Tony said as he left his chair. "Make your order, Charles. I'll soon be back." Then he followed the guy, and they disappeared into the door behind the bar.

Charles ordered beer.

It took almost an hour before Tony returned, and when he eventually did, he had a small box with him.

"We have a special package," he said as he led Charles in another direction to an empty room. He dragged the heavy metal chair, making a screeching noise with it, to the only table in the room, dropped his buttocks into it, placed the box on the table, and opened it.

"What's this?" Charles asked.

"Wait till you see."

Then he brought out the contents of the box one after the other: a syringe with a needle and a bottle of white powder and a spoon with a fire lighter.

When he had taken a shot, injecting himself, he closed his eyes slowly and rested on the chair, drifting into oblivion, as Charles watched in amazement and with interest. After a while, Charles repeated the same procedure for himself without any supervision. Charly closed his eyes and smiled to nothing in particular as he drifted off.

They woke up randomly and took a shot more each and went off into the land of fantasies that they now enjoyed and they never wanted to vacate.

When they woke up again, it was almost dawn. It was Charles who woke up first.

"To, To, Ton, Tommy," he said quietly and incoherently.

"Yeah," Tony murmured.

"It's almost morning. Can we go?"

"Yeah sure," he replied as he tried to stabilize himself and stood on his feet. They felt so heavy that they thought they needed help to get to their feet. They supported each other as they made their way, saying a lot of rubbish, as they staggered along to Tony's car.

"We need a drink now, man, that's all we need to feel better," Tony said as he drove on. So when they got back into town, they stopped by a store, and Tony told Charles to get the beer.

"Here, try this. I just got it yesterday. Think it belongs to some rich guy," he said as he handed him a credit card. Charles took it, looked at it with his watery eyes, and staggered into the store. He bought two bottles of beer and a pack of cigarettes. He brought out the credit card and handed it to the old man behind the counter.

"Here," he said.

Without a word, the old man took it from him, swiped it in, and gave it back to him.

Charly looked at him with contempt. "Dumb fucking old man," he said as he walked back out. On getting to Tony's place still in high spirits, Charles picked his car and drove home gently but still in his drunken state, enjoying the effect of the drugs in his veins. He managed to get home without a ticket but drove into their lawn, knocking off the wooden fence. He got out and staggered to the house smiling. He banged on the front door hard and repeatedly. Then he kicked it hard again as Elina was opening it. He stormed in, pushing her aside. Elina followed him, saying, "I will not have you around my baby in this state."

"Where is my baby?" he yelled.

"Don't touch her!" Elina shouted as she ran past him to pick up the child.

"Give her to me."

"No, never!" Elina said.

"Give her to me now, Elina, now," he said, his eyes expressing the increased anger he was beginning to feel.

He grabbed the baby with one hand and struck Elina across the face with the other; he also kicked her in the rib. She collapsed to the floor with a shriek and did not move. Charles lay on his back with the baby on his chest, and he slept off. About fifteen minutes later, hearing the baby's cry, Elina painfully opened her eyes. She felt so much pain in her side that she could not move. She closed her eyes again to remember all that had happened. She took her time and mustered the strength to get to the phone, dragging herself, because she couldn't stand on her feet. When she got to the shelf where the phone was, she could not reach it, so she pulled the cord, and the phone dropped on the floor. She called the police.

"Help," she said, then she paused a moment for the pain. "Ten Cadbury Street, Cadbury," she repeated and fainted again. Two minutes later, there was a knock on the door. When there was no answer, two policemen forced their way in, pulled out their guns, and walked in cautiously. Checking one room after the other, they heard a sound and moved toward it. They saw Elina on the floor; one of them stopped by her, and the other moved toward the bed, pointing his gun at Charles who was still sleeping with a smile on his face. The officer with Elina placed two fingers on her arm to feel her pulse; the other still focused on Charles. The officer with Elina left her and came to his partner. He now pointed his gun at Charles while the partner with one hand holding the gun tried to get the wailing baby out of Charles's entanglement with the other. When he had done this successfully, he put her in her cot and resumed his position beside his partner. He motioned to his partner, who now sheathed his gun again, climbed on the bed gently, and with one grab took Charles by both hands and placed them on his sides, turned him facedown, pulled his hands behind his back again, and cuffed them.

He pulled him to his feet and pushed him to the door. Drowsily, Charles went on without resistance. The officer took him to the car and locked him in the backseat. The other officer with Elina picked up the phone and called for an ambulance; afraid to move her in case of broken bones, he stood by her watching her till the ambulance arrived. Some paramedics came with the ambulance, and one of them picked the baby up, while the rest of them put Elina on the stretcher and took her to the ambulance. When they had driven off, one of the policemen made a note on his pad and locked up the house, and they took off with Charles who was now gradually coming to his senses.

Charles was detained. After two days, he was tried in court and sentenced to three months in jail. He got to find out in the court that Elina had suffered two broken ribs, temporary blindness, and a skyrocketing high blood pressure. She could not appear in court. A month later, Elina was discharged; she went home with her baby, packed her things, and left the house. When she noticed Charles's car, she went over to it, stopped, and thought for a moment. She took her baby to her car, went back into the house, brought out a keg of gasoline, and emptied it all over the car; then she stopped and thought again, looking at the house and back to the car. She realized that it was too close to the house. So she opened the car, released the brake, and let the car run down the road; and then she pushed it to the roadside again and set it ablaze. She left town with her baby, leaving no trace.

The car pulled up in front of the police station. The officers stepped down and brought Charles out of the backseat after a long drive from the prison. He was led in and saw offices to his left and right. *This is quite different from the police station I was in three months ago,* he thought. He was led down the lobby, and one of the officers opened a door to his left. He walked in to see two men apparently waiting for him; the other two officers who brought him turned back at the door and closed it behind them. Charles saw the door closed, and he felt as if he had been lured into the lion's den, betrayed.

"Have your sit, Mr. Ooo," said one of the men in there, with a questioning look on his face so that Charles could pronounce his surname properly.

"Ogbu," he said nervously, looking into their eyes randomly for a clue as to why he was there.

"I am Agent Vick," said the one sitting at one end of the table, facing Charles at the other end, "and standing there is Agent Douglas." He pointed to his partner standing against the wall. Douglas was chewing the frame of his glasses, so he just lifted it to Charles in salute.

"If I may ask you, Mr. Oobuu, pardon my pronunciation, do you remember this credit card?" He held it up for him to see. When Charles was making efforts to see from across the table, Officer Douglas took it from his partner and handed it over to Charles. Afraid to touch it, Charles looked at it inquisitively and shook his head. "No, I can't," he said.

"Did you ever have a credit card?" Vick asked again.

"If you meant to ask if I ever operated one, no, I never did."

Vicky was now looking at him from above his glasses, as his glasses now rested on his nose. He was silent briefly and then continued.

"Mr. Charles, this card was found on you the day you were arrested, and records have it that you paid for two bottles of beer and a pack of cigarette earlier that morning at a store out of town. Am I right?"

Charles started rubbing his forehead, trying to remember something.

"Am I right, Mr. Obuuu?"

"I don't know, but I think I can remember paying for some beer or something with a card I got from a friend I was with that morning, but I don't know where he got it from."

"Mr. Obuuu, again, pardon me, this card was stolen from a senator, two weeks prior to that day, and it had a balance of over fifteen thousand dollars on it then; but by the time we retrieved it from you"—he looked up at Charles and hesitated—"it had just two hundred dollars left on it."

"Oh my god, I don't know anything about it. I swear I don't. I only bought the beer. I swear, I'll take you to the guy that gave it to me."

"Tony is no more in the country, Mr. Obuu. He fled, so you're in this alone."

"Please help me," Charles said, almost crying. "I'll cooperate. Please, just don't send me back into that place, please."

"Where, Mr. Obuu?" asked Vick.

"Prison!"

"You won't be going back to prison, Mr. Obuu," said Vick as he and Douglas exchanged glances.

Charles looked at them, wondering.

He was on the next flight to Nigeria.

CHAPTER FOUR

"Which one of you is Koja?" asked the prison warden, clad in his dark-green trousers and light-green shirt.

"Get out of here, you fool!" shouted one inmate.

"If I lay my hands on you, I'll kill you, you idiot!" shouted another.

As the whole cell D was in an uproar, every one of them rained curses on the warden on duty.

"You will all die in this prison. I promise you. Which one of you, I ask again, is Koja?" he yelled this time.

"I am," said a voice from behind the crowd at the entrance of the cell.

"Get out of here before I change my mind on your case, you criminal," said the warden.

"Where are you taking him to, or do you want to go and kill him?" asked one of the inmates.

"He's dying already, so why bother," another one suggested.

"Shut up, you criminals, I wonder why you all were not given death sentences. You're real dirt in this society."

Again the whole cell began to erupt into noise.

"I'm calling all these names once each, and if you're not out by the time I shut this gate, I'll make sure you die in there, okay!"

"I have completed my term here. Shouldn't you free me to go?" another inmate shouted.

"Koja? Daolu? You have completed your term, but have you completed your lesson?"

"Yes!"

"Daolu?" he continued.

"Akeem?"

"Yes!"

"Moses?"

"Yes!"

"If I have called your name, I want you on a single file behind this gate, now, and if I didn't call you and you come out when I open this gate, you're a dead man. I'll just raise an alarm that you're trying to escape, and you know what, I want you dead quicker than anybody else in this world." He opened the gate, and all the inmates he called filed out.

He locked the gate again. "Follow me," he ordered, as he walked on ahead of them down the corridor to the door next to the chief warden's office. He opened the door, and they filed in; he stepped in behind them. The chief warden himself was sitting behind his desk; he was still busy writing for another two minutes before he looked up.

"Hello, guys," he said expressionlessly, and before they could answer him, he continued.

"As you are aware, the head of state just passed on, and there has been a new government," he said, looking at them one after the other, then he hesitated.

"So the new government, the newly sworn-in head of state, has granted some prisoners freedom. The well-behaved ones among you and those of you who have completed their sentences. Anyway"—he paused again—"we have checked your files, and your behavior so far has been impressive, so the four of you have been released."

He then watched their faces for impressions and, disappointed by their lack of euphoria, asked them, "Are you not happy? I just told you, you've been freed." He was surprised.

"Of course, we are," said one of them, smiling, and the rest also murmured the same thing in unison

"All right, your papers will be arranged immediately, and you can take your leave, but first I will like to employ you all to start a new life as good citizens of this country when you get out there and live rightly. I can assure you the society you left some years back is not the same anymore. It has changed, and for the worse, if you care to know. You could be back here in a week or two. So I wish you all happy new lives and good will in your entire endeavors. God bless you. You will follow the warden now, and the clerk will prepare your papers. Bye and I don't wish to see you again, at least not in here."

The warden opened the door for them again as they walked out of the chief's office.

"The chief is so funny. Did he just say he hopes not to see your faces again? Ah ah ah," he laughed. "I bet you all won't last two weeks out there, you damned criminals. I don't know why the government should allow you people back into the system, you crime-infected people. Left to me, I'll just let you rot in here. Get in there," he said, pointing to another room. They entered another room with wardrobes all around it.

"Take off your real clothes and put on the fake ones in the wardrobes. Just pick your size; and I advise you, don't roughen the prison uniforms which, of course, are your real clothes. I'm very sure you will be back soon to pick them up again!" he said with a chuckle and left them in the room. "Join me in my office when you're through. The earning scheme has some change for you," he said at the door.

The prisoners were wondering what had just befallen them.

"Why are they releasing us?" one asked, looking confused at the others.

"What do you mean by that? Don't you want to go home, I mean, live a normal life again?" another argued.

"I don't have anywhere to go. I can't go back to my family. I've been disowned," answered Daolu.

Without saying a word, and after the shock of the news of the release had lessened, Koja opened one of the wardrobes. He saw some rather old but clean clothes there. He picked a shirt, and looking at it, it was too big for him and did not fit. He picked another one and noticed it was torn. He dropped it and searched for something more appropriate to wear. He eventually settled for a black jean trouser that was just a little longer and a short-sleeved shirt. The rest of them were looking at him all the while.

When he was through changing, he looked back at them all.

"Guys, I don't understand why you're standing there not doing what you're told to do. I'm sorry about how you all feel about this news. The prisons are too damn congested, and the government feels like letting some people go. So you see, it doesn't matter if you have a place to go or not. I'll advise you to change your prison clothes now before that demon of a being comes back, because you're leaving here today."

And just as if they were waiting for his motivation, each of them opened the wardrobe nearest to them and started changing. About ten minutes later, they all walked into the warden's office.

"And for god's sake, who the hell told you to walk into my office like that? You animals, on a single file, now, and let me tell you, until you leave the gates of this prison, you're still under my authority. Am I understood?"

"When I call your names, I want you to step forward to collect your papers and money." Ten minutes later, he was through with them.

"And lastly, boys, go ahead and let the government regret releasing you, okay, because I know they will. Crime is in your blood. Bye for now, and I will be expecting you back soon," he said, grinning at them with such hatred that they had grown to know and lived with. They folded their papers in their hands and walked out of the office in a single file, almost afraid he would change his mind concerning their situation. When they eventually walked out of the main gate, Koja looked back at the prison that was shielded completely by the very high walls that surrounded it. He shook his head.

"I can't believe I've spent the past eight years of my life behind these walls," he said, looking at the gate, like someone admiring a work of art.

"Stop exaggerating, boy, what about the times we went working on the field at the back of the premises," said Akeem.

"You won't believe it, guys, I never got out of these premises with you when you went cutting, man. I don't know how it happened, but that wicked pig of a warden never realized he never took me out for work," replied Koja.

"You are so lucky you didn't do all the hard cuttings with us," said another.

"Did you say lucky? Ah ah," Koja laughed briefly. "You called being locked inside for eight years luck. You call seeing nobody else apart from inmates and wardens for eight years luck. Ah ah ah," he laughed again. "I don't see it as luck, my brother, I see it as torture. Somehow anyway, I know it was divinely arranged because I don't think that bad news Warden Ajayi ever noticed. He would've killed me before today. And I think my not doing any hard times is due to God not wanting me to suffer for what I did not do," he said.

"And talking about what you did or did not do, you never spoke about what brought you in there in the first place," said Moses. "I robbed, that was how I got in there. Daolu killed somebody even though he said it was by mistake. I've never heard of killing by mistake, but that was what his lawyer said, and with that, he escaped death sentence. If I were the judge, I would order your execution right there in the court," he concluded, looking at Daolu with such disgust, he almost spat on him.

"Do you hate him that much all this while?" Koja asked.

"You ask me? Didn't you hear how he killed the person he killed? I've never heard anything so stupid," Moses said, looking at Daolu as if he were some mountain of dirt. "The idiot almost killed himself trying to kill the guy."

Koja looked into the eyes of the other guys inquiringly if they knew what happened.

"Koja," one of them said, "he ate out of the food he poisoned while trying to lure the guy into eating the food. He only didn't eat as much as the guy, that's why he's alive now. He was hospitalized for about two weeks himself."

"What!" Koja exclaimed. "I've never heard of such a thing in my life. You could've killed yourself," he said, looking at Daolu.

"But I didn't, and I achieved my aim. Now I'm a free man," Daolu said, looking guilty.

"How I wish the doctors could not revive you," Moses said distastefully. "So, as I was saying, let us know how you got in prison?" Moses asked.

"Are you in a hurry?" Koja replied.

"In a hurry? Did you just say hurry?" asked Moses. "Ah ah ah," he laughed. "If any one of us still has that word in his dictionary, the person must be a fool," he added as they all swore in unison.

"Out of my own allowance, I invite you to have a drink at the nearest bar we see, so I'll tell you my story as we celebrate our newly found freedom." They walked into the society again and were surprised to see that only a few changes occurred since they left it. They perceived the breeze of freedom; they felt life enter into them again, as if they were being reborn, and without knowing it, they all beamed with smiles. They stood there studying their new society, watching people head in different directions, vehicles in different grades, commuters, taxis, trucks, and motorcycles, all of them constituting nuisance to the environment.

"Guys?" Koja startled them, his voice breaking their different lines of thought. "We are going for a drink. Don't worry, we have the rest of our lives to watch the whole world. Shall we proceed?"

They looked left and right before crossing the road, and the traffic was so fast at the "gate area" in Ibadan. They were so close to each other looking from their right to their left, waiting for the break in traffic that would enable them to cross the road. Moses, who was the shortest among them, was in the middle and so could not adequately stretch out his neck to check both sides. When they moved, he was so unready that he took off late and so was caught up in the middle of the road by a fast-approaching car. The car slammed on its brake with a loud screeching sound, just a foot from Moses, and he fell down as though dead. The man behind the wheels came out and rushed to his side with his hands on his head. Koja and the rest of the group also rushed back as other cars approaching came to rest at the point of the supposed accident. When Koja had knelt down beside Moses, he said to him, "Moses, Moses, you're not dead, okay. Rise, the car did not hit you."

"Are you sure?" Moses asked, still with his eyes closed. "Are you sure I'm not dead? Are you sure the car did not hit me?" Then he opened his eyes and looked around at the faces surrounding him, and Koja and Daolu helped him get up.

The moment he stood on his feet, he shook himself free from Daolu. "Leave me alone, you fool. It was your entire fault. You are too tall, that was why I could not look well. You were blocking me!" Moses said, looking up and down at Daolu's frame.

"Guys, let's leave here before this crowd gets out of hand and they start suspecting who we are and where we're coming from!" Koja murmured audibly, enough for them to hear.

"Please don't leave like that. You might be hurt. Let me take you to the hospital," said the man who drove the car.

"He's totally fine," Koja quickly cut in. "He's going to be all right. You can go."

"Not so fast!" shouted Moses before the man could turn back. "Some money for drugs will do. You know, I still feel the effect of the shock. I think that should be cheaper than taking me to the hospital," he said, stretching his hand with his palm wide open to the man.

"All right, that won't be any problem at all." The man produced his wallet from his back pocket and counted twenty fifty naira notes and handed them to Moses. "Will that do?" the man asked.

As Moses was mumbling, "Ehm ehm ehm," Koja cut in again, "It will. You've really tried. Thanks a lot. You can go now." He walked the man back to his car before Moses could say any other word. Koja joined the rest of the guys and rushed them on, and Moses kept murmuring and making inaudible sounds.

They settled into the first bar they saw and ordered drinks. "Koja, we don't have to drink on your allowance anymore. Let's do it on our just-earned money" declared Moses, and they all cheered. "Shall we hear your story now, Koja?" Moses asked.

"Yeah, but I wonder what Daolu is busy thinking about," Koja said, gaping at Daolu who was apparently lost in thought. They all turned to face him.

Moses murmured something and added, "What is it you're thinking about? I hope I won't regret asking you that question." He lifted his cup to his mouth without looking at Daolu.

Daolu beamed at them all and said, "Now I have a very good idea of what I will do now that I'm out of prison, and that has been a point of concern to me since all these years, you know. This thinking of where I'm going to start all over from. Just now, barely an hour after I'm out, I got it. It must be by divination, I presume."

"Let us know what this idea is and stop dreaming. What is it?" asked Akeem.

"Don't you guys get it? Moses just made one thousand bucks without sweat and without getting hurt. I know you guys have not thought about it, but isn't it a bright idea? I mean, you can jump in front of an incoming car, and before it hits you, you fall to the ground as if it had already hit you, and that way you get paid, cool easy cash," he said, smiling to the rest of the guys, who apparently, except Moses, were all staring at him with their mouths open in disbelief.

Moses turned to Koja. "Would you tell us your story now?" he said in frustration.

"You don't see any sense in what I just said?" Daolu queried. "I know it's a mistake telling you guys about my idea. I shouldn't have. I should've just kept it to myself, lest you steal it."

"Yeah, do just that and die alone," said Akeem.

"Amen," Moses added quickly. As Koja burst into a round of laughter, Akeem joined him. And after their laughter had subsided, he began.

"I was working for this company, at Iwo Road, NEE. You know it?"

"Yeah, I think I do," said Akeem.

"I was in my office at closing hours one particular day when the deputy general manager walked in. 'Mr. Omosu,' he said, smiling as he entered, 'busy as always, isn't it? Doing everything for your boss. I doubt if you ever let him do anything by himself!'

"'Good afternoon, sir,' I said, smiling to him, because he was right, everybody knew that I stayed long in the office after closing hours doing, most times, things my boss should do.'

"'And that is why I like you,' the deputy general manager continued. 'You see, a lot of our staff here do not have the spirit of dedication to work like you do, and they exhibit so much negligence in their duties. You are a very industrious man, Omosu.'

"I said, 'Thank you very much, sir.' But by then I was getting uneasy, wondering what the DGM was doing in my office, chatting with me like that and at that odd hour. Besides, he and my direct boss, the executive director of finance, were not on good terms then. So I was really suspicious of his visit to my office, which was, again, unusual. When I could not summon the courage to ask him what I could do for him, not out fear, but I just don't know why, I became afraid of him all of a sudden. I kept quiet. My silence grew so intense within a few minutes he got to the point.

"'As I was saying, Mr. Omosu, you are a very hardworking man, and I think you deserve more than what you get from this company for all these long hours of what I call intense labor.' I was now looking at him seriously as every word that followed sank into my heart. He continued, 'Koja, since we are going to be more familiar from now on, I have a request to make of you, which is going to benefit you, and I mean really benefit you.' He stood, talking to me since he entered my office, so I offered him a seat, but he declined. He then brought his left hand from his back, and that was when I noticed he had it there all this while. He was holding a paper that he placed in front of me and told me he would like me to get my boss to sign it. Afraid to touch it, I looked at it, and all I could gather from it was that it was a list of equipment.

"'Koja, please pick it up and go through it. It won't bite you.' So I picked it up, with my gaze still on the DGM. 'Sir, I don't see any reason why this document should not be submitted to my boss's office directly. It is definitely his to sign,' I told him, feigning ignorance of what he had implied.

"'Koja, the list of things in there never transpired. I mean, none of those transactions were ever made.'

"'Then the release of this money would be illegal, and so the director will cross-check and will never sign it,' I pointed out almost in rage. 'Good you jumped the illegal part of it to where you're concerned. You know, Koja, that your boss will not cross-check whatever you have already checked. Both you and I know that your boss trusts you far more than that.'

"'So what makes you think I want to betray that trust, sir?' I said.

"'Koja, it is needless to mention the ridiculous pay you get as salary, but in this, Koja, in this you have a million naira.' At that, he turned to leave, but at the door, he stopped and said, 'If you're not interested, let me have that paper back by tomorrow morning. Otherwise, I will like it back after work tomorrow, signed.' I forgot to tell you that I was in the account department, and even though we have never made such a large procurement before, it was not outrageous."

"And did you give in?" asked Moses. "I mean, did you do it?"

"Yes, I did, but I thought about it all through the night. The next day I packed it with some other papers my boss should sign and gave it to him. He signed them all through without checking. The truth is my boss really trusted me. The next day the money was released."

"What happened next?" Daolu asked.

"Do you have to ask that question?" Moses yelled. "He's getting there."

"What is wrong with me asking? You asked him if he did it, didn't you?"

"And that is why you must ask a question too, stupid or not?"

"It's okay, guys, let me finish. My boss was arrested about three months later. By then I had been transferred to another branch of our company. Auditors had come over the following month, and the fraud was discovered. I was called forward too, but I had little to answer." He paused. "I had to confess later when I could not bear my boss's predicament anymore."

"You what?" Moses asked.

"My boss was a very good man, Moses. He loved and trusted me. Why should he pay for that?"

"So what happened to the money, and how much was the whole thing anyway?" Akeem asked.

"The whole money was ten million, and I got 10 percent of it, and of course, they got the money back from the bank I kept it."

"But I think they should let you go after you had confessed and they got their money back. That's unfair," Akeem added.

"Unfair? The case was already in court, and that was exactly why I got ten years. The DGM and the rest of them got twelve years each."

In silence, they all picked up their cups and gulped the content. "You're telling me you spent eight whole years because of some conscience thing. Why did you get involved in the first place when you knew you had that kind of problem?" Moses broke the silence.

"You are not any less stupid than this corpse here," he said, pointing to Daolu.

"Ah ah ah," Koja roared in laughter. "I knew you would say something like that. I knew you would."

"Koja, I'm sure that was then anyway," Akeem said, "I'm very sure you smoked enough *igbo* in there to burn away all the conscience left in you."

"You had better do that," Moses said as he downed the last of his drink, and the rest did the same thing. They rose and left the bar. When they got to the main road, not knowing which way to go, they stopped there just looking at the traffic again.

Then Koja spoke up. "Guys, here we are at a commencement, that is, the end of one thing, the beginning of another. I don't know what your plans are, that is if you have any, but I sure don't have. But one thing I do know, take a good look at this society. You don't belong there anymore, now that is reality. I don't have anywhere to stay in this Ibadan. My family disowned me when I was sentenced. Throughout the eight years I was in there, I never had a visitor, not once. My fiancée did not even come to the court the day I was sentenced. I have to go on to Lagos, guys. That's my best shot." They all listened and looked at him soberly. He stretched out his hand to Akeem and shook him, then to Daolu who instead pulled him into his embrace and gave him a hug, and then he turned to face Moses.

Moses told him, "Koja, it's been eight good years. You can't just leave like that. Come, stay with me."

"I have to go to Lagos." They then hugged, when they disengaged. "I pray when we meet again we have better stories to tell," Akeem said, and they all said amen.

"Better stories don't come easy, my brother," Koja said. "And that is if we ever see again. But if we do, may it taste like honey." They watched him as he took the next taxi and left for Iwo Road where he took a bus to Lagos.

CHAPTER FIVE

It was Idumota, Lagos, rowdy as usual, and the noise was also deafening. The blaring of motor horns, the yelling of various vendors and bus conductors, and the zooming of numerous vehicles of different shapes and sizes. It was a whole different world under the bridge, located right in the middle of Idumota. The people of the hustle and bustle of the business world, at the end of the day, left for where they came from. But the world under the bridge and its surroundings as it was during the day, so it was in the night. In reality, when it was dusk on the bridge, it was dawn under it. Callous, dirty, and as stinking as it might be under the bridge, from there have come some most beautiful, bold, and brainy people.

Miide had been caught cheating while gambling and angered the group. As he yelled back at them, they surrounded him; and being skinny, they overpowered him and beat him up, kicking and punching him as he covered his vital organs in defense. By the time they finished with him, he had a bleeding nose and a swollen mouth and was limping. All through the beating, he held on to the money he won; and when others tried, to no avail, to get the money from him, they gave up and kept beating him, until some older men of their world under the bridge pacified them. That is one of the daily experiences living in the environs of the Idumota Bridge.

Miide had always been the best in picking pockets and stealing among his group because he was never caught or seen when doing so. At the end of the day when they were counting their proceeds, the rest of the group marveled at what Miide always brought in, which is usually about three to four times their own proceeds. Miide always had money—another reason he incurred envy and hate. Because of his frugality, he saved a lot. So even though they all lived under the bridge throughout each day, he had a rented room apartment of his own. He appeared every morning and disappeared at the end of the day, only to reappear the next morning again. None of the rest of the group ever knew where he lived or where he slept; as a matter of fact, they never knew he did not sleep under the bridge with them. This was because before he left in the nights, they would have been drunk to stupor and as high as heavens from smoking cannabis, all from the money they made from stealing and picking pockets. And he would have arrived early enough in the morning to buy them breakfast, as usual, as they would have been broke again.

Miide grew up at the orphanage. He had been told the story that he was found between his mother's legs at birth, kicking in blood, under the bridge as she had passed away. It had taken him time to really digest this story as he grew up at the orphanage. He was a very brilliant lad, he got enrolled at the primary classes at the age of ten, and he performed brilliantly. He finished his primary education and got into high school. On his first day in school after school hours, he was expected back at the orphanage at lunchtime, but he wasn't seen, and for some time, nobody seemed to be really bothered. The proprietor of the orphanage was thinking he must be back in school somewhere studying, but when it was getting late, the proprietor took it up and went to the school to see if there were any students left, but there was none. The school security men informed them that even they had left the school at about five o'clock. Just then the proprietor looked at her wristwatch and saw that it was seven o'clock.

Then the proprietor asked the men if they had seen any boy who met Miide's description, but when the men heard he was a first year student, they said it was not possible they knew any new boy of that age. The proprietor and the two other young women who followed her thanked the security men and left the school for the police station closest to the school and the orphanage. At the station, they filed in a report of the missing boy and wrote their statement. After one of the two officers on duty that evening had filed their report, he advised them to come back in the morning, that it was getting late and that there was nothing that could be done that evening. He then asked them to bring the boy's photograph to the station when they returned the next morning. As they returned to the orphanage that night, they looked and searched every nook and cranny of the roadsides that led to the school from the orphanage, all to no avail. On getting to the orphanage the proprietor called a general prayer on behalf of Miide.

Meanwhile, Miide was at a friend's house. He had followed him home after school hours. When it was getting late and everybody was dispersing, Dapo, one of Miide's classmates, invited him to his home. He had promised to walk him back to the orphanage that evening after dinner. Miide had seen it as a good idea before Dapo even finished talking and consented delightedly. It was getting dark when they got to Dapo's house, and knowing Dapo's mother would not welcome Miide at that hour, they both agreed that he should be sneaked in. Dapo took him to the back door to wait while he went back to the front door. He knocked on the front door, and after a while, his mom opened the door for him.

"Where have you been?" she demanded, returning to the kitchen from where she apparently came.

"School, Mommy," he answered.

"At this hour?" she exclaimed. "I know you've been playing football all day, that's why you're home late. Your father is going to hear about this when he comes, if you don't stop this late home coming."

He went into his room and changed from his school uniform. He started watching out for his mom to leave the kitchen. After a while, his mom moved to her bedroom, and Dapo moved swiftly, almost sprang to the kitchen; he opened the door for Miide who, almost shouting, demanded, "What have you been doing since?"

"Shuush," Dapo said, putting his finger to his lips to tell Miide to be quiet. "Inside, inside!" he said, only audible enough for Miide. He stepped in, and Dapo pushed him toward his room and locked him inside.

"Dapo?" his mom called just in time as she made her way to the kitchen.

He murmured, "Yes, Mom," and followed her to the kitchen. His mother served his food and handed the plate to him. He took it and went back to his room. When he opened the door, Miide hid behind it, and Dapo looked around the room in shock, and then he saw him. "Why are you hiding from me in my house?"

"I thought it was your mom." They both sat on the floor to eat the *eba*.

"What about your daddy?" Miide asked when they were finished.

"He works outside of town. He only comes home fortnightly."

Dapo squatted on the floor but got up and left for the kitchen to get them water.

"When you took your food, didn't you take water? Meaning you haven't taken water since you started eating?" his mom queried when she saw him carry only his plate without a cup. "Have you finished eating already?" she was surprised.

"Yes, Mommy, I ate fast. I've been very hungry." He headed for the kitchen, avoiding eye contact with his mom. Back to the room, they both looked at the clock on the wall at the same time and looked back at each other. It was late, and Dapo knew his mom will not give any chances for Miide to move out. Dapo didn't have to say a word, and Miide knew he was sleeping there for the night. Dapo persuaded his younger brother to go and sleep in their mother's room, and he obliged. He locked himself and Miide in so his mom would not bump into the room unexpectedly.

The next day was a Saturday, and they had planned that when they finished breakfast, Miide will go out through the back door and pose as if he was just coming in through the front door on a visit. Right before they could carry out their plan, Dapo's mom sat in the living room all through the day and shuttled just between the kitchen and the living room. The few times she went to the bedroom, they didn't have enough time to move out. Before they knew it, Miide had his lunch and later his supper. The next day was Sunday. Miide thought his sojourn at Dapo's place had come to an end, but by the time they were ready for church, they still had not been able to manipulate their way out the back door. Dapo's mother seemed to be all over the place. "I think you're going to be locked in till we come back from church," said Dapo.

"Why, can't I go out through the back door while you're gone?" Miide asked.

"Don't even think about it, and who will lock the door from the inside when you're gone? When I get back, we'll think of a way to get you out of here."

"You talk as if I came here of my own will. What do you mean by 'getting me out of here'?"

"Of course, you came here of your will, even though I invited you! Now, let's make use of the time we'll be in church. Take off your dirty school uniform and put on any of my clothes. There should be some detergent in the bathroom. Wash your uniform there while we're gone, then hang them in my wardrobe here when you finish. And please do everything quietly. Our neighbors don't go to church," Dapo ordered.

"You know, I'm happy I am out of the orphanage for a change. I only wish I was freer because I don't get this caged at the orphanage home. I don't mind spending a week here, if only we could be out all day having fun, playing football and all sorts," Miide confessed, grimacing. Dapo looked as if he was going to shout when he heard his mom call.

"Dapo! Dapo!" his mom screamed before he could reply to Miide.

"Yes, Mom. I'm coming," he replied.

"Are you not going to church anymore, or do you want me to lock you in?"

"Wow, that would be the brightest idea I've had in two days," he mumbled as he rushed out to his mom. He watched as his mom locked the doors and dropped the keys in her bag. *I hope this boy leaves no clue for my mom to notice!* he thought.

"Dapo?"

"Yes, Mom."

"I've been getting really uneasy with your attitude these last few days. You've been acting rather strange. Is anything wrong with you?"

"No, Mom, I'm fine, completely fine," he answered, looking away from his mother.

"Are you sure nothing is bothering you? You seem distracted. You know you can tell me if something is wrong."

"I know, Mommy, but really, nothing is wrong with me!" he said convincingly, still avoiding eye contact. His mom looked at him from behind and shook her head in worry.

By the time Dapo's family came back from church, the rest of the day was no different from the previous day. Dapo's mother sat on the cane chair at the main entrance of the house facing the kitchen door. When Dapo told Miide of this development, Miide asked, "Does your mother ever sleep?" At supper time, as Dapo was taking the plate containing his food to his room, his mom called him.

"Dapo?"

"Yes, Mom."

"We don't need to talk about yesterday and the day before yesterday, but would you tell me why all of a sudden you have started eating in your room?"

"Mommy, tomorrow is Monday, and I have not done my homework. I just want to look through it while I eat."

"Okay, I didn't know why, dear, but it's not a good idea trying to study and eat at the same, you know."

"I know, Mom, I'll be fine," he said and went into his room. The moment he got in, "Fast, get in there, get into that wardrobe fast," he whispered at Miide who was always sitting very close to the wardrobe. Miide went quietly into the wardrobe. Dapo then put his plate of food on the table and quickly withdrew a book from his bag and waited. Nothing happened. Miide was running out of patience. "Just wait!" Dapo whispered, and five minutes later, Dapo's mom walked in quietly. Dapo pretended he didn't notice, looking seriously at his book. When his mom had looked round his room well enough, she spoke.

"Dapo, why don't you finish with your food before you start with your homework? Your food will get cold."

"Okay, Mom, I'll do that." The mom left, smiling to herself. "Come out, boy, she's gone."

Miide slowly pushed the wardrobe door open, and when Miide came in to Dapo's full view, he asked, "How did you know she would come?" His mouth was wide open.

"That's why she's my mom. I know her."

"If I had a mom, could I know her this much?"

"Come and eat, boy, it's getting cold. Talking about your mom, you've never told me anything about your parents. Were you told anything about them?" Dapo asked.

"No, nothing. I don't know, and I wasn't told anything. Can we concentrate on our food, please?"

For the rest of that day, they could not think of any way to move Dapo's mom from her sitting position, so they gave up hope for that day. They were thinking of the next day, which was a Monday, when they both had to be in school. Miide sat at the edge of the wardrobe door. All he had to do if Dapo's mom showed up suddenly was to pull in his legs and lean back into the wardrobe. They both sat together and kept thinking on how to get Miide out the next morning. And after a long silence, Miide came up with a plan.

"What time does your mom wake up?" he asked.

"Six o'clock. Why?"

"When will she take her bath?"

"Why do you want to know?" Dapo asked, frowning.

"What's the problem with you! Just answer my question. When does she get into the bathroom?"

"She gets up six, quickly puts something on fire after her morning prayer, then I think she wakes me around six thirty to do some sweeping, and then she wakes my little brother and bathes him. After that, I think she goes to the kitchen to check on her cooking, and then she comes to take the broom from me to finish up the sweeping while I go take a bath. As soon as I'm done, she would take her bath while I and my brother get dressed. I think that should be around seven. So?"

"Good. I won't be taking my bath tomorrow. I can't anyway even if I want to. As a matter of fact, with the kind of bath I had this morning after missing my bath yesterday, I don't think I should be needing another bath for a day or two. So the moment she gets into the bathroom tomorrow morning, Dapo? How many ears do you have? I'm out of here. Only if your mom would not be taking her bath tomorrow will I not leave your house, and I don't think that would happen." He made a funny face. "Or can it happen?"

"Watch your mouth, it's my mom you are talking about."

"Sorry."

"And you've been eating her food for the past two days."

Their plan worked out. The next morning, Miide left for school earlier after promising Dapo that he would not expose what happened to anyone if asked at the school or at the orphanage.

Miide got to school before anybody else, and as he showed up at the school gate, the security men wondered why a boy his age should be out of home that early morning. When school eventually resumed, he was summoned to the principal's office and was questioned, but Miide never said where he was for a whole weekend.

The police were informed by noon that same day. Different people had so many questions targeted at Miide, but he stood like a statue before them and didn't say a word. Afterward, he was taken to the police station and was really threatened to tell them where he had been for almost three days. He was detained there for the rest of the day but without any results. At the end of the day, at the orphanage, a prayer was said for him. He wondered what his homemates would give to live in a real home with a family and to see the outside world, being as free as anybody else in society.

I can't stay in here, he thought and closed his eyes as the prayer came to an end. Barely a month later, he visited another friend whose parents were not in, so it was his friend's elder brother who took charge of the house. He was gladly welcomed and went about freely, having all the fun he never had at the orphanage as they visited a lot of places; and before he knew it, he had spent two weeks out of school. When he eventually returned, he was punished severely; and afterward, he told himself, *One more time and I am gone.*

Despite his nonchalant attitude toward education, it was as if he was becoming more brilliant. He had two double promotions even in high school. The school had no choice. After the first term in every class, it was apparent that he had gone beyond the syllabus and that he was otherwise being drawn back. So at age fourteen, he sat for the General Certificate Examination and made all his papers. The night he got his results, he left the orphanage. He believed he needed to be free, and he took to the streets to get his freedom. It was rough for him at first, but he fought, and he survived. Now a young man at twenty-two years, he had his reputation and was respected for it.

So after that thorough beating, he got up to his feet and looked at his wristwatch for the time, but his wristwatch was gone; he staggered a little, trying to steady his head with his left hand. He then looked at the content of his right hand and for a moment grinned and started walking away slowly, avoiding looking around. He knew the guys were still watching him, and when he got out of sight, he arranged the money and put it in his pocket. He looked up to the sun.

"I should go and see Kachi now," he said as he walked on, a little faster now since the guys were no more in view.

Usman had been waiting patiently on his hospital bed for the doctor, so the moment the doctor walked in, he didn't waste any more time. He attacked him, yelling, "Doctor, Doctor!" He kept calling as the doctor walked toward him smiling. He stood in front of him, looking at him without saying a word. "When I came in here, you told me I wasn't in such a bad shape, and so I won't be staying for long. Now it's been two weeks. Did you lie to me then or you have forgotten me here?" he asked.

"I didn't lie to you then, and I've not forgotten you either!" replied the doctor.

"Why am I still here then," he demanded again.

"Because we were not through with you then, that's why," the doctor said.

"You were not?" he asked again.

"Yes, we were not, but now we are through with you, and you can go home."

"Do you mean that?"

"Of course, I do."

"Then how about this POP on my arm?" Usman asked.

"You can get back here in about three months if you can. Otherwise, you can go to a chemist, and the pharmacist can get it off for you. Do not take it off before two months please."

"Thank you, Doctor," he was saying as he stepped down from the bed, "and I don't think, Doctor, that I would be needing these crutches anymore."

"The physiotherapist told me you're doing well with your legs. He said you can now walk without them, but I will advise you still continue on them for a while, maybe two more weeks, and later you can switch to a walking stick." The doctor looked round at the other patients, turned, and left the ward. "I wish you a wonderful reunion with your family, Officer," the doctor added as he walked out.

Usman sat still at the edge of the bed at that instance, as if he had just been reminded of something dreadful. He bowed his head looking at the floor; then after a while, he reached for his sack bag, opened it, and looked through but not for anything in particular. He called on a nurse and asked for his clothes that he had sent to the laundry. The nurse left to get it. When she returned with his clothes, he took them, and the nurse covered him with the hospital demarcations so that he could change into his clothes. When he was ready, he checked if the money he had could get him to Okene, Kogi State, where he hoped his family will still be in one piece in their home. Then one of the nurses called from the end of the hall, "Officer, when you're ready, let us know so we can sign you out."

"Okay," he replied moodily. He took another look at the bed and started walking down the hall to the nurses' desk, and after signing the papers, he walked back through the ward where the other patients bade him farewell. *If only they knew how much within the past ten minutes I have felt like not going home anymore, they would not be wishing me any good-bye.* He was in deep thought as he found his way out not responding to their greetings.

He reached for the bulky envelope in his bag and checked the money again. He still had more than twenty thousand naira, and so much people had told him, "Nobody hits you on the Maryland–Ojota road and stops to pick you up. It's always a hit and run, so you're lucky to have been hit by a good Samaritan." The man had packed immediately, and as people rallied round him, they picked him up together and put him in his car. He rushed him to the nearest private hospital, and after about an hour, he had gained consciousness. After another hour, all test results were ready. The doctor had told the man who had hit him that he wasn't in such a bad shape, that he would be okay. The man explained to the doctor that he was in a hurry when the whole thing happened, and he still had to get to where he was going. So the man asked the doctor how much his treatment would cost, but the doctor wasn't really specific and had asked for an initial payment of ten thousand naira. The man gave him twenty thousand naira and his complimentary card. He apologized greatly to Usman who wasn't sure what he was saying and explained things to him, hoping he understood. He came back two days later and then a week later again, making sure he was being fed. So when he came the second time after he had tried to help Usman trace the address he was coming to in Lagos to no avail, Usman spoke to him. "Mr. Osintola, I know you are a very busy man, and it is rather unfortunate this incident happened to you. I must confess you have really tried for me. After all, the accident was really my fault, and I've also been told you are a very nice man to have picked me up and brought me to the hospital. I have been told it doesn't happen. Now the doctor has told me of all the down payments you have made and that you are going to cover my treatment till I leave here, so I beg you to stop coming. Face your business, and I pray you are repaid for your kindness. When I leave here, I'll find my way home."

Mr. Osintola at first refused the offer but later obliged. He gave Usman another twenty-five thousand naira and his complimentary card. He told Usman to see him when he had fully recovered, then he prayed for Usman, and that was when Usman knew he was a Christian. He kept the money back in his bag and wondered what was happening at home as he had been away for two weeks. He walked out of the hospital compound and took a taxi to Ojota, getting in as slowly as he could. When he got to Ojota, he boarded a bus to Kogi, his home.

CHAPTER SIX

Kachi had been working all day. Since she resumed in the morning, she had felt her boss's stares on her every step she took. She kept doing all the work she could find around the canteen, taking every order, clearing the tables, and cleaning them and even doing some other extra work. If she had waited to take just a deep breath, her boss would tongue-lash her for trying to take any break from work. At times when some customers noticed her running around, they tried to caution her for fear that she would get weary and faint one day because she had become so thin and frail. But she dared not stay long enough to listen to them or her boss would think she was trying to flirt with the men. And when the men called the attention of her boss to her excessive hard work, the madam gave them the insults of their lives.

She told the men that nobody gave her the money to start her business, and nobody will teach her how to run it. Her cruelty to Kachi was so conspicuous that the rest of her waitresses took it as an excuse to be lax, knowing Kachi would not dare to leave any work undone. She had started working at the Paput Food Canteen for about two months, and she didn't find it easy compared with the other places she had worked. She had been jinxed, she thought, because none of her bosses ever liked her in all the places she had worked. In total, she had worked at two hair salons and three food canteens. She preferred the food canteens because of the tips she got from the customers. This new madam usually cursed her and her parents.

This caused her to often reminisce on the sad event that deprived her of the joy of growing up with her parents. Eight years ago, she lived with her parents in Kaduna. Her dad was a teacher and a part-time pastor, and her mom was a trader. She was very tiny in stature at age ten, and she was the only child of her parents. Being an only child and because of her unique beauty, she was loved very much by her parents and friends. She had a very likable demeanor, the more reason she wondered why she was hated now that she was grown. Her father taught at the Sunday school, but she usually went late to church with her mom, always wanting to sit at the back unnoticed. Kachi's mother was Igbo and her father, Hausa, a union both her parents' families never consented to. Hence, her mother lived far from the reach of her people, and this was the reason why Kachi never knew anybody from her mother's family in the east. This alienation extended to Kaduna where they lived. Kachi's mother wasn't liked very much, even in the church. Kachi grew to be very God loving and industrious, a quality her parents cherished in her so much. She would wake her mother up early in the morning with the sound of her sweeping, and as her mom was then pregnant with her second child, she cared for her mother well. She was anxious to have a sibling so she could have someone to care for.

Kachi attended a primary school not too far from home, so she walked to school with the other children from the neighborhood. Before she left every morning, her mother would say to her, "God go with you," and she would make Kachi reply, "God remain with you." And so they said to each other that day, and after she had gone, there was an uproar. Before they knew what was happening, it was rather too late. It was a religious riot, and every clergy in the city became a prey. It happened so fast that Kachi's parents were trapped in the house and could not go out. Her mother wanted to run to her school for her, but her husband held her back and comforted her, telling her all they could do was to pray for her and hope the riot didn't get to the school. But while they waited, since they lived in the enemy's territory, the rioters broke into their house, killed them both, and burned the house down with their bodies in it. The riot eventually got to the school, and some of their teachers were killed, but the pupils were spared since they didn't know which ones were Christians or Muslims. Before then, one of Kachi's aunties who taught at her school had sought her out and fled with her. By the time she got out of the school and saw what the city looked like, she knew there was no home either for herself or for Kachi to return to. She had to join the crowd, and she ran in the same direction everyone else ran. As they ran, she saw, not too far away, Kachi's home; and every other house in that neighborhood all burned down. She then realized she was holding her. She stopped to pick her up and carried her on her back so she could run well. With tears in her eyes but not a sound, she thronged along with the stampede in the direction of the motor park. As she ran, she was going too fast and suddenly stumbled, falling directly on the sharp edge of a broken bottle. It tore into her stomach by her side. She screamed, and Kachi's weight further pressed her on the bottle. For a moment, she lay still. She remembered she was fleeing, so she got to her knees first, and very swiftly without looking, she pulled out the broken bottle and let it drop to the ground.

Kachi's auntie feared that she could be trampled on by the stampede, so she quickly jumped to her feet and continued running. She was bleeding, but she didn't know it. As they got to the bus park, she sighted a lorry that was almost full;

not knowing where it was bound for, everybody mounted the back of the lorries that were there. Any other place was better than Kaduna that sad day. Now settled at the back of one of the lorries, she held Kachi to her side and held her stomach with her other hand. "Kachi, everything will be okay." she said, agonizing. She did not say anything more to Kachi. She held her to her side tightly; it was a long and quiet afternoon at the back of the lorries that were in a convoy, loaded with people who had survived the Kaduna mayhem. The lorry they boarded, unknown to them, was a goods truck headed for Lagos.

After all the series of police roadblocks and checkpoints, the convoy arrived in Lagos at 1:00 a.m.; and when it pulled to a stop, Kachi woke up at her auntie's side. The door was let down, and people were alighting from the vehicles. Kachi shook her aunt to wake up. She shook her again and again, then her auntie's body slumped. She still held on to her auntie's clothes, shaking her. "Auntie, the lorry has stopped," she said to her auntie in Hausa dialect. When she got no response, she kept repeating herself, and she shook her even more. A woman then approached Kachi and said to her, "She's dead. Your mother is dead." Thinking she didn't understand her, she repeated herself in Hausa, "Yaya mutu," and she rubbed her head and left her.

Kachi looked back to her auntie and continued shaking her, starting to cry. Just then she thought she heard someone crying, and when she turned in that direction, she saw a woman crying over her dead husband, and then she realized what the woman had told her. She held on tightly to the corpse of her aunt and cried quietly but profusely, wondering with angry eyes why her auntie had taken her away from her parents in such a hurry. *At least we could have gone to call my mommy and daddy at home so we can run away from the trouble together,* she thought. The driver and some men came and carried the two corpses out of the truck, gathering them together with the other dead bodies from the other trucks. The truck driver then collected his fare from the passengers he had brought, but when he came to Kachi's turn, he had to exempt her seeing she was with no one. The people gathered together at first, and Kachi, not knowing what to do or where to go, just stayed by them, and when they eventually fell into groups as they knew each other, she sat with a group. It was still dark, so she was not noticed, and everybody had to stay in the Lagos Park till daybreak. All over the garage that night, there were moanings and wailings of anguish, but Kachi found solace; she slept.

By the time she woke up in the morning, a quarter of the people had dispersed. She saw that she still had her auntie's handbag by her side, then she looked at the group she had slept with and realized it was half of a family, and they were mourning the rest of their family they had lost in the riot. What was left of that family was the mother and two sons. The people became fewer as many had left the park. When the family she was with was leaving, she knew she had to leave too. She carried her auntie's handbag, fell on her knees, and said her prayers. She felt bad sleeping off without saying her prayers before she slept. Most Lagosians were arriving already, including the National Union of Road Transport Workers, the petty traders, and the travelers. After her prayers, Kachi began walking behind another group, pretending she was following them so that she would not be noticed to be alone. She walked on and on and on, until she became tired and hungry. She didn't know where she was; all she knew was that she was in Lagos. She saw a market ahead and walked on toward it. She saw a lot of things she would have loved to eat, but she had no money, or so she thought until she felt her auntie's bag by her side again. There were a bunch of keys, cosmetics, handkerchief, and some money. She counted the money; and it was sixty naira, two twenty naira, and two ten naira notes. She took a ten naira note and bought some biscuits and yogurt, and she had some change left. She left the market by the back where there was a bridge not too far. She walked there carrying her meal and then settled down to eat, away from the noise in the market.

She sat on the pavement of one of the pillars of the bridge, looked around, and started eating her biscuit. As soon as she started, she saw two long legs in front of her, very worn-out jeans, and slovenly looking boots. She stopped chewing on her biscuit and slowly started raising her head. When her head was fully raised, she was terrified by what she saw. She had not seen anybody or anything aside from the violence she witnessed in Kaduna that was as scary as what was before her. The rest of her biscuit and yogurt fell to the ground; she looked into his eyes, afraid and confused.

"What do you have in that bag?" the man asked her, but she did not reply. "I said what do you have in your bag?" he repeated. When she did not answer again, he pulled the bag away from her; and as she had worn the strap of the bag, she rolled over when he pulled it. He looked through, took the rest of the money there, and threw the bag back at her.

"Where is your mother?" She did not respond, so he asked again. She nodded her head as if to say yes and murmured something in Hausa. She was terrified. Then she tried to speak English, but it did not make sense to the young man.

"If you or your mom knows what's best for you, you won't be where you are, or do you see anybody cross over from the market to this place?" he said and started walking away. He stopped and went back to her. He looked her over for a moment and again asked her about her mother. Then he started walking away again, then he stopped and looked back. "Where are you going?" he asked. She shook her head. "Where will you sleep tonight then?" he asked again, and she shook her head again. The boy looked up and looked down, rubbed his head, and bit his lower lip. He looked at her again and again, and then he turned and went back to her. "Have you eaten today?" She shook her head again. "I actually thought my mom was heartless. I say your mom is worse. If she wanted you to live under the bridge, she should have abandoned you since birth instead of letting you grow to know her before she abandoned you. Come on now, let's go, but you have to really promise me you won't give me any trouble till I have the time to take you to the orphanage. I don't think it is the best place for you though, but being here will be worse for you." Then he took her by the arm, and she followed him.

"You want to know the real reason I'm doing this? Looking at you, I could tell that you have no mother anymore," he said and giggled. "What's your name?" he asked and looked down into her face as they walked along, "Kachi," she replied, feeling a bit elated. The boy looked into her face with surprise as if he wasn't expecting an answer to his question.

"What is your name?" she asked back timidly. The boy laughed out briefly, raising up his chin, and looked down at her eyes again.

"Miide, Miide, that's my name," he said. "First thing, let's go get you some food, then we can hear your story later. I know with enough patience I can listen and understand you, because I know you understand me."

Later that day, after Miide took Kachi to eat, he got into a fight; he cheated while gambling and was beaten up by the guys he played with. All the while he sat Kachi down at a corner to watch from there. After the guys were done beating him and he lay there almost unconscious, she went over, tried her best to raise him to his feet, and helped him to his bed space under the bridge as he directed her. There she took care of him.

Miide's bed space under the bridge had only a torn paper carton, and it was not big enough for two people, so that night he left it for Kachi and slept on the ground while she slept. He wondered why she fell asleep so fast and so early. He looked into her face and observed her beauty. She was thin, seemed fragile, but strong, he deduced. *I will listen to her story tomorrow. Everyone that comes here always has a story,* he thought.

He grew to like her and afterward grew to love her as his sister. He taught her a few things, like training her to spy on opponents' card for him while gambling and using her as a distraction for the market women while he stole from them, but Kachi wouldn't learn. After about two years that Kachi arrived, Miide saved enough money and got a room in the slum of Idumagbo. There he lived with Kachi as his sister to keep her safe from harm under the bridge. Miide got her a job at the hair salon and took her away from the salon because her boss was always beating her. He got her another job, and she complained about the same thing. Miide knew beauticians had a bit of problem with beautiful trainees because they thought they were all flirts. This was why he thought the food canteen would be different, but it wasn't, a little better though, but Kachi still complained, so Miide made it a point of duty to always check on her at work.

It's been eight years now since they met under the bridge. They had been living together for eight years; they had dined and wined together, laughed and cried together, sorrowed and rejoiced together. When Miide got to Kachi's place of work, he walked straight to the kitchen through the back door. When the other staff saw him, they became uncomfortable as usual. This was mainly because of his reputation. Now aged twenty-six, he was tall, and people dreaded looking at him. Knowing what they made Kachi go through at work, he made it a duty to always frighten them whenever he came around. Kachi, who was eighteen, was elated to see Miide; apparently she was the only one who felt happy by his arrival.

"How are you?" Miide asked her. "I hope that witch has not beaten you today?" he added, looking into the eyes of the rest of the staff, ensuring they heard him.

"No," she replied, covering Miide's mouth with her hand before the rest of the girls could hear him refer to their boss as a witch.

"I'm fine and almost through. Will you wait for me outside?" she asked him.

"No! I'll wait for you right here."

"No, don't get me into trouble. My boss will kill me later when you're not there," she protested. So when she looked like she was going to cry, Miide left to wait outside. While waiting, he saw a man alighting from a taxi, paying the taxi driver from his wallet. From where Miide stood, he could see the contents of the wallet; it was stuffed with money. The man walked on after he had paid. Seeing the direction he was going, Miide crossed to the other side of the road and ran ahead of the man; he ran far beyond him. He looked back and saw the man walking leisurely. He then crossed back to the side of the road the man was and started running toward him. He ran fast and ran into the man as if he was in pursuit or being pursued. The man fell to the ground, and so did everything he was carrying: his folder under his arm, a leather bag, and a cellophane bag that he carried in each hand.

"I'm very sorry, sir. I'm very, very sorry, sir. I was only running after a man that left with my change," Miide apologized and started helping the man to his feet. When the man was on his feet and steady, he began picking his things for him before the people passing by could trample on them. When he had picked all the things, he brought them to the man and apologized soberly.

"That is okay. I think I'm fine. Thanks for picking my things," the man said.

"Once again, I'm very sorry, sir, I didn't mean to—" The man then cut in.

"I know, but I'm actually impressed by what you did. You stayed to get me up and picked my things. Some other children would have just run away without looking back," the man commented, collected his things, and left.

"Thank you, sir. Bye-bye, sir," Miide said, turned, and started walking away in the opposite direction. He brought the man's wallet out of his pocket, took the money inside, and, without looking back, tossed the wallet back on the spot the man had fallen.

"He might need the other contents of his wallet," he said and left. When he got back to Kachi's workplace, she had been waiting for him. "I didn't say you should go and come back. I only said you should wait outside," she complained. Miide did not reply, but he brought out the money he just got out of his pocket and gave it to her.

"Keep that for me, will you?" he said and walked ahead of her. Surprised, Kachi looked from the contents of her hand to Miide. "Where did you get this from?" she asked, not moving.

"Are you coming or not?" Miide demanded, and Kachi started catching up with him still shouting.

"I said where did you get this from, henn . . . hen? I'm asking you a question. Where did you get this from? Is this what you went for just now, hen . . . ?" Then she started pulling him to stop, but he didn't oblige.

"Miide, please, I thought I told you to stop this? We can live on whatever I make." She was now holding on to his clothes and very close to tears. "Whatever you make indeed!" He looked at her helplessly and held her close. "Come on, let's go. Okay, I'll stop. I mean it this time around. I'll stop, okay? Now stop crying in public and let's go home."

When they got home, Kachi was still very upset with Miide; she sat alone and did not venture to prepare anything for them to eat, knowing that was what Miide was expecting.

"Kachi?" Miide called her, but she did not answer. "Kachi?"

"Yes! What is it? Leave me alone!" she replied furiously.

"There are still a lot of things you don't understand," Miide said. "We live on the streets, Kachi, and you can't deny that. We live on the street, by the street, and for it! What else can we do? I'm doing all this for you. I can starve to death but not you."

"I know you're doing it because of me, and that is why I hate it! I'm no more a little girl now, and I can endure if we decide to live on what I make, Miide." She was staring at the floor. "Hmm, hmm, the reason, the reason is, I'm scared, Miide, I'm scared. What if something happens to you someday? What if, Miide? What if? With all the burning of thieves and armed robbers in Lagos, you're the only one I have, my brother, the only one." She started crying, reaching out to him; he hugged her.

"We have only each other, but nothing will happen to me, I promise you. I won't leave you alone, never. That's okay now. Let's find something to eat please," Miide consoled her.

"Miide, you know what?" She started wiping her eyes. "I could talk to my church pastor. He's been praying well for me lately. Perhaps he could help you get a job."

"Oh my god! I hope you've not been talking to that pastor of yours about me?"

"No . . . o . . . o, I've not . . . oh, it's just that . . ." She trailed away.

"That what? That what, I ask? If you know you want to keep going to that church, better stay clear of that pastor, okay?" he shouted angrily at her, and she knew better than to get him angry.

"Yes, I've heard you."

"Prayer, prayer, the same prayer that did not save you when you needed help most as a child: the same prayer that has refused to feed you and the same prayer that cannot help you retain your jobs. I wonder when you'll get tired of praying to the same god, or whomever. I am sure you bore him."

"No, I don't! He hasn't complained yet, and he hears me!" she shouted and stormed out of the room.

"Thank you very much, my sister, I appreciate it," Ben said to the waitress who was now busy attending to other customers and so could not hear him. *I hope my landlord would be sleeping by now or at least in bed,* he thought. *This is nine thirty, and I have to get home before they lock the front door. I will have to call on the landlord himself to come and open the door for me, and that means I will be sleeping outside. Let me just go. I'll sneak in from the back.* He walked on slowly.

He got into his room as he had planned and quietly locked the door behind him. He hung his jacket, loosened the button of his shirt, and kicked off his boots. He fell on his buttocks on the mattress and reached to the corner of the room, pulled out a small bag containing *garri* (cassava grains), emptied it into a small bowl of water, and left it for some minutes. He was looking at the bowl as if some magic was going to come out of it.

"This garri doesn't rise well at all," he complained and picked up a spoon from where his bowl had been. He started scooping the garri into his rather dry mouth, at first slowly and then very fast. When he was through, he gulped the rest of the water and fell on his back. A few minutes later, he was snoring.

CHAPTER SEVEN

"Ladies and gentlemen, in a few minutes the aircraft would be landing at the Murtala Muhammed International Airport of the Nigeria Airways, Lagos. Please be seated and fasten your seat belts. Once again, you're welcome to the Federal Republic of Nigeria. Thank you for your patience and patronage." Charles was startled and awoke from his sleep. He had been lost in thought and had slept off since he left the shores of America, the country he had lived in for eight years and had served as his homeland. He had worked, had gotten married, and had a child in America. He never thought of returning to Nigeria. Even if he had, he definitely didn't think it would be this soon and in this manner. Worst of all, he wasn't allowed to pick anything from his home, that is if he still had any; he had no single luggage, no bag, nothing. He was empty handed.

Where do I go? He resumed his deep thoughts. *To the same family I betrayed when I left? They mustn't see me. If they do, it will be worse than all I've been through already. My uncle and cousins will kill me for selling the family house! And to which friend will I go? When I've not made a call to any of them since I left?* He sighed deeply, holding firmly to the armrest of his seat as the plane touched the ground.

As he walked out of the airport into Nigeria that evening, he wondered how he would move from the airport if he eventually thought of a possible place to go. He checked the time; it was 7:30 p.m. He stood aside and watched the orderliness at the entrance of the airport, how families were being reunited as they saw each other again after long periods. *How sweet it would have been to have people welcome me today,* he thought and put his hands in his pockets. He felt something in his left pocket and quickly brought it out. It was two hundred and twenty dollars. He wondered how it had gotten there and then realized he had not put either of his hands in his pockets since he was released about twenty-four hours ago. *It must be the money left in my pocket since the day I was arrested. Of course it is.* He smiled. He checked the rest of his pockets, but they were empty. So he folded the money and kept it in his pocket again. He was in deep thought for a while and then brought out the money again, took the twenty-dollar bill from it, and returned the rest into his pocket as he walked toward the car park. There were the Hausas, the money changers. They were whistling to him, beckoning on him.

"You wan change money?" one of them asked him.

"Yeah, how much is a dollar?" Charles asked.

"Na ninety naira for one dollar."

"Ninety? The naira gone that bad?" he exclaimed, bewildered.

"Oga, the naira done bad o, e don bad very well," the Hausa man replied.

"All right then, can I have the twenty dollars changed then?" He showed him the money.

"Na small denomination and small amount, e no be good business—," the Hausa man began to say when just before he could finish his statement, Charles cut in, "Don't give me that crap now. You just told me the damn thing is ninety. How come you saying bullshit again? You are a thief."

"Oga, I no be thief. Small denomination na bad business. If you get more make you bring am make I change everything for you now. I fit change am for eighty-seven."

"Forget it, I'll go ahead and change my money in town," Charles declared, and just then another money changer joined them, still a Hausa man.

"Oga, any *froplem*?" he asked with a very concentrated Hausa intonation.

"Yeah, your friend here is trying to cheat me!" Charles jabbed his index finger at the man he had been speaking with, so the man turned to the other guy and spoke to him in Hausa.

Smiling and turning slowly to face Charles, the other guy said, ""Oga, now I understand. You see, when your money is a small denominash-ion, it lowers the value, and when the amount is small, it lowers the value in the market. So it's not our fault. It's the system, but I will plead with him to change it for you at eighty-seven naira to one dollar if that is all you want to change. But if you have more, I will advise you change it now because this is the best market you can get in Lagos."

He looked at the two of them suspiciously and held out the twenty dollars. "This is all I want to change."

"Thank you, sir," the man who joined them later said and walked away.

"How much will that be?" Charles asked.

"I dey come, sir." He brought out his calculator and punched it a number of times.

"Na one thousand seven hundred and forty naira."

"Let me have it now." He got the money, and as he was about to leave, the man called him, "Oga, the time I tell you say one dollar done turn ninety naira, you do as if say you no happy, and as I wan change am for you for less you vex, why now? I think say you for happy to change am for less to help the economy of Nigeria since you no happy say e don bad." Then he grinned and kept quiet.

"Was I the one who made the naira bad in the first place? Was it not you guys who have been around? And besides, who should be blaming who? Who sells the naira? You stupid fool."

He took the next taxi he saw and headed for town.

"Where to, sir?" the taxi driver asked.

"Just into town. I've not really made up my mind where I am going."

"Sir, it's getting really late, so I'll advise you make up your mind quick. This is Lagos, and you don't want to keep late nights," the taxi driver advised.

"Sorry, mister," said Charles, "but if I may ask, I cannot but notice your good command of English. What's your qualification?"

"Ah, I have my first degree in chemistry and my second degree in computer science."

"What did you say?" Charles almost shouted. "You have two degrees and what do you do for a living, you drive a taxi? Is this country getting worse or better?"

"For ten good years I have searched for a job, but I could not lay my hands on even the least of jobs. I was dying of hunger, and so I first started with Okada, you know, the motorcycle transport. I rode Okada for about two years, then I got someone who gave me this taxi to drive for him."

"You mean this car is not even yours?" Charles asked in dismay.

"Mine? Did you say mine? Who dash monkey banana? Where am I supposed to get the money to buy one? As a matter of fact, if I get the money to purchase my own automobile, I will just drive it myself doing the same thing because it pays more than having a monthly paid job. Now it is the owner of the car that enjoys my labor. I have to deliver my daily due, and whatever extra change I'm able to make is all I have for the day."

"My god, I didn't experience much of this. I left the country immediately after I finished my first degree, and I can't just believe it. You don't have a family, do you?" Charles asked.

"Why won't I? I am not a kid. It's stress and suffering that is making me diminish in size. I'm getting old. I will be forty in about two months, and I have two kids already."

"Oh my god, I can only imagine how you're coping."

"I will advise you not to settle down in this country. If you don't already have what you want to work with to engage yourself, just go back to wherever you're from and make enough money to establish a business that you can call your own."

They were both silent for a while as if they both needed time to ruminate on the taxi driver's last statement.

"We've driven around long enough, sir, and, it's high time I parked the car. I know a small hotel that will be convenient enough for you at least for tonight. Should I take you there?"

"That will be perfect," he said as he looked out of the window in silence. The driver took a few more turns and drove through a gateless fence. "Here we are, sir, Sunset Hotel. You'll like it here. It is cheap and comfortable. I actually suggested it since I noticed you don't have any luggage. I guess you won't be staying long in this our country."

"Yeah, you're right. I-I-I don't intend to stay long. I-I-I-I"—he looked around and at the entrance of the hotel—"I'll be going back very soon, yeah, very soon. Thank you very much, Mr. . . . ?"

"Obe, Mr. Sugun Obe."

"Well, Mr. Obe, thank you very much. I'm grateful." He shook the taxi driver's hands and turned to leave, but he noticed the driver held on to his hand, his other palm stretched.

"Oh my god, I haven't paid you. I'm sorry, how much did you say your money is?"

"Four hundred naira."

"Four hundred naira!" Charles shouted. "I didn't know it would be that much. You should have told me," he lamented, looking into the stone-cold face of the driver.

"All right, you can have it." He brought out the money he just changed and paid him. The driver collected it and recounted as he went back to the car and sped off. "He thought I would forget my money? Or he thought I spared him the fare just because we got familiar?" Mr. Obe said to himself. Charles stood there looking at the rest of the money in his hand; he returned it into his pocket and walked into the hotel.

There was a table and a chair, and that was supposed to be the reception.

"Hello here, hello, hello, hey, hey, anybody here?" He paused a moment. As he was contemplating walking out, a side door flung open, and a stout man walked in. On seeing him, the man ran up to him.

"Good evening, sir," he said, passing by Charles to get behind the desk. Charles moved aside for him. "Can I help you, sir? Room dey, very good rooms with convenience. We have two-thousand-naira room, then the ones for short time. Those ones you no fit use. The one for two thousand naira is okay for you." Then he looked up better to find that Charles wasn't listening to him but staring at him. He was looking at him like he was actually shorter than he really was.

"I bet you're the shortest guy I have ever seen. You're from Eskimo land or something? Damn!"

"Oga, wetin you talk." Charles spoke so fast, and with his American accent, it was difficult for the guy to understand him.

"That table must be so short, for you to be taller than it."

"Oga, wetin you talk," the man called again.

"How many of the two-thousand-naira rooms do you have?"

"Heeeey, na only one dey down now, that is good. E e only one is good now, but we have more than one. You can come and see that one."

"Wait, do you have water?"

"Yes, I go go fetch am for you. No problem with that."

"You have TV?"

"Ah nooo, we no get TV o o, but you can see we have light well well."

Yes, you do, obviously. With that deafening noise from behind the building, they have a generator set there, he thought.

"Oga, you go check that room, abi?"

"Shut up, will ya?" Charles snapped and walked out slowly.

Charles walked into the night, down the road; he checked his watch, and it was 11:30 p.m. It was getting quieter.

"For god's sake, I can't even see well. No streetlights, and even if there were, I still can't see into these wide drainages." His voice trailed away when he thought he heard footsteps approaching him; he wasn't sure from which direction. At first it sounded a bit far away, and then the footsteps started sounding closer and closer. Charles took to his heels and ran as fast as he could. He kept running into the darkness of the night. He wasn't afraid of the drainages anymore. Now, he was only afraid of the footsteps closing in on him. He kept running. *Looking back wouldn't make any sense,* he thought since he was sure he would not see whoever was after him in the dark. He thought of shouting, but again, it wouldn't make any sense; who would rescue him at this hour of the night? And that could even enrage his pursuer the more if they eventually caught up with him, he thought. He wasn't sure for how long he'd been running now, but he was sure it wasn't getting any easier for his pursuers than it was for him. The steps started fading away, but not stopping. He kept running, trying to increase the distance between him and the people behind him. He thought he saw a glimpse of brightness, dull though, to the right side of the road far ahead. He made it his target, and as he moved closer, it became brighter. It was light, and more like a lantern. He ran faster now. All his focus was now on the light. He wasn't even listening to the footsteps anymore. He was seeing an entrance; there was a wide doorway. He made the bend to the right. Heading for the entrance, down he plunged, falling into the drainage. He climbed out in a rush, as if nothing happened, running inside.

"Please help me, help me please!" he shouted, looking back.

"Yes, yes, what is it?" asked one of the men inside. He had calmed enough to notice they were in uniforms. He looked around quickly to discover he was in a police station. He held on to the long and high concrete desk, leaning on it to steady himself, regaining his breath, his chest rising and dropping.

"What is the matter, mister? What can we do for you? What was pursuing you?" another one of them asked, while another took a rifle and went to the door, his gun pointed, ready to shoot.

"Take it easy, mister, okay? Take it easy. You are in a police station now. Nothing will harm you in here," the policeman talking to him assured him. They left him to calm down, with their eyes fastened on him.

When he was calm enough, he looked at the policeman who talked to him, and he said, "Did you say relax when I ran in here?"

"Yes, because you are now in—"

Charles cut in, "Not even Daniel with all his experience in the lions' den would relax with what I've been through tonight!"

I've never done anything so energetic and unnerving in my whole life. I should have gone to the National Youth Service Camp before I ran away from Nigeria. I certainly regret it this day, he thought. Then another policeman emerged from a back office, and it was then that Charles counted them, and they were five.

"Are you only five in here? There is no way you could've been able to contend with those people chasing me if they had ventured to come in. No way!"

"But they didn't come in, did they? No! And that is because they know this is a police station."

"What if they had guns? How many guns do you have in here? I see only one, okay, and that one"—he pointed to one against the wall at the corner—"making two."

"Mister, if they had guns, I don't think they'll bother themselves this much before taking you down," another police said. Charles bowed his head a little as if trying to remember something.

"When you said 'take me down,' did you mean shoot me?"

"No, I meant romance you," the policeman said sarcastically, hissed. and walked away.

"Now," continued the man standing in front of him, "I want you to tell me all that happened tonight. What are you doing out this late and around this vicinity?"

Charles slept at the police station that night.

Kachi had been waiting for Miide for the past half hour. She didn't realize that she would be closing early from work, and she knew Miide would want to come over to walk her home as usual. To avoid missing him she decided to wait for him just outside the canteen while she looked at the flow of traffic of both people and motors. A Mercedes-Benz E-Class car pulled over by the side of the road where she was standing. At first, she didn't notice it, and then she saw it, and she thought the occupant was one of their numerous customers at the canteen. The occupant got out, and Kachi thought he beamed at her. He walked round the car and toward her. He was tall, dark, and slim but with the handsome face of a boy. He stood right in front of her and smiled down at her. He was patient, apparently shy, before speaking.

"H-h-hi, ah, ah." He scratched the back of his head with his car key. "Sorry, I mean, I-I drove past here about twenty minutes ago, and I thought I saw you standing here then." He paused, looking at the ground smiling. When he raised his head, he was looking at people passing by, or his eyes moved toward the traffic or his car; he wasn't nervous but shy, very shy. "And when I saw you on my way back now, I thought I should check if there is anything I could do. Hope there is no problem?" he asked in his very polished English, looking briefly into her eyes and backing off, still smiling. Kachi was looking into his eyes. She wasn't sure she heard all he said. She just wasn't sure what this kind of person was doing talking to her.

"I mean, what are you doing here, if I may ask?" He was still smiling.

"I work here," Kachi replied, pointing her thumb over her shoulder to the canteen.

"Oh, I see." He looked over Kachi's head at the closed door of the canteen. "It looks like you're closed for today?"

"Yes, I'm waiting for my brother."

"Well, you can't stand here all day. If you don't mind, I would like to take you home, I mean, to your own home, so I can know where you stay. By the way, my name is—" A very loud call interrupted him.

"Kachi, Kachi!"

Kachi looked in the direction of the voice and saw Miide beckoning to her from a corner. His signal seemed urgent from the distance, so she ran.

"Bye-bye, sir, that is my brother. I have to go," she looked back to say. When she got there, she could not see him anymore.

"Miide, Miide," she called out, then suddenly he grabbed her and pulled her into a corner.

"Miide, what is wrong with you? You look terrible. Where are you coming from? What is the problem?" she went on and on trying to get all the questions out at once. She was petrified.

"Nothing is wrong with me." He was bleeding on his right ear, but Kachi hadn't seen that.

"Just let us go home," he said, and they moved out, then Kachi noticed he was not walking well and his ear was bleeding.

"My god, you're bleeding." She held him close to give him support.

"I . . . I can walk." He cringed, breathing slowly. Kachi thought he must have felt a sharp pain when she held him. He was carrying something under his shirt at his armpit. Kachi walked on toward the road.

"No, not that way!" Miide yelled. "This way, we'll go behind these shops, through those houses, bypassing the bridge."

Kachi kept quiet and followed his orders, following him by his side with her tear-filled eyes fixed on him.

When they got home, Miide brought out what he had under his arm. It was a cellophane bag, portably wrapped. He gave it to Kachi. "Keep this, and please get me some pain relievers," he ordered, fell on his back, and lay down. Kachi unwrapped the cellophane bag, bringing out its contents. It was money, four bundles of crisp fifty naira notes.

"Miide, what is this?" she asked.

"My share, my share," he said and slept.

In front of the canteen, the young man watched Kachi as she ran away and could not believe it.

"The very first time I want to get a lady for myself and she ran away. At least this is the first time one would listen to me. Damn! How am I supposed to see her again?" He touched his head and started walking to his car. As he grabbed the door to open it, he faced the canteen, and he remembered.

"Oh, she works here, yeah, yeah, yeah, she said something like that." Excitedly he got into his car, slotted in the keys, and turned on the ignition.

"And what is that name again? I heard the so-called brother call her, oh my god. What is that name?" he said and held his forehead. "Nkechi, yeah, yeah, that is it, Nkechi." He turned on his car stereo and drove off.

Very early the next day, before the cock crowed, Ben was up. He wanted to quickly make arrangements for a bath. Sneaking out of his room into the passage, he quietly opened the main door that led to the back where the bathroom was. Holding the wrapper around his waist with his free hand, he grabbed the only bucket he could see in the bathroom and headed for the well at the back of the next house where people were gathered already, fetching water. He put his bucket very close to the mouth of the well, and the people he met there started murmuring, but they could not speak out, as most of them were young girls.

"You," he was talking to the girl, who was fetching, "I say you, put water in here for me, do you hear me? I say put water inside this pail for me right now."

"At least you'll wait and let me finish fetching, then you can come here and take the drawer to fetch, but you still meet some people here, you know," the girl replied.

"Chei!" he said, putting his finger to his mouth. "Is it me you are talking to like that? You girls of nowadays have no respect anymore. You mean you would stand there looking at me fetch water and not take the drawer from me to fetch for me? Now let me come and see which one of you who will draw any water here today without filling my bucket first." Then all the girls started jeering at him and moved away from the side of the well.

"Why do you always come here to make trouble every morning, trying to get water before all the people you meet here, and even if that is the case, then do it yourself, or if you want somebody to do it for you, then go and get your own children," another girl lamented.

"Is it me you're talking to like that?" Ben exclaimed as he picked up an empty bucket to throw at them, and then they dispersed.

"You foolish girls, no home training at all!" he yelled and took one of the already-filled buckets of water on the ground and emptied it in his own bucket. He cursed them one more time and left. He took a bath and quickly left home before his landlord woke up to see him and remind him of his debt.

"What time is it?" Ben asked the man walking by his side.

"Three o'clock," he replied.

"My god!" he exclaimed. "I've been walking for three hours, bless my soul." The last time he asked the time, it was twelve o'clock. "I just hope I won't drop dead walking one day." A vehicle sped past him and splashed mud water from a pothole on him.

"You are mad! You this stupid, rich people, should I not walk on the road anymore because of you? My god, look at me, and this idiot did not even look back to say sorry," he lamented, looking at his trousers and back at the car.

"And look at the car, is it Mercedes? No, it looks like BMW. My god, am I going to drive this kind of car ever, heen, am I? I will o o, I swear I will. I will drive one even bigger than this no matter what it will cost me," he declared, brushing off the water from his trousers, then he straightened up. "It's past three. I think I should be moving towards that canteen now. My friend must be getting hungry wherever he is."

He walked slowly to the canteen so he could make it there around four o'clock. On getting there, he met the woman who owned the place at the entrance where she sat looking after the affairs of her business.

"How are you, madam, and how is business today?" he asked, beaming at the woman who was wondering why he was fraternizing with her. From her countenance, it was clear she could not recognize him, that is, if they had ever met.

"Fine o, we thank God," she replied, staring at him in a funny way. "You wan eat?"

"Oh yes, of course, what else would I be doing here, eh, eh?" he asked and giggled.

"Go sidon, dem go serve you soon," she told him, and he obliged. A waitress came to him.

"What will you like to eat, sir?" He looked at the wall clock and thought for a moment, *Quarter to four, hmm, hmm.* "Okay, my sister, you see, you see, I have not eaten anything today, so I may be eating twice. So give me some appetizer to start with, you know, something like rice and chicken, eh, eh, hm, hm."

"How much, sir?" the girl asked.

"Oh, the way you sell it per plate. Ah, money is not the problem, ahhh, at all," he said, beaming and smiling as the girl left. *It's better that way since am not sure that the man would be coming. That is wisdom,* he thought. The girl brought the food, and before she could place the plate on the table, he was almost eating it from her hands. He raised his head at a point and looked at the wall clock. It was five minutes past four. He looked at the door and back at the other people busy eating and continued with his food. After a while, he looked at the clock for the second time, and it was 4:20 p.m. Then he started getting restless as he finished his food. He looked down into the plate he had just emptied. *I don't even know how much they sell the plate of food. I should have bought it in bits,* he thought, then he looked at the entrance again and back at the wall clock.

"I hope there's no problem?" an elderly man sitting in front of him asked.

"Oh me? Not at all. I'm only expecting someone, and the person is keeping me waiting. No problem at all, no problem," he answered nervously.

"By the way," the elderly man continued, "you look so much like a nephew of mine. The resemblance is so much that for a moment while you walked in, I almost shouted his name, and then I could not just believe my eyes when I discovered you're not him. As a matter of fact, you could have been twins. Ah, ah, it's too much. He is Lanre by name, and he is in the United States."

"Really, so goes the saying that there are two of every one of us on earth, sir," replied Ben.

"Yes, yes, you can say that again. If it won't be a bother, may I suggest you please allow me to pay for your meal on behalf of my nephew? I'm sure he would be glad I did when I tell him I found someone that looks exactly like him."

"Oh no no, sir, I should pay for you, as you are older," Ben protested.

"Yes, I know, but my nephew in question is younger. I mean, you are older than him, so he should be paying for you, okay?" the man explained, smiling.

"Ah, ah, I shouldn't agree with you o, but if you insist, sir," Ben said.

The elderly man then called the waitress and asked for his bill. The girl told him, and he paid. It wasn't until then that Ben realized he hadn't taken water. He took a cup from the set of cups at the center of the table and grabbed the jug of water. He filled the cup and gulped it all almost at once.

"Shall we?" the man asked. "Unless of course you still want to wait for your date."

"No, I really don't think he will be coming again. We can leave," he said, rising from his chair. He joined the man, and they walked out together. At the door, he met the man he had been waiting for, who paid for his food the previous day.

"Hello, sir," Ben called on him.

"Hello," the man replied and rushed in, obviously not recognizing Ben immediately.

"Sir," Ben said to the elderly man, "that's the man I've been expecting. I' have to go and meet him."

"I see. He is really in a hurry, but he didn't seem to see you?"

"Yes, sir, that is why I have to go and meet him."

"All right, see you then. Bye."

"Bye, sir, and thanks a lot for the meal."

"You're welcome." The man waved and left. Ben went back inside and sat on the table opposite the man who paid for him the previous day.

"Hello, hello," Ben called again since the man did not hear. He was busy talking to the person he actually rushed in to meet. "Hello, sir," and this time the man looked his way, a little confused for a moment, and then he beamed.

"Oh sorry, I didn't quickly recognize you. Pardon me please."

"I just wanted to say thank you for my meal yesterday."

"Oh, you're welcome. That's nothing anyway," the man replied and faced his date, continuing with their discussion.

"In fact, that is why I've been waiting here since," Ben continued, but the man was not listening anymore, "and their food here is very delicious too, eh, eh, hm." Then he quickly beckoned to a waitress, and when she came to him, he said, "Please, quickly give me four wraps of pounded yam and *egusi* soup with bush meat and fish with a bottle of soft drink."

"Sir, I thought you just finished eating?" the girl asked.

"What's your business? Are you counting the number of times I eat? Or am I eating it into your stomach? Or are you the one paying for me? Idiot, go and get me the food. Stupid children of nowadays, thought I told you earlier I might be eating twice." He looked the way of the man again.

"I think your office is not too far from this place, sir?" The man did not hear. "Sir, sir," Ben continued with his fraternization.

"Me?"

"Yes, I said your office is close to this area, I guess?"

"Something like that," the man replied and continued with his discussion. Just then Ben's food was brought. He washed his hand and started eating. Ben was halfway with his food when the man and his companion rose to leave. The man did not eat. His companion only paid for himself, Ben noticed. As he was swallowing a ball of pounded yam and almost choked, he asked, "Are you going?"

"Yes," the man answered and rushed out. For a moment, Ben froze, then he came back to himself. He didn't know what to do. His hand hung limp. He was like that for a long while when one of the waitresses walked by and noticed he wasn't eating.

"Why are you not eating, sir, is the food not good?"

"Eh, eh, I will eat, I will eat. Of course it is good. Why will your food here not be good?" he replied soberly and continued eating. By now the food had turned bitter in his mouth. Slowly he ate it. For almost an hour after he had finished eating, he could not get up from his seat. The girl came around and asked for her money, and he could not pay, so he was reported to her madam. The madam came to meet him. As he was the only person left in the hall, they rained curses upon him. The madam and her girls slapped him around except for one of the girls who stood away looking at the whole scenario pathetically. He was made to split wood for cooking using the axe for almost two hours before he was let go, after the madam had left for the day. Kachi, the girl who did not join in while he was being beaten, offered to finish splitting the wood for him. He then picked up his shirt and staggered home.

CHAPTER EIGHT

It took about two hours for the bus to get to the bus garage at Yaba since it had left Ibadan. When it eventually got to Yaba, the passengers alighted fatigued. Hence, Koja craved for a bar where he could relax and refresh his soul with a good beer.

He walked down the road looking on and feeding his eyes, unconsciously satisfying his desire to see the world again with the same elation that had kept him awake throughout the journey from Ibadan to Lagos while almost everybody else in the vehicle slept.

He stared at everything, conspicuously turning his head in the direction of every sound or shout he heard; he walked very slowly. At a point, he stood and watched how the motorcycle transporters passed by in their numbers, screeching and filling the atmosphere with exhaust fumes. By the time he came back to himself, he noticed that he aroused suspicion around as people were beginning to look at him strangely. He later found out that he had been standing almost at the center of the road; this was why the motorcycle drivers had to split up their convoy to bypass him on both sides. He ignored those staring at him and walked on by the side of the road until he noticed a signboard with the inscription "Faaji Restaurant and Bar." He went in and ordered for a bottle of beer as he sat at one corner of the beer parlor, eavesdropping on the conversation of the other people in the bar.

He took another bottle of beer and then a third one. He was feeling drowsy and a bit drunk after three bottles. "What's happening? At least I should get to the eighth bottle before I start feeling anything, or have they increased the alcoholic content in this beer since I have been away? How can I get drunk this early?" he complained. He took one more bottle and staggered to his feet. He gave out a loud and long belch and started walking toward the door when the waitress approached him.

"Sir, sir, you have not paid for your drinks," she called out.

"Who? Me? Have not paid ke? Ooohps," he belched again. "Okay, how much is your money?" he asked.

"Hundred and fifty naira," she replied.

He brought out some money that was left from his fare to Lagos and paid her after he had fumbled with it for a while.

"Take," he said, "I say take, take your money." He was still holding tight to the naira notes as the girl tried to rid him of it. He walked into the night and darkness of Lagos City, and out of the semblance of sanity remaining in him, he thought he should steady his steps so it won't be apparent to all who saw him that he was drunk. After walking for a while, he started seeing some ladies and women who could pass for his mother all dressed skimpily, hawking sex. He stopped right in front of them and started staring at them, blinking his eyes, trying to adjust his dim sight.

"You," he called one of them, "you come." A young and pretty but arrogant-looking girl moved close to him.

"Oga, na me be this. Na short time you want or sleep over?" she asked him in pidgin English.

"I want to sleep," he said blurrily. The girl turned and started walking into a narrow way in between two bungalows. When she looked back and saw that Koja was still standing there, she signaled to him.

"Oga, make we go now," she said.

"Where are we going?"

"You no dey go again, abi, na on the road we go do am?" she protested, and Koja followed her. She turned another corner to the right, and they were in the middle of a roll of small doors to the right and to the left, like shops in a complex. The young lady brought out a key from her waist and opened one of the doors to her right. The moment they got in, Koja settled on the bed while the girl stripped herself of her clothes and got into bed with him.

"You have not taken off your clothes o, and please you have to use condom. If you don't have, I'll give you one here to use."

"Oooorrrr," Koja snored and slept off.

It was as if Koja's head was being hammered as the girl lightly tapped him to wake up the next morning.

"Oga, oga, oga, wake up now, wake up, morning don come," the girl shouted and watched Koja with disgust as he dimmed his eyes, holding on to his head with his left hand. "Oga, I say come and be going. It is morning already, abi. Please get up from my bed," she said as she pulled him up from his lying position to sit. He held his head in his two hands, resting his elbow on his knee.

"Oga, pay me my money and go. I'm almost late for work."

"What work?" he asked. "Do you have some office you are going to, or is this not your office, that is if you have one?" he asked, sounding rather abashed.

"I have another job at a supermarket, and that is where I'm going now. Give me my money," she asked again as she fixed her earrings and snapped on the gum she was chewing ferociously.

"What am I paying you for?" he asked, rubbing his temple. He raised his head to look at the girl for an answer.

"What kind of question are you asking me? What did you come here for?"

"But, but we didn't do anything, did we?" He looked confused.

"So you can remember you didn't do anything? It doesn't matter. Just give me my money now before I begin to shout and the guys around here come and beat you up. What do you mean you didn't do anything? How come you slept here then? Stop wasting your time and pay me my money because nobody will believe you," the girl lamented, gradually raising her voice. Koja rose and started for the door.

"I am not giving you a dime. That will be fraudulent—," he began to say, but before he could finish his statement, the girl had started shouting, calling on the remaining occupants of the brothel, "*Ole, ole, ole, ashawo,* thief, thief, thief, help me, help me! He doesn't want to pay me after sleeping with me." By the time Koja opened the door, there were four hefty men and a crowd of majorly women gathered already.

"Mister man, what is the problem?" one of the four hefty men asked.

"Is it true you are trying to run away?" asked another.

"Pay the *ashawo*," said another one of them, referring to the prostitute.

"Pay her for what exactly do you mean? I didn't touch her. I just slept off since yesterday night as soon as I came in. So why should I pay her?" he protested.

"We have heard this kind of story many times, mister man, why didn't you go and sleep in your house when you know that is all you want to do, or did you rent any room here? Please just pay the lady and don't waste our time or else we will beat you like crazy now, and believe me, that is not the option you want to opt for," one of the big guys said kindly enough. Koja looked round the crowd and realized he was in another world entirely. These ones would take sides with their kind, he thought, and there was nowhere the issue would be heard that he could be vindicated. He made up his mind to pay. He dipped his hand into his left pocket where he had kept the money he had left. When his hand didn't touch any money there, he tried the right pocket, then he asked, "How much is the money anyway?" When he got no reply, one of the big guys again called the girl.

"Monica."

"Yes."

"How much is his money?"

"Five hundred naira," she replied, and her cohort murmured she should have increased the pay to one thousand naira. Koja had checked all his pockets, including his back pocket and his shirt pocket, and could not find the money.

"Ah, ah, what's happening?" he asked himself, then he turned and went back inside the room. He checked the bed, ripped off the permanently stained white bedsheet, held it straight up, and shook it, thinking the money could be hanging somewhere in it. He dropped it back on the bed and got on his knees to look underneath the bed, all to no avail. Then he got up and went to look for the girl outside.

"Are you sure you didn't take any money out of my pocket while I slept, or did you see any money on the floor in your room at any time since I came?" he shouted.

"What do you mean did I take any money out of your pocket while you slept? Mind the way you talk to me, this madman. I may be a prostitute, but I'm not a thief. Just pay me my money, you this liar," the girl countered.

"Anyway, I was just about to tell you I don't have up to five hundred naira, but now as you can see, I don't even have anything," he said as he waved his hands and dropped them to his sides. He wanted to continue speaking again, but before he could complete his sentence, *parrrr*—a slap was dealt him by one of the big guys, and another slap followed that. Before they went too far, a voice rescued him.

"Hey, hey, hey!" the voice yelled. "Don't beat him, don't beat him. I'll pay for him." The minicrowd parted for his "rescuer" to come to the front. It was a young man. "Yes, how much is your money?" he asked, smiling, almost laughing. He made no effort to conceal his euphoria. He brought out money from his pocket and started counting.

"One thousand naira," the girl declared again, and Koja was about to erupt when the young man paying for him motioned to him to keep quiet. He counted one thousand naira and gave it to Koja to give to the girl himself. He collected it and gave it to the girl, cursing her as he did. He and the young man then walked out of the brothel together. The young man was still smiling when they reached the main road, still musing over the whole scenario.

"Thank you very much, my brother, I'm really grateful. Thank you very much. I still wonder why you came to my rescue that way. Apart from the fact that you don't know me, your enthusiasm in the whole matter still surprises me," Koja confessed.

"You don't have to be surprised. You don't have to be at all. Three years ago somebody rescued me the same way. I got drunk one night like that, and I had ended up with a girl in this same brothel. Immediately I got on the bed, and I had slept off. First thing in the morning, she asked me for her pay after robbing me while I slept. I was about being lynched when somebody I didn't know who was just passing by rescued me and told me the same story afterwards. So I promised myself that I must rescue someone too. Hence, I've made that my pledge ever since."

"Could that be the same girl that robbed you then?" Koja asked.

"Of course not. She no longer stays there. I took care of her sometime later," the young man replied with a grin.

"You took care of her later . . . ?" Koja repeated, eyes wide open "I see, I think this Monica girl too requires the same."

"Good you feel that way, and even better you remember her name. I have to go now, but let me give you some money," the young man said. He brought out the rest of the money in his pocket and gave Koja a thousand naira. Koja hesitated. "No, I can't collect that. I just cost you a thousand naira early in the morning, when you should be making money. Please, thank you very much, but I can't collect it," Koja lamented.

"Look here, I'm not trying to be nice to you. Is it not apparent that you need it? The truth is you'll regret it if you don't collect it. Please take it." Koja then collected the money without further objection.

"Thank you very much. I must confess you're an angel today."

"Every life on the street needs money. I believe we'll be seeing more of each other?"

"I hope so," replied Koja. "Of course we will. In case you don't know, the life you live now is really low, and we would always see each other in it. See you," the young man said and walked away. It took Koja another five minutes before he realized he didn't ask the young man for his name. He looked at the money in his hand and put it in his pocket.

"Good morning, Officer," Charles greeted the first officer he saw the next morning as he stretched.

"Good morning, Mr. Ogbu, how was your night?" the officer asked in response.

"It was okay," Mr. Ogbu said, still sitting on the bench. He continued sleeping and rubbed his face with his hand.

"But I'm sure sleeping on that bench wasn't a very pleasant experience."

"At least I slept safely, without fear," Charles replied, trying to clean the corner of his eyes with his forefinger, forcing himself to wake up. Then the rest of the team of officers started coming out of the inner offices, and they all exchanged greetings with Charles.

"Mr. Ogbu, how was your sleep? I guess sleeping on a bench after such a long time abroad wasn't very easy, was it?" another officer said, and all the men roared with laughter.

"Excuse me, I'll like some water to wash my mouth and face," Charles said, heading for the door.

"Please don't stay long. There are still some questions I want to ask you concerning the statement you wrote last night, and I will also like to hand you over to the morning-shift guys, okay?" He lifted his voice to be sure Charles heard him as he exited the building. The officer joined the rest of his team as they discussed more about Charles and laughed at his predicament over and over again.

When Charles came in about an hour later, there were already new faces in police uniforms, the morning-shift officers.

"Ah, Mr. Ogbu, ah, ah, I thought I told you not to stay for long. You said you only want to get water."

"Yes," Charles cut in sharply, "and I decided to while away my time. Have you any problem with that? Come on, stop treating me like a prisoner! I walked in here myself, remember? And if you had a water system here, I wouldn't have needed to go anywhere, would I?"

"Aha, that is not what I mean. It's just that I should have gone home after handing over to the men from this shift, so let me just call the head of the morning team to join us in this brief examination of your statement. Sergeant Vincent, please." The officer walked over and sat beside another officer. He nodded his head at Charles who replied, "Good morning."

"Good morning, mister."

"All right," the officer continued. Pointing to the new officer, he said, "He has looked through your statement before you came back from your walk, and he raised the same questions I raised. You said you just got back from the United States last evening. Don't you have any luggages or handbags, you know? I mean, don't you have any baggage?"

"Of course I do, but they have not arrived. I think they should be here in about a week or so, because I have a lot of things coming," he answered presumptuously.

"I see," the new officer said, nodding his head. Can I see your passport please, your international passport?"

"I kept it in my pocket but have been looking for it since I got here. I think it must have fallen off while I was being pursued by those people. Only God knows who they were," he replied, looking confused.

"Really?" the new officer said.

"All right, when you leave here, where are you going? I mean, where will you be staying?"

"Ahhh, really, I don't know yet, because I've lost contact with home for a very long time, and the last place I lived before I traveled is Lagos, but as I sit here before you, I don't have a single address of any of my family. All the same, I'm still going to look around the city if I can still locate or manage to trace out any of my folks here."

"And what if you don't get to see any of your family members at all, what would you do? Because Lagos is not a place where you just walk about and stumble on people you know, and neither is there any library or DA's office like you have where you are from where you can check through records to look for lost ones."

"Then you'll have to bear with me a little here for me to speed up my return."

"What do you mean bear with you here?"

"I mean, to stay here till I go back. I can't feel safe anywhere else."

"There are safe hotels in the city of Lagos. You can't stay here," the officer argued, and before Charles could say another word, the new officer cut in, "How are you thinking of going back, Mr. . . . ? Sorry," he said, looking at the other officer for assistance.

"Ogbu, Mr. Ogbu is his name."

"Ogbuuu, sorry, sir, it just eluded my mind."

"Yes, what did you say?" Charles asked, pretending he didn't hear what the officer had said.

"I asked how you are thinking of going back, when you don't even have an international passport anymore?"

"Oh, the embassy will take care of that. I'm an American citizen as well," he lied.

"Oh, I see."

"Oh yes, I am."

"That will be all then. You are free to go and come in anytime you want. The police are the friend of the people. The only thing is that we are responsible only for your security. I will advise you make your stay here as brief as possible. This is a police station, not a hotel."

"Of course, absolutely, thank you very much," he said as he took a very heavy but quiet breath of relief after the policemen had turned their backs to him.

The nearer Usman got to the house, the more afraid he became. When he eventually got out of the taxi in front of his house, fear had fully resumed and taken a permanent place in his heart. He gently got out of the car, his crutches first, then his bag followed by his legs. He began to walk toward the door to his house when he heard a shout from inside; it was his daughter.

"Daddy, Daddy, Daddy!" she shouted and emerged at the door running toward him, and the person who followed her made Usman freeze, and for a moment he could not feel the weight of the POP on his hand and leg. His bag fell off his hand, and he almost let go of his crutches when his son caught him in an embrace.

"Jubril, is it you? Is it you? Tell me!" Usman demanded.

"Yes, Papa, yes, Papa, it's me, Papa," his son replied.

Usman held firmly to his crutches, else he would have fallen because of the weight of both his son and his daughter hanging on to him, but he still stood there limp, not believing what he was seeing. His wife ran out of the door with a broad smile that disappeared as soon as she set her eyes on her husband. She halted and stood staring at him in disbelief and terror. When their eyes were affixed, tears emanated from her eyes. He released his bag to his son who was too dumbfounded to say anything than cry. He held her close as she sobbed on his chest, then they went into the house. Usman narrated his ordeal to his family. His wife listened, half attentive as Jubril and his sister fumbled with the snacks their father bought for them on his way from Lagos. Usman, who since he came home never really took his eyes off his son, asked his wife again after he had finished his story, "Is it him?"

"Yes o, yes, it is Kuku him. Thanks to the Almighty that will not allow me to sorrow twice on my children," his wife answered, raising both hands upward and bringing them to rest on her head and down to her chest.

"What happened?" Usman asked again with his eyes still on his son.

"It was just God, that's all I can say for now, and it is the same god that has delivered you from death and me from sorrow again. I didn't want you to go to that Lagos remember, he heh. I didn't want you to go oo. See now, see now," the wife lamented as she began to cry, and her husband consoled her. Then she rose to her feet.

"Come, let's go inside. I will not want anybody to see you like this. I even thank God none of the neighbors were outside when you came. Let me help you up," she offered as she put her arm under her husband's shoulder.

"I don't think I really need any help to walk," he said as he rose from where he sat. "At least I came down from Lagos by myself."

"Jubril," his mother called, "have you laid the bed I told you to lay?" and before the boy could answer, his father cut in, turning to look at the mother.

"Are you sure he's that strong already?"

"Of course he is. You've been gone for two weeks, and he has had enough time to rest since he came out of the hospital," she replied carelessly.

"Yes, Mommy, I have laid it," Jubril replied. Usman got into bed with the help of his wife, and after he was settled in bed, he again demanded from his wife how his son finally made it home from the hospital.

"It was nothing but a miracle, just the miracle of God. It was on the day you left. In fact, I almost wished there was a way I could make you change your mind and come back that same day. It all happened so strangely, I was scared. You remember by the time you left he was asleep, and I asked you to wake him to let him know you were leaving?"

"Yes," Usman answered with keen interest.

"He slept for long that day," the wife continued, "slept for so long that he skipped his lunch. When I woke him up to take his lunch, he felt so tired that I decided to leave him to have all the rest he wanted to get. I forgot to say that this happened after I went to the doctor when I could not bear my curiosity anymore. I went to demand him to tell me what he told you about my son. He hesitated at first, but I prevailed over him, and he obliged. So I cried until it was time for his lunch, and it was since then I kept watch over him as if he would die anytime.

"But one thing I noticed but wasn't sure of was that shortly before he woke up, like an hour before then, I had noticed that his breathing had steadied, and when he woke up, he spoke well and asked for food. After eating, he told me he felt better. He sat up in bed and was breathing normally, then later he got out of bed and walked to the window and around the room. Just then the doctor came. He could not believe his eyes. 'What is this?' he exclaimed. 'What are you doing out of bed? Do you want to kill yourself?' he asked him, then he turned to me and asked me the same question. Jubril then got back into bed, and the doctor was still wondering how it was possible for him to be on his legs. 'Where did he get the strength from?' the doctor asked. He checked his heartbeat, his eyes, and his pulse. He then stood back and stared at him and asked me, 'What time did this start?'

"'Start what exactly, Doctor?' I asked him, then he said, 'When did he start walking around?' I told the doctor he just finished eating, and he told me he was feeling better, then he got out of bed and was moving around. The doctor then asked again why I didn't come to tell him, but I simply told him that perhaps if it had been a negative development, I could have thought about it, but it did not occur to me at all to do so because I was so caught off guard by my son's actions. The doctor suddenly said he could not believe what he was seeing. I asked him what it was, and he told me that it's just as if nothing was ever wrong with Jubril before that time, then he ordered for another X-ray which I took Jubril for. The X-ray came back negative and the result confirmed that my son is in perfect health."

"Just like that?" Usman asked.

"Just like that, but the doctor still kept him for another two days for observation and to conduct more tests. He even called some specialists to examine him, and they verified it."

"Verified what?" Usman asked in disbelief.

"That nothing is wrong with his heart," the wife affirmed. "Should I prepare you anything to eat?" she asked her husband. "Or will you like to rest first?"

"Yes, I will like to have some rest first before I take anything. Jubril, come here," he called his son, beckoning to him; his son came to him and sat on the edge of the bed.

"Is it true you are okay now? Are you well? You don't feel sick?"

"Yes, Daddy, I'm fine."

"Are you sure?"

"Yes, Daddy," he assured his father with a weak smile.

"You don't feel pain when you breathe anymore?"

"No, Papa, I don't," the boy said and beamed with an even bigger smile to his father who stroked his hair and rubbed his shoulder, finding it very hard to believe what he had just heard.

"Let me take some rest now, and when I wake, I'll eat," he said, turning on his side. His wife rose and left with the children. When they were gone, he turned and lay on his back again in deep thoughts.

What happened? Could he have heard me when I called on him that day in the hospital compound? Did he hear and answered? Who heard and answered? Maybe the doctor was not even sure in the first place? Perhaps my son was never really sick? No, but the symptoms were there, his breathing, the pantings. Perhaps he was sick, but it probably was not as bad as the doctor had painted it. He looked up at the ceiling and turned on his side again, trying to take his mind off the issue, then after a while, he looked up again.

"If it is you," he said, "whoever is responsible for this, I just want to say thank you very much." He closed his eyes; then after a moment, he opened his eyes again, looked up, and said, "Thank you, God," after which he slept.

Three weeks later and about a week after Usman had removed the POP on his hand and leg, he reminded his wife of his intention to go to Lagos to start work.

"Aisha," he called out to his wife as he walked into their sitting room with the walking stick he had been using since he took off the POP. He sat opposite his wife like they usually do since they only had two cushioned seats in their two-room apartment. "I will like to leave for Lagos as soon as possible," he emphasized.

"Aha, why the hurry? At least you should get completely recovered before you travel again. I think you should get ready and be fit enough for any job they might offer you in Lagos," his wife argued.

"I'm fit enough for any job. I can walk and run without the stick. And when I said as soon as possible, I didn't mean today or tomorrow."

"Then when will you like to leave?" his wife asked.

"Sometime next week."

"What is the difference if you leave today or next week?"

"Seven days! Seven whole days makes the difference, and remember, I'm not going on vacation. I'm going to make a living for this family."

"Of course I know, and I also know that your health should be first, and you should spend time with your family too," the wife countered.

A week later, he left for Lagos.

CHAPTER NINE

Kachi walked leisurely as she returned from her boss's errand. She had bought some groundnut and popcorn to eat as she walked back to the canteen. The young man waiting for her had seen her from afar. He had been on the lookout for her since he was told inside by one of her colleagues that she had been sent on an errand by the madam. Though he had only seen her once, the moment he sighted her coming down the road, he recognized her immediately. As she moved closer, the young man started smiling, thinking she had seen him. He didn't bother to call her name, and Kachi almost walked past him to enter the canteen when he realized he had to catch her attention, so he called out to her.

"Nkechi, Nkechi." When Kachi did not answer to it, he waved to her. "I'm calling you," he added with his shaky voice but smiling face.

"Oh, sorry, sir, I didn't know . . .," Kachi replied innocently.

"You are Nkechi, right?"

"No, sir, but I don't know you."

"Hee, yeah." He grinned. "I was here a few days ago, if you can remember," he said, pointing to his car. "We were talking here when your brother called you," he added, seeming nervous, yet he did not stop smiling.

"Oh yes, I can now remember, sir. Do you want to eat now?"

"No, I've actually come to see you." Kachi looked toward the canteen, hoping her boss wasn't watching her.

"Why do you want to see me, sir? I have to go into the canteen now to give my boss her message. She earlier sent me on an errand," and before she finished, "Kachiiii, aaagh!" her boss called. She came out and saw her chatting with a man. "So you have been back since and you went your own way to see your useless man friends. Can I have my message now?" She spread her palm out to Kachi; and Kachi, looking extremely scared and nervous, stood at arm's length to give her the money she went to collect for her. "You will come and meet me inside," her boss said to her as she stormed back inside.

"Ah ahaaa, I'm in trouble. I'm in trouble. My boss is going to kill me. Please go." She then ran inside cautiously. The young man was confused, not comprehending why the boss should be mad with her. He walked back to his car miserably, and as he wanted to get in, he started hearing Kachi's madam beating and slapping her with loud curses. Full of regret and embarrassment, he got into his car and drove off. When Kachi could not bear the beating anymore, she ran from her boss. Her boss pursued her, beating her as she ran. So she ran out of the canteen and left. As she cried along the way covering her face with her hand and sobbing, she met Miide who was coming to check on her at work as usual; he could not believe his eyes.

"What happened to you?" he inquired, raising his voice in rage. "Just don't tell me it's your boss again or I'll kill her today," he added as he drew Kachi close and asked her what had transpired between her and her boss. Amid tears, Kachi began to explain to Miide who was fuming as he listened.

"Is that all that happened?" he asked Kachi, staring at her intensely.

"In fact, it doesn't matter anymore what happened. I think I've told her many times not to ever beat you when you do anything wrong. She should just send for me and tell me. Let's go anyway," he said as he took her by her arm and pulled her along. "Let's go!"

"No, no, Miide, don't go and cause trouble there, please." Kachi hesitated as she held back from following him. "Please don't go, Miide, please," she said, crying.

"Shut up now before I get angry with you. Follow me," he said, trying to pull her along,

"Miide, please don't go, please don't go," she kept saying, and Miide turned back and asked her, "Why shouldn't I go?" Kachi flinched.

"Just don't go. I forgive her. Since I was the one who made her vex, I have forgiven her."

"If you don't want to go, you can stay." He let go of her hand. "But I will still go to teach her some lessons so that if she ever sets her eyes on you, she will tremble with fear," he said and marched away.

When some of the other girls who worked at the canteen saw Miide coming, they took to their heels through the back door.

"Where is your madam?" he demanded from the door as he entered. "I say where is your madam?" he asked again as he paced round the kitchen and stood in front of the only girl left who had not run away on seeing him approach. "She has gone out," she answered.

"Don't lie to me. She couldn't have gone out so soon. She just finished beating Kachi now, or were you not here then? Answer me before I break your neck."

"She has gone out. She was actually going out when she saw Kachi with the man, then she came back in to wait for her, and immediately after she finished beating her, she left," the girl explained.

"Fine, if she's not here so I could inflict physical pain on her, I will cause her financial pain, and she will come and meet it when she comes." He walked to the three massive pots of different stews that had been cooked and turned them over. "That does it. Tell her the next time she sees my sister, she should not cross her path, and as for you, I only spared you. The next time you see me anywhere in this kind of mood, don't you dare stand around to look me in the eye, okay?" he declared and stormed out the way he had come.

As Mike drove away, he felt so abashed. He held the steering wheel with his right hand and rubbed his temple with his other hand, resting his elbow on the car window. A lot of thoughts flashed through his mind as he sped on; paramount of them was the sudden hatred for Kachi's boss.

That's what I'm going to do. I'll get her arrested, he thought. *Why on earth did she have to beat a human being like that? That was so cruel of her, and an abuse of some sort. And I'm going to make sure I close down that canteen of hers.* He approached the gate of Moses International Corporation, the massive building that housed his office, the head office of the Moses group of companies.

Moses Ventures, as it was formally known, was established in England in 1952 by Jeremiah Oluseun Moses, the tallest man the Moses family had ever had. He had moved to England in 1949 to find greener pastures, leaving his wife and son. He first worked at a clothing factory where he served as a manager and made a reasonable amount of money that enabled him start up a furniture shop. This was the original thing he had been involved with in Nigeria before he left, and in five years, his shop was the second biggest in England. He married a Briton and had a child shortly before he came home for the Nigerian independence in 1960. He met a group of Americans who came to England. They dealt in solid minerals, such as steel and tantalite, and they needed these minerals in large quantities. At that time, he didn't know much about these minerals, but he knew Nigeria was rich in them.

He got to Nigeria, and to his surprise, he got these minerals easily and at very cheap rates. Thus, this enabled him to export them at very cheap costs.

He reunited with his family in Nigeria while accumulating wealth as his export business prospered. It took him another three years before he could tread the soil of England again. Even though he kept in touch with his wife and son while he was in Nigeria, his Briton wife wanted to leave the marriage, and so she filed for divorce. The court ruled that they split everything he had worked for in England. So his manager at the shop bought his own half of it. Three months after, he finally left England, his wife taking custody of their only child. His manager married his ex-wife. By 1971, Jeremiah Oluseun Moses had established three other businesses in Nigeria: a soap manufacturing company, a roofing sheet producing company, and a cement company. He had two other companies abroad: one in the United States and the other in China. At this time, his son, Abiola Moses, was twenty-two years old and was studying in the United States.

By 1980, Stephen Abiola Moses and his Nigerian wife, Felicia, in the United States gave birth to their first child, Michael Oludare Moses. And two years later, they had a girl. The children lived with their parents in Los Angeles in the United States. Their parents ran the U.S. offices of the now-renamed Moses International Corporation while their grandfather took charge of the home office in Nigeria. On the first of May 1985, Stephen Moses got a phone call that his father had slumped. Jeremiah Oluseun Moses died at the age of sixty. After his father's demise, Stephen Abiola Moses had to move to the home office of the corporation in Nigeria with his wife and left the children in the United States, but he made sure he visited them every month.

In 1990, on the fourth of July, as Stephen Abiola Moses and his wife returned from a ceremony held in their honor at their Asia office, they lost their lives in an accident that killed them instantly. Catherine Atinuke who was eight years old was at the mercy of her aunt and her uncle-in-law, who was now in charge of the business as he had always been working with their father as the group general manager.

The children remained in the United States with their aunt till Mike completed his studies. In February 1998, Mike celebrated his eighteenth birthday; and later, he moved to Nigeria for the first time in his life. He resumed work two days after he came into the country. His uncle-in-law thought it wise that he got into the business system at an early age so he could grow with the ethics of the business.

On the same day he resumed work, he was ushered into the office his grandfather and his father had used while they had occupied the position inscribed on the door: "President, Chairman, and Chief Executive Officer." Mike's uncle had been the chief executive officer since his father died and still occupied the position, but he had a separate office. Mike saw the grandeur of the office and was astounded. It was bigger and more exquisite than the U.S. office, and he suddenly really understood and had a better perception of the vast empire he had inherited. After about six months that he'd been around, he had learned a lot, gotten used to the Nigerian society, and managed to find his way around Lagos City. It was during one of such drives around the city without his chauffeur that he had met Kachi a few days before.

He drove through the corporation gate on high speed and halted, making a whoosh sound with his wheels. He got down from the car, slammed the door, and marched angrily toward the entrance of the building. His grandfather had laid the foundation to this building. The two security men who stood by the entrance flung the door open for Mike as he almost flew past them. He went to his personal elevator along the corridor and ascended to the tenth floor where his office was located. He got out of the elevator, and the members of his staff on that floor basked him in adulation of greetings as he walked past them.

"Good afternoon, sir," a few of the staff chorused.

"You're welcome, sir," some others said.

"Good day, sir," another group emphasized, but oblivious of them all, he walked to his office door, and his personal assistant who was always on standby opened the secretary's door for him and quickly ran ahead to open the main door that led to Mike's office.

"You're welcome, sir," his secretary, a middle-aged woman, said, apparently not expecting any response. She quickly picked up a few documents and followed him into his office. Mike's personal assistant stood aside after he had opened the door and walked in. Mike suddenly stopped and looked back at his secretary.

"Get out of my office," he said sternly.

"Yes, sir," the woman said and briskly stepped out.

"And please close the door after you," he added. He walked ahead to take his sit behind his desk. The secretary and the assistant stood still in utter awe of their boss and just noticed another side of him that they had never seen, unlike his usual passive, shy, and gentle side they were just getting used to. About twenty minutes later, the intercom on the secretary's desk buzzed.

"Yes, sir," she answered as she pressed down the button.

"Get my PA," Mike ordered over the intercom and cut off at once.

"He wants you," the secretary hissed to the PA who was already halfway to the door. He knocked and went in.

"Pius, I want to get somebody arrested, and I want you to call and report the case to the police," he spat, a little calmer than he was when he came in. He was busy putting some papers together on his desk and didn't bother to look up at his PA. When he didn't get any response from Pius, he raised his head to look at the rather timid PA.

"Did you hear what I said?" Mike said.

"Yes, sir, I was just wondering what exactly the case is about, so as to know what to tell the police."

"All right then, I witnessed the maltreatment of a fellow human being today, or rather should I call it an abuse of human right. I saw a canteen owner, I mean one 'madam,' as you call them, that owns an eatery beat up one of her waitresses, mercilessly, in an unjust manner, and I think the police should call her to order. Besides, I will like to file charges against her on behalf of the girl," Mike stated.

"Sir, may I suggest something?" the PA asked timidly.

"Yes of course, that is perhaps why I called you," Mike said.

"Sir, I would rather advise we just probably report the madam's inhuman treatment of her girls to the police first and let them take up the case as best they know. And also, sir, I think we might have to find out the actual situation of things from one of the girls . . . sir."

"Mmmm, I don't think it would make any sense to argue with you on your suggestions since you know the system better than I do. But on just one of your remarks I agree with you, that I should go back and inquire from the girl how she has been faring working at the canteen."

"No, sir, I don't mean you, sir, you should not be found in places like that, sir. Just tell me the place and I'll go and do just that, sir," the PA cut in.

"No no no, you're not familiar with the place," Mike said, raising his forefinger to stop him from interrupting him further. "I think the girl should be closed now, and besides, I don't think she would be in the mood to entertain any visitor for the rest of today after such beating, so I'll see her tomorrow, better still on Monday."

"Do you have any particular girl in mind, sir?" his PA asked.

"Piusss?"

"Yes, sir."

"Get my driver. I am going home."

"Yes, sir," he responded, straightening his new tie, one of his latest purchases. He usually did that when he got really nervous waiting on such a young man like Mike. "I don't know what goes through his mind most times, and judging by the way he looks at me, I fear he could just fire me at any time," Pius had one time confided in Ellen, the secretary. She had laughed and assured him. "That's the way all CEOs look," she encouraged him.

Ben lay on his back, looking straight up at the ceiling. He had not moved from that position for the past hour. His two hands were crossed under his head serving as his pillow; he blinked, and tears flowed freely down the corner of his eyes into his ears. This gave way to a little tremor, and he closed his eyes again, trying to fall asleep. He had been indoors for two days with severe body aches and very hungry, not having much to eat. But thanks to the woman selling cassava grains in the next building, she usually gave him credit on his purchases because they were both natives of the same hometown; this was coupled with the fact that she claimed to have fallen in love with Ben. Thus, aside from the times that he needed her favor, he absolutely ignored her, the more reason why it was usually difficult to get the next credit. He felt renewed hunger pangs in his stomach after about an hour, and then he woke up. He sat up on the mattress, resting his back against the wall, and rubbed his naked protruding tummy. He looked around the room, and his eyes settled on the covered bowl that usually contained his cassava grain. Even though he knew it was empty, he lifted the lid as if expecting a miracle to have taken place, but he realized he had even washed the bowl clean.

He lifted his right knee and rested his right elbow unto it, holding his temple in his hand. He got up after a while and put on his shirt. He picked up his broken piece of mirror and looked at his reflection. He then rubbed off the dry tear on the side of his head with the edge of his shirt. He picked a nylon bag and squeezed it into his pocket, rehearsed a little smile, and exited his room.

"Marris, Marris," Ben called out with a wide grin as he approached her kiosk in front of her house, "how are you? I was greeting you this morning, but you didn't hear me. I think you were going to the market to get more of your goods." He came to stand in front of her kiosk. Marris didn't say a word. She was dressed in her native blouse with a matching wrapper. Ben thought she was overdressed. She was going about her kiosk, not minding Ben at all. "Marris, answer me now," he said, putting his hand around her neck, a gesture he had never tried before, and gave her a smile.

"I won't answer you, I won't answer you. All the time I come to your house for my money, you refuse to answer me, making me think you're not inside, and your next-door neighbor would always tell me you were in the house all those times I came, hen hen," she complained.

"Aaha, that is a lie o, that my neighbor knows I'm never in o. They know and you too know that I go out to look for job always now. You know, don't you? Don't mind my neighbors o. The thing is that they don't like the way they see us together, so they are jealous, heen, they are jealous," Ben defended.

"Eeenh, I remember now, again, why didn't you come that day you said I should be expecting you?" she asked, still looking from the corner of her eyes, now grinning naughtily.

"Which day was that?" Ben asked deceitfully.

"The last time you came for a bowl of cassava grain and I gave you for free, you promised to come to see me at home that day, or have you forgotten?"

"Ahaaa, yes, I remember now. I'm so sorry I didn't come. I should have come to explain things to you when I got back. You remember I said I was going out later? It was for a job interview, and they kept me till very late there. Ah, I'm so sorry, and I didn't even remember that when I thought of coming to chat with you today o."

"Hen e, so you have come to play with me today? I thought you have come to beg for garri again." She was emptying her new carton of biscuits into a large basin where it is easily accessible when customers come to purchase it.

"Ah, ah, Marris, you mean even if I have come to beg for garri, you will not give me?" he asked with a teasing guilty face as he picked up a wrap of biscuit, and Marris's eyes followed his hand, but she had a weak smile. Then Ben said, "Or will you make me pay for this one too?"

"No o o, if not for the way you behaved to me, I would have been giving you all your foodstuff for free, since I know your condition, but you never give me face or even look at my side. You always make all the women in my house here mock me because they know that I like you," she lamented now with a sad look, gesturing with her hands. Ben, who was dumbfounded by her revelation, made a funny face behind her.

"Marris, don't mind your neighbors, ehen. I really like you, and they know it, that is why they are jealous," he was saying when she broke in.

"Let us go in now since you said you like me so my neighbors will see you with me," she said excitedly.

"Not now, Marris, give me time. You see, by the time I start coming to your house, I will be spending a lot of time with you, okay, so don't let us be in a hurry. By the way, I still have to go out very soon." He excused himself. "You are angry with me again, abi?"

"No o, since you have explained to me well today, I can see you done dey give me face small small." She smiled and shrugged.

"But I don't believe you, I don't, except you do something to show me you are not annoyed with me."

"What do you want me to do now eh, eh? Okay, I will give you some foodstuff, or is it money you want? Do you even have any money at all since you don't even have a job yet?"

"No, I don't o, but whichever you want to give me, I don't mind. It's just to be sure you are not angry with me again, that's all." He watched her as she innocently filled three nylon bags with raw grains of rice, beans, and two bowls of garri. "Now, I know you are not annoyed with me. Thank you very much," Ben said. Not replying to him immediately, she brought her money bag out from beneath her wrapper around her waist. Ben looked away as she counted out ten fifty naira notes and gave them to him. While she was still tucking in her money bag, Ben didn't know what to do in response to this barrage of gift surprises, whether to cry or jump for joy. It had been an extremely long time that he had held that much money. He quickly thrust it into his pocket as if afraid she would change her mind.

"So when should I come and see you now, or will you come to me?" she asked suddenly. Ben, caught off guard, didn't know how to refuse her.

"I-I will be expecting you," he said soberly.

"Hen hen, I should come?"

"Hen, yes, now why not," he replied, forcing a smile.

"Okay, I will soon be there. Immediately I pack and close, I will come."

"Okay, let me quickly go and prepare for you," he said. Ben dropped the bags of foodstuff in his room, looked himself up in the mirror one more time, straightened his shirt, and went out in a hurry.

When Miide got home, he saw the door locked. He knew Kachi was not in; so he let himself in, halted, and looked round. Agitated, he started looking around for where Kachi kept the money, but he could not find it. He searched everywhere but could not find any money and was frustrated.

"Where for god's sake could she have kept this money now, and I've always asked her to tell me where she keeps money, but she refused, heh," he hissed. "And where on earth is she?" He looked beside the pillow where Kachi kept her Bible. "This girl, this girl, she has gone to church again. What am I supposed to do about this girl, for god's sake?" he added, putting his right forefinger to his chin and his left hand to his waist. "All right, I know what I will do, mm, mm." He started changing into another shirt because he had spilled some of the stew on himself when he had overturned the pot in the canteen. "I just hope she has not been giving out my money the way she gives out her clothes in the name of charity, or else I'll teach her the lesson she'll never forget in her life. I don't know what my business is with charity. The rich at Ikoyi and Victoria Island are not doing charity, why should it be me, a lowlife at the back side of the city, heh, heh," he continued as he buttoned the fresh shirt.

"Ah, clothes that I picked at Oshodi at the cheapest prices, she's giving them out, someone that should be stealing clothes all around town. She should virtually be stripping people's clothes off their backs, and she won't even follow me out once," he complained. Miide paused and then continued talking aloud to himself, "I don't even want her to follow me, and now she's been fired again." He stood arms akimbo, staring into oblivion; he shook his head slightly and left the house.

When Kachi got home later, she knew Miide had been there, but he didn't eat the food she left for him. She then discovered his stained shirt in the pail by the foot of the bed.

"Oh my god!" she wailed. "Oh my god, blood, blood, Miide, what have you done to yourself!" she shouted as she picked up his shirt. "Ooooh, okay, thank God. I thought it was blood. Thank you, Jesus, but what is this?" She spread the shirt out well. "Stew, this looks like stew, but he has not touched his food. Where did he spill stew on himself? Maybe he ate out," she deduced and later dropped Miide's shirt. But just as she walked away, she shrieked all of a sudden. "My god, my god, the canteen, the canteen, ahaaa!" She started crying. "Miide, what have you done? Ah, Miide, has killed me o, I'm in trouble. How can I go back to work? Ah ahaaa ahhh." She cried for a very long time, lamenting as she did.

"Miide, just come and meet me here today o, hehh. I'm waiting for you. You'll get me another job tonight. I swear, you will. Anytime you like, come back tonight. I will be waiting for you, aaah haaahhh." She wailed all night sitting on the edge of the bed, waiting for Miide to come home. When it was ten o'clock,

Miide still hadn't come back. She reclined on the bed, resting her back on the wall and stretching her legs before her. When it was eleven thirty, she lay on the bed, forcing her eyes to stay open. "I will not sleep today. I will wait for you till you come back and we straighten everything out tonight," she grumbled. Thirty minutes later, she cuddled up in bed and murmured something as she fell asleep.

When she woke up, it was daylight already. "Ooh my god! I'm late!" she exclaimed and ran out of bed. "Miide! He didn't come home last night." She was silent for a while as she tried to remember the things that had happened the previous day. She walked back to the bed and dropped her buttocks on the mattress. *What could have happened? Where could he be? Of course this is not his first time sleeping out, but he didn't say he was going to sleep out,* she thought. She curled her legs up to herself so her chin could lean on her knees, and after thinking for a while, she said, "I can't even go to work because I don't know the situation of things there." She peeped at Miide's shirt in the bucket.

She decided to wait for Miide to come home. She thought of taking a walk to the canteen, so she dressed up even though she knew she won't venture going too close to the place. She went all the same. She hid in a corner, about a hundred meters from the canteen, and watched the day's activities. It was actually nothing short of the normal daily routine. The normal flow of customers, the usual faces of the few customers who ate every morning at the canteen measured against the mass of people who came for lunch.

Kachi maintained her distance from the canteen as much as possible, but she could still observe what was going on there. She still thought that whatever happened yesterday at the canteen after she left could have something to do with Miide's whereabouts now. But at the same time, she believed that Miide could not be held down by anybody there. Besides, she thought, he had been home afterward, and nobody knew where they lived anyway. All these thoughts went through her mind as her interest was lured away by the variety of people who, because of their quest to keep their "body and soul" together in a society of uncertainty, a country basking in its delusions of grandeur, the perpetuation of a glory long lost, have subjected themselves to slavery. This slavery was out of obligation though, not captivity. What should have been for people different "interests" of life had now become different "works" of life.

And as she dove a little deeper in her thoughts, she understood Miide's points even: that the lowlife has no class and that the middle class is almost scrapped out. The government and its friends, being the minority, monopolize every sector of the economy; even common salt in the market goes for the price affordable only to the same importer of the product and his kind where his license for importation came from. Hence, the crux of Miide's contention is that the rich and powerful, by their indifferent attitude and the hardship they had imposed on the poor, coupled with their flamboyance and oppression, are indirectly or directly unconsciously calling on the masses that make up the majority to, by all means that they could, find their way up the ladder. It was only there, up the ladder, that there was hope, life, and future for them.

Kachi all of a sudden came out of her thoughts, and looking forward, she almost fell from her position as she saw her madam looking in her direction from a distance. She quickly withdrew into the corner, breathing rapidly out of fright, and then started walking away, not looking back. She walked briskly at first, then she started jogging; and when she was sure the canteen would have been out of sight, she slowed down and looked back.

"Kachi!" a voice called her, and she was startled, and shrieked. "Aah, hope no problem?" the voice added as Kachi turned to see their next-door neighbor Mama Seri.

"Heh? What? Heey, no problem, am only surprised. You know I wasn't expecting to see you."

"Okay o, your brother has been looking for you o. I heard him shouting your name now before I left home," the woman informed her.

"Heeh, thank you. I'm on my way home too. I will go and meet him." She passed the woman, who stared back at her suspiciously and shrugged as she walked away.

"Okay o, me have gone to shop sha," but she didn't get any reply from Kachi.

Kachi burst into the room and found Miide lying on the bed. He immediately turned her way as she came in.

"Where are you coming from?" he questioned

"Where have you been?" she countered. "Miide, I was scared. I didn't know where you were!" she shouted, her voice shaking, and she faced the floor as tears flowed from her eyes.

"Sorry," Miide apologized with his hands under his head as he lay with his right knee raised. "Sorry," he repeated with a grin on his face. "I didn't know I would not be coming home. You know I would have told you. I'm really sorry. It won't happen again." He was smiling to her now to pacify her; but she ignored him, spread a mat on the floor, and sat on it.

"Kachi, I said I'm sorry. Look, I have another surprise for you," he said excitedly as he sat up on the edge of the bed.

"I don't want your surprises. Just leave me alone," she said with a scowl, but Miide smiled and pulled out a bag from under the bed and unzipped it, and there were money and jewelry in it. Kachi leaned over to see the contents of the bag and was startled.

"Miide, what is this again? Oh my god, Miide has killed me o." She quickly rose to her feet and shut the door because she had left it open since she entered the house.

"Heeh, what did you do at the canteen yesterday?"

Miide's face changed immediately as he also asked Kachi in response to her question, "What happened? Have they come to bother you again? Or did you go there?"

"No, I didn't. I just want to know what you did there," Kachi inquired, looking straight into his eyes, but Miide waved her off.

"Don't bother me. I have taught the woman the lesson she deserved. I remember I told her never to lay her hands on you, that is the reason why I took you out of the other places you had worked previously. Look, I don't even want to talk about it."

"What do you mean you don't want to talk about it? I don't know what you did there, and only God knows if I still have my job!" Kachi yelled.

"What job?" Miide asked. "Even if they want you back, you are not going there anymore."

"Heeh?"

"And that reminds me, the reason I was coming to the canteen yesterday before I met what I met is that I've been noticing that a few of my old shirts have disappeared. While I was looking for them, I also noticed some of your clothes are not in the house. You wouldn't happen to know anything about the missing clothes, would you?" Miide added, but Kachi kept quiet and was a bit calmer.

"Did you hear what I just asked you?"

"I took them to church," she murmured.

"What did you say?" he asked, straining his ears and moving closer to Kachi.

"I said I took them to church," Kachi said audibly and looked away.

"You took my shirts to church? For what?"

"I thought they were old and you don't use them anymore."

"Old? What do you mean old, Kachi? I'm a street guy, I grew up under the bridge, and I sustain myself on the streets. No shirt is old for me," he explained, moving toward Kachi as he did.

"You have money to buy more."

"And so what? Even those ones I bought then were fairly used. And I don't want to start living like that yet, at least not until the big money starts rolling in."

"What money are you talking about? Don't think you will be bringing any money that I don't know the circumstance surrounding it into this house," she shouted. "Miide, what is wrong with you?" she continued as she rose to her feet and held on to his shirt. "Heh, please, you know you promised me that you will stop this dangerous means of living. Please, Miide, I spend the whole of my time praying for you whenever I go to the church, heh, because I'm always afraid, Miide, I'm always afraid one day I will wait for you to come back and you will not. I'm afraid one day I will go out looking for you and I will find the remains of your body burned. Miide, you remember the last time you came home wounded? I was so scared. Miide, if anything happens to you, what do I do?"

"Nothing will happen to us, don't worry. I'm doing this more because of you, you know—"

"If it's because of me, I want you to stop, stop," she cut in, but he drew her close to his chest.

"Look, let me tell you today, the reason I don't let anybody know this place is because of you, so they won't have to trace me here one day. And that is why I give you all the money to keep, so listen to me now. The day you hear anything that could get you into trouble about me, whether I'm here or not, just get all the money and leave. Just the money o, or else you could be suspected," he instructed, and Kachi cried all the more, hitting him and asking, "Why are you so hardened, Miide, why?"

"That's okay. I promise you nothing will happen to me, okay? That reminds me, where did you keep the money, the one for our upkeep? I looked all over for it yesterday, but I could not find it. I want to believe it's not in this room, else you're one hell of a cunning lady."

"It's in the stove."

"Which stove?"

"That one on the cupboard."

"My god, that was almost the only thing I did not check. I couldn't have thought of that place, he, he."

"Again," he said as he rose to go to the stove, "Kachi, don't go giving my money to the church o."

"I can't even take that kind of money to the church. I still keep my pay separate, remember, and I do get tips from customers. That is what I take to church," she countered and picked up the new bag of money. "Miide, we are now having too much money. What do you want me to do with it?"

"I was just about asking you where you have kept the rest of the money."

"They are all over the room."

"In this same room and I didn't stumble on any of those hideouts yesterday? I think I should consider recruiting you," he said and laughed. "So what do you want us to do about the money, dig a hole in the ground and keep it there or go give it all out?" he said, still laughing.

"Funny," Kachi taunted with a frown. "I've been thinking, I feel we should go and open a bank account." She looked at Miide who turned sharply to look at her too.

"What account? What money? You must be joking. Just leave my money alone if you know you can't keep it. You want me to get robbed? Have you forgotten how I got it myself? My money in a bank?"

"No, it's not like that. It's safer there."

"What if they want to know how I got it?"

"They don't concern themselves with customers' businesses, if you don't want them to, and it will even yield interest. I mean, increase if it's in the bank instead of keeping it here where it rots away in heat."

"I can't go to the bank. How am I supposed to do that? And how did you come to know this much about banks?"

"I take money to the bank for my madam almost every day of the week. I'm the only one she trusts with her money. The rest of the girls steal her money."

"She trusts you so much with her money and she still hates you so much. She's crazy. Let her go and deal with the rest of the girls with her money now."

"Miide, what is this?" Kachi picked up something wrapped in black nylon with two fingers, but before she knew it, whatever it was fell back into the bag because of its weight. Miide rushed to her side and took it before she had touched it again. He pulled up his shirt and tucked it into his belt strap at his waist, covering it immediately with his shirt.

"We take the money to the bank tomorrow, all of them, and save them in your name."

CHAPTER TEN

"Good afternoon, I'll like to see the general manager."

"Who?" asked the seemingly confused receptionist who had a telephone in each hand. "Who?" she repeated while she was trying to speak into the two phones at the same time.

"The general manager, Mr. Osintola, please," Usman replied.

"Hold on please." She motioned to Usman to take a seat. He sat on one of the beautiful long couches at the reception where some other people were waiting. After calling about two people who obviously came before him, the receptionist called him, "Sorry, sir, who do you say you want to see?"

"Mr. Osintola," he answered but was shocked by the surprised look on the woman's face.

"From where, sir?" Before he could answer, she asked him, "What is your name, sir?" And just as he was on the verge of answering, she asked again, "Do you have any invitation?" She lifted the intercom as she listened to him with her eyes on him. She spoke so quietly into the phone that Usman couldn't hear a thing she said as close as he was to her. Just as he was producing the card that he was given by his guest, a man approached the receptionist.

"Where is the man?" the man in a blue suit asked the receptionist. She in turn pointed to Usman who was now almost regretting not heeding his wife's advice to stay longer at home.

"This man will attend to you now, sir," the receptionist told Usman who was still holding the card. The man offered Usman his hand and shook him, collecting the card in return.

"How did you get this card, sir?" the man asked him.

"Mr. Osintola gave it to me," Usman answered nervously.

"When, sir?"

"About two months ago."

The man then picked up the phone beside the receptionist and punched in a few buttons. "What did you say your name is, sir?"

"WO2 Usman," he answered, trying to sound as important as possible. "Yes," the man said into the mouthpiece of the phone, "is there any name by WO2 Usman on his list of visitors today?" He pursed for a while, obviously waiting for a reply while whomever he was talking to checked. Usman kept studying the face of the man, checking for any expression. When the man eventually said okay, he knew the reply wasn't positive; the man dropped the phone and faced him.

"Your name, sir, as I have been told now, is not on the list of names for today, I mean the list of names of people that are to see Mr. Osintola today. But what baffles me is that this card, even though it's his old card, is not just a complimentary card, it's also a special invitation. This means that he must have forgotten to notify us that he gave one of these out as it is his custom. But I will beg of you, sir, to come with me into my office so we can serve you tea while we try to get hold of our boss. And by the way, sir, Mr. Osintola is our group managing director," he said as they walked on to his office. They went down the lobby and turned a corner. He stopped at the first door on the left, inserted the keys in the door, and opened it.

"You can have your seat there, sir," he offered Usman a seat and walked to his desk. "Pardon me please for not introducing myself to you earlier. It eluded my mind. I'm the chief security officer here. My name is Mr. Okafor. Let me order some tea for you while we wait for the call from upstairs, if and when they locate the GMD. I think he's most likely not in the office. He's been very busy of late with our new chairman. After punching the buttons on the phone, he communicated with the person at the other end, "May I have tea for two here please? What? Oh no, not at all." He laughed lightly into the mouthpiece. He then replaced the phone. "Yes, as I was saying—" The phone buzzed again. "Hello," he said as he snatched the phone handle. "All right, all right, right away then, thank you." He dropped the handle with a smile. "Our GMD just came in. He has been informed about you, and he requests to see you immediately."

"Really?" asked Usman, who had hardly spoken since he got to the office except when he moaned or mumbled a few incoherent words.

"I'll walk you to the elevator." The CSO got up from his seat and led the way to open the door. "If I may ask, sir, how are you to our GMD?"

"We're friends now," relieved, he answered with pride.

Usman had been sitting for another twenty minutes in the secretary's office, and he still hadn't finished feeding his eyes on the opulence of the office. The secretary beckoned to him.

"You can go in now, sir," she said.

"Oh, me? All right." He rose, straightened his shirt, and went straight for the door. He opened it, stepped in, and almost forgot to close the door behind him. For what he saw before him, he had not envisaged, not even after seeing what the secretary's office looked like.

"You should close the door after you, sir," whispered the secretary who obviously had peeped in to see what Usman's reaction will be on seeing the GMD's lavishly furnished and beautiful office. She had earlier realized he had been dumbfounded by the beauty of her own office.

"Officer Usman, here you are. It's so good to see you again," exclaimed a voice from the far corner of the vastly spacious office, and for a moment, Usman could not figure out where the voice was coming from. When he eventually did, he had to walk forward fast to catch up with Mr. Osintola's outstretched hand, as he stood behind his desk.

"Good afternoon, sir," he said with a wide smile and gripped Mr. Osintola's hand.

"I'm really delighted to see you in this form. Thank god you are well and up and doing now. I'm really happy. Please have your seat." He pointed to the chair behind Usman.

"Thank you, sir," Usman still managed to say amid his amazement. He sat.

"How is your family?" Osintola asked.

"They are fine, sir, back there at Kogi State."

"Oh, that's true, you did say you are from Kogi then. I hope they were not too devastated when they saw you in the state you were in then, with all the bandages and stitches."

"Of course they were, sir, but with some explanations, they actually realized that I was very lucky. We then began praying for you and your family, and I want to also, on behalf of my family and myself, say a very big thank you for the money you gave me even after I was discharged at the hospital."

"No no no," Osintola cut in, "I only did what was appropriate for me to do, and besides the fact that I caused you so much pain and fractures, my faith teaches me to do good when I am in a position to do it."

"But what I mean, sir, is that at home, we found the money useful for many other things even after I got better," Usman added.

"It doesn't matter," he said, waving the issue off, and scrambled on the papers on his desk. "You are quite lucky to have come today. You know, I've been really busy for a long time now. As a matter of fact, I have been very busy since the time of the accident. At first, it was the preparation to welcome my chairman, then later on his arrival. We had a tour of our factories. So I actually just came in this afternoon to see what requires my attention, and I was informed of your presence."

"I hope you didn't have a problem remembering my name?" Usman asked.

"No, not at all. As a matter of fact, they were just about to go ask your name when the receptionist said she kind of heard you tell the security man a name with a military title. This was coupled with the fact that you came with an old card of mine, it didn't take me time at all to remember. I will soon be rushing out again, so I want us to quickly discuss. Officer Usman, I didn't quite get what you say you do now being retired?"

"Basically, nothing for now, sir, since I got retrenched from my last place of work about a year ago. I was a storekeeper at a local factory then. I have not been able to secure another job," Usman explained.

"When did you leave the army, and was there no sort of gratuity or at least anything at all for compensation?"

"I left the service eight years ago immediately I came back from the ECOMOG."

"Did you go to the ECOMOG?" the GMD cut in, astonished.

"Yes, sir, I did, 1988 to 1990."

"Really, you're a hero then. It's just a pity how little is the reference given by the government to the ex-military men in this country," he said, shaking his head slowly and staring at Usman pathetically.

"And the gratuity came very much later, after a tug-of-war, going to the directorate of military pensions almost every day when we could not rely on their promises anymore. And by the time I got it, there was more debt on ground already to deplete the whole money," Usman confessed.

"This is rather incredible. I just don't know what to say any more than that because I'm sure your family has not been finding it easy ever since."

"We have not, sir. We have only been surviving by my wife's petty trade and some very good friends and neighbors. That is the real reason I'm here, sir. If there is any assistance you can render regarding my getting a job, I won't mind at all. I will be very happy."

"Hhhmm, to get you a job is not the problem," Osintola said and smiled. "But the only problem is that we don't have any office in Kogi State, and I don't know if it would be convenient for you to leave your family and work in Lagos."

"Ah, sir"—Usman flashed his dentition in a broad smile—"that is exactly what I'm looking forward to, sir, to work in Lagos."

"Then that does it! But I guess you still have to go and inform your family about the development, right? Or else I would have just handed you over to the human resources over here now."

"No, I'm not going anywhere again, sir. I've already informed my family of the possibility, and they are not expecting me anytime soon. I already have some change of clothes here and a few basic things I would be needing."

"If I may suggest, I would say a kind of job that goes with your professional background would be the best, and I'm thinking of finding you a place at the security department. What do you say?" the GMD asked him.

"That will be fine, sir, I like it," Usman consented.

"Let me call in the administrative manager then so he can arrange for you with the head of security. Also, may I let you know that it may not necessarily be

here at the head office? It could be in one of our numerous factories in Lagos."
He then picked the intercom. "Call me the administrative manager," he ordered.

"Good evening, Officer Akilu," Charles greeted as he entered the station
after another day's combing of the city in search of some free accommodation or
a God-sent helper that had been elusive for the past few days that he had arrived.
He had managed to pick up an extra shirt and trousers at the fairly used market.
He walked more and made sure he avoided any means of transportation as much
as possible. When such was unavoidable, he took the bus.

"Good evening, Mr. Charles, how was your day? Any luck?" the officer
responded, looking into a very large book in front of him.

"No, not really, but I think I'm making progress. I hope the divisional police
officer is gone home for the day, because Officer Banjo warned me not to let him
see me, that is why I left very early in the morning and came back late so that he
would have gone."

"Yes, he's gone home," the officer said, still looking down at the book, and
then he looked up. "The DPO is the reason you should have left here to find
whoever you say you are looking for. You know you can't live here forever. I even
doubt if we'll allow you here by the weekend. So you better get your bearing
right," he thus scolded Charles. Charles, who stood still while listening to him,
now walked over to the bench he usually slept on and sat there. He kept mute
for a while, peeping at the policeman at intervals, out of shame; then he humbly
asked, "Officer?"

"Yes," he answered, just raising his eyelashes, his head bowed.

"I was just wondering if there is any way I could, hen, hen, take my bath
around here. I've not really enjoyed a good bath since, though I manage to wash
my hand and mouth when I go out, but I will like to take my bath if there is water
anywhere around here. I don't mind taking it somewhere around the back."

With disdain, the officer looked at him, hesitating to speak at first, and looked
back into the book he was holding. He let time pass a bit before responding,
obviously trying to avoid speaking in the mood he was in. Then he murmured,
"There is a bucket in that next office, and there is a well in the next compound."

"Thank you very much." Charles went into the office.

"Thief, thief, thief, ole, ole, ole! Somebody help me! He has snatched my
bag! Help me!" shouted a woman who was just coming out of the premises of
the Trust Gate Bank on Lawson Road. She was still looking around, not sure
yet who snatched her bag in the midst of the normal heavy flow of people that

crowded the road because of the local market around the vicinity. The main reason why the bank opened there was so that the market men and women could easily lodge their money at the end of each day of business. "My bag has been snatched o!" the woman shouted again and started crying. The bank security men approached her.

"Madam, what is the problem?" The two security men stood by her, holding her by the hands.

"My bag, my bag is gone," she said faintly and started falling on her back; one of them held her while the other ran through the crowd onto the road and shouted, "Thief! Thief! Thief! Ole, ole, ole!" Immediately, some volunteers, on hearing this, quickly ran in different directions of the road trying to catch up with whoever looked like a suspect. The security man went back to join his colleague who was pacifying the woman. She was now sitting on the ground, crying profusely. They both tried to get her on her feet so she could move out of the bank's way.

"Oh, two hundred thousand naira, ah, I'm in trouble o. I'm in debt o," the woman kept wailing as she went on.

Meanwhile, the shout of "Thief, thief, thief!" extended. More people who knew what happened also joined in the chorus, shouting, "Thief, thief!"

Miide walked faster, holding the bag to his chest so people coming behind him would not see it; then as the shout drew nearer, he started running and increased his momentum even more. A group of security men who were by a factory gate saw him run past them suspiciously, and just almost immediately, they too started hearing the shout of "Thief, thief!" They got suspicious of him and one of them ran after him in pursuit, and his colleagues were trying to call him back.

"Usman, Usman, Usman!" they shouted, but they could not follow him because the gate would be left unguarded. Usman ran after Miide and started closing in on him when Miide, who was almost relaxing, realized he was being chased. He veered off the main road and ran into a slum neighborhood. He kept looking over his shoulders at intervals, still holding the bag firmly to his chest. He turned another corner and was now at the back side of the neighborhood. When he deduced that the pursuer wasn't ready to desist, he ran across a railway line and stopped running. He turned to look at the man pursuing him, who hadn't seen him ahead standing still, and waited for him. As the man drew closer, he unzipped the bag and, seeing that it was full of money, put it on the ground between his legs. He looked up at his pursuer who, now having seen him, started walking slowly, breathing heavily from exhaustion. As he drew closer, Miide said, "Old man, I can see you have been very zealous and for no just cause, I would say. Wait there now and listen. I could go away with this money, yes, I could go away. All I have to do is keep running till I get to where my guys are, but on second thought, I considered two things. One, these guys are very mean guys, and they can kill you, and I don't want your blood spilled anyhow. It's not as if I care o. Two, I think it is better to share the money with just one person and not with only God knows how many of my guys will be there waiting for me now." He looked down and pointed to it. "I don't know how much is there, but just looking at it, I can tell it's not less than a hundred thousand. So how would you like you to go home with fifty thousand naira today, just because you ran?" Miide stood arms akimbo, having been satisfied by his own exhortation. Usman, who was still trying to steady his breath, was looking from Miide's eyes to his legs; he then found his voice.

"What, hm, hm, do you mean?" he said, pointing to Miide in the face and trying to talk in between his gasps and breath. "Do you think I'm a thief like you?"

"Story," Miide taunted sarcastically.

"I'm an ex-soldier, if you don't know. I'm WO2."

"Story," Miide cut in again.

"I'm arresting you, and I'm taking both you and the bag to the police station."

"Story," Miide said again, and before Usman could continue, he added, "Look, wait, wait." He raised his hand to shut him off. "I've told you I could go away with the money, and I will. So if you don't want us to do it my way, the easy way, fine, but I have to tell you either of us is going to die right here and now." Out of nowhere, Miide produced a pistol and pointed it to Usman.

"Do you still feel like stopping me?"

Usman slowly stretched out his hand and, trying to conceal his fear, nervously said, "No."

"Fine," Miide said and picked up the bag. He pulled the zipper shut and held the bag under his arm. "It's just that you're a fool. You should have accepted my proposal and you would have gone home happy with a whopping fifty thousand naira. Your wife would have given you at your old age a very good sex tonight for making a good decision. But if you dare tell her about this, she would pack out first thing in the morning." He took two steps backward and waved the gun at him. "You can go." Usman didn't move, so he repeated himself.

"I'm sorry, but can I still have the money?" Usman requested.

"What?"

"I asked if I could still have the money."

"Oops!" Miide sighed and rubbed his temple with the back of his hand that was holding the gun. "Man, I love your guts. I thought you said you didn't want it."

"I didn't say exactly that."

"Oh yeah."

"I was going to take the offer."

"Really?" Miide put the bag down, opened it, and took ten wads of five thousand naira notes out of it and threw them at Usman's feet. He picked the bag up again and put it under his arm. "It is because you are an old man. That is the only reason I gave you the money, plus your guts to still ask for it," Miide commented and tucked the gun away again as Usman picked the money.

"I have to go now before any of the managers notice my absence. Bye." And Miide looked on, not knowing what to say. "It's nice doing business with you," Usman added.

"Oh, you see it as business, not favor?" Miide asked. Usman ignored him as he walked away.

"Ah, ah, Usman, where have you been, and why did you run after that thief like that?" asked one of his colleagues as Usman approached the gate of the factory.

"You saw me when I ran after the thief, didn't you?" he replied.

"Of course I saw you, and were you able to catch him?"

"If I did, you would have seen him with me, wouldn't you?"

"Why, what happened?"

"He got away. He was too fast for me. Apparently he's younger, wasn't he?" He entered the security post carrying a black nylon bag.

"You shouldn't have taken that long o. The supervisor just came in from the head office."

"What did he say?" Usman asked sharply, looking at his colleague sitting on the pavement.

"He didn't notice you're not here. He drove down straight, but you can be sure he would check in when coming back. By the way, what is that?"

"What?" Usman asked nervously.

"The bag you're carrying, what's in it?"

"Vegetables, I bought vegetables on my way back." He opened the mouth of the bag and exposed the bunch of vegetable that was only at the brim of the bag. "Let me just quickly take it to my quarters. I will be back before the supervisor gets back." He walked out briskly toward the security quarters that were in the factory premises where he lived.

"Pius, you still don't get it, do you? I've been to that canteen for the third time now, and I've always been told the same thing. That she doesn't work there anymore and nobody knows where she lives, and the worst part is I'm beginning to believe them," Mike confessed.

"That is the way such people live, sir," Pius said, standing in front of the old Italian but ever-beautiful wooden desk in the president's office. "I mean, those lowlifes, they hide their address or give fake ones so when they eventually carry out their mischief at their places of work, they just disappear and are untraceable," he added convincingly, and when he saw his boss's countenance, he bowed and gazed at the floor.

"We are going to find her," Mike ordered with a tone that suggested that they had no other options.

"Yes, sir," answered Pius, standing alert.

"You and I will roam that road and every other road that leads to it, every day as from today. Aside from when we are in the office, irrespective of our schedule or location, we must go by that road, and I believe one day we'll find her, and I mean very soon."

"Yes, sir."

"Get my driver."

"Yes, sir." He turned and left.

Ben looked up at the blazing sun, eating groundnut and popcorn. He wiped the sweat from his forehead with his forefinger and looked around the road. He filled his right hand again from the cone-shaped piece of paper in his left hand full of groundnut and popcorn and threw it into his mouth at once. He had given up search for a white-collar job now, so he had stopped carrying around his folder that usually contained his credentials. He now dressed as casual as possible. He left home very early in the morning, though now, he had been able to pay part of his rent, courtesy of Marris. He walked to the next bus stop and waited with the lot who were waiting to catch the bus. He raised up the paper cone in his hand and turned it into his mouth, emptying it there. Just then the bus arrived, and he panicked, joining the rush as everyone struggled at the same time to enter the bus. Some people alighted and had to jostle their way through the mob going in. A young man was among those disembarking, and Ben felt he was particularly close to him as he got down, so as he stepped in, he felt impelled to check his pocket, and his money was gone.

"Thief, thief, thief!" he shouted, pointing at the young man who was now running. He got down from the bus and started pursuing him. "My money, my money! Ole, ole, thief, catch him please! He has picked my pocket!" He ran as fast as he could with his fat body. Miide ran into a corner, and by then Ben was getting tired already. Miide looked back and saw that the man could not run anymore, so he slowed down and eventually stopped when he noticed the man had now bent over, holding his knees with his two hands. Ben fell on his buttocks and was trying to catch his breath. He placed both hands on his chest to relax himself, and Miide saw he was helpless. He started walking back toward him cautiously, ten feet away from him, and he saw that there was no way Ben could have matched up with him. He was too big, and without a word, he knew he was lazy.

"When you know you can't run, why did you try it?" Miide said and shook his head. "Abi, why do you want to kill yourself because of money? Abi, how much is the money *sef*?" he asked and pulled out the wallet, a very old one, opened it, and counted the few notes inside. It was two hundred and fifty naira. "Is this why you want to kill yourself? Heh? Because of two hundred and fifty naira? You're not serious at all," he said, waving the note at him and then thrust it in his own pocket. He threw his wallet back at him. "You could be needing that, and, man, you're such a stingy idiot. See your wallet, can't you change it, mmh?" Miide turned his back on him and left.

"Okay, let's drive around one more time, and then we can come back here and wait a little more before we go back to the office," Mike ordered the driver. Pius sat in the front passenger's seat of the Mercedes-Benz jeep, and Mike sat in the middle of the backseat so he could look out of all the car windows and even through the back screen conveniently as the driver drove around. They had been waiting in front of the canteen for one hour after they had gone around twice, driving slowly through the road and turning into every street one after the other; and since neither Pius nor the driver knew who they were looking for, all they did was listen to Mike and quickly pull over anytime he saw somebody who looked like the lady they were looking for. Agitated and somewhat apprehensive, Mike gazed out as they moved on.

"Sir, maybe she's out of town," Pius said, almost shouting out of frustration, and he immediately came to his senses. He quickly added gently, "I mean, I think she could be, sir." When he got no response, he waited until they had gone into another street before he disguised his next complaint.

"Or probably, she does not even stay around here, sir, maybe she stays quite far from here, and she only could find a job here." When there was still no reply this time, he did not wait for long to introduce his next line of discouragement.

"Sir, I honestly think the weekend would be the best time to find somebody in this kind of environment. I think by then it will be calmer around here, and most people will be home then." But before he finished this time, Mike cut in gently.

"Pius."

"Yes, sir."

"Do you know that you should never give up on a dream just because it will take time to accomplish? The time will pass anyway . . . So the next time you ever try to discourage me, I will discourage you first," he said without any change in his posture, still looking around.

"Stop," he exclaimed all of a sudden, "stop, stop, pull over!" Before the car could come to a halt, he opened the door, and Pius shouted, "No, no, sir, don't juuummp!" He tried to reach out for his boss from the front. "Pull over, you idiot!" he shouted to the driver.

"I have, sir," the driver cried.

"You should have pulled over faster. Can't you see he's trying to kill himself?" Pius looked out to see Mike running into a street. "Oh my god! This young man is going to kill me!" he exclaimed and ran after him.

"Sir, sir, wait!" Pius shouted as Mike took a bend and turned into another street following the lady he saw. He caught up with her and touched her on her shoulder lightly. The lady turned to see him breathing fast and heavily. She shrieked. Mike could not believe his eyes as Pius joined them; it was not Kachi.

"Oh!" he said in amazement. "I'm sorry, please, I'm sorry," he said in between his gasps and breathing. "I actually thought you're somebody else. Please, I'm sorry."

"You can go," Pius said to the young lady who looked every inch like Kachi in terms of her body shape but nothing like her facially. Pius took Mike by the upper arm and started going back to the car. Mike shook himself free of him and walked faster, ahead of Pius to the car.

"To the office," he said as he settled in the back of the jeep again.

Usman finished eating, picked a toothpick, and stuck it into his mouth. He picked up the napkin and started drying his hands. One of the service girls in the canteen where he had just finished eating, which was down the street where he worked, came and stood beside him waiting to collect her money. Deliberately ignoring her, Usman brought out some money from his pocket, looked at the amount on his bill, and dropped it on the table where he ate. Resentfully, the lady picked up the money and walked away briskly as Usman rose and started walking out.

He froze as he got to the door when he saw a face he knew. Miide also stood still and fixed his gaze on him.

"Good afternoon, sir," he said, and his eyes left Usman's face to quickly survey the people in the canteen. When he did not get any reply, he repeated his greetings, not knowing what Usman would do if he turned his back on him and left. He boldly walked past him, but Usman grabbed his hand, and Miide quickly turned to face him.

"We need to talk," Usman said in his commanding tone. "Meet me here tomorrow at this same time." He stared into Miide's eyes a little longer than was necessary. He released his hand and left as Miide remained there with a dreadful look and watched Usman walk away.

"He's really a soldier," he said, smiling and massaging his wrist with his right hand. "He almost bruised my hand," he added as he proceeded to a table to make his order.

Usman had been waiting for thirty minutes after his lunch for his appointment with Miide, and already he was beginning to doubt if Miide heard him when he had said they had to meet at the canteen.

Could he have forgotten? It's just about twenty-four hours ago. He must be very dumb if he really has forgotten, he thought. He checked the front door again, and his eyes went to the wall clock. He was supposed to have been back at his duty post at the second gate, the back gate of the factory, about ten minutes ago; but he thought of waiting another five minutes as his eyes kept oscillating from the door to the clock on the wall. He rose from the chair. It was apparent that he was apprehensive of something because he almost staggered as he drew back his chair to walk out of the canteen. He walked to the door and lingered a little with his hands in his pocket. He was conspicuously restless. He then left and started walking away swiftly. Just about a hundred meters away from the canteen, he heard a whistle, but he didn't answer, and then it came again. He looked around and didn't see anybody, so he walked on, and when he heard the whistle a third time, it came with a call.

"Baba soja, baba soja," Miide whispered and waved his hand when Usman looked around to find out where the call came from. When he saw him at a distance taking a drink at a kiosk, he walked up to him angrily. He looked into his eyes for a while and spoke up.

"Look, young man, agewise, you are like a son to me, so you should be more respectful in your dealing with people old enough to be your father. When I said we should meet in that place"—he pointed to the canteen—"today at a particular time, I meant it. I left my duty post to be here, mind you," he gushed out, arms akimbo, with a scowl. Miide, who looked around suspiciously, took another gulp of his drink before he answered.

"I've been here before you came. I saw as you went in, and all the while you waited after you finished eating your eba and egusi, I was waiting here."

"What," said Usman in surprise, "and you just decided to waste my time? Are you crazy?" Miide took another gulp and dropped the bottle in the drinks crate with a slight noise. "I had to be sure you're not trying to set me up," he said, looking at Usman straight in the eyes. "Follow me," he added. He walked on ahead of Usman to a nearby restaurant and sat at a table. He gestured to Usman to do the same on the chair opposite him.

"Go straight to the point," Miide said.

"If you had been waiting for me at that kiosk while I was eating, how did you come to know—"

"Get to your point." Miide was sounding more nonchalant each time he spoke.

"There is money at my workplace, and I want you to come and steal it," Usman said.

"Steal? Are you calling me a thief?"

"No, I mean come and rob the place."

"My god, you just called me an armed robber again," Miide complained.

"No no no, I mean, whatever! Just come and get it!" Usman said, confused, as they both stared into each other's eyes.

"How much are we talking about here?"

"Honestly, I'm not sure, but every day from Monday to Friday, these dealers and customers from different states and cities come with their big trucks for our product, and they pay cash in our office here. But this money is taken to the bank at the end of each week, so they keep it in the account department safe vault till Friday when it would have accumulated. By then the office requires the assistance of the bank with a bullion van to convey this money to the bank."

"So what makes you think we can rob this place you're talking about and take the money?" Miide asked.

"I think it is quite simple."

"Simple? Fine, go do it yourself then," he said and started rising when Usman caught his hand.

"No stealing is simple," Miide said, "let alone robbery, mind you." He sat again.

"What I mean is the security there is not so tight. That's where I work, and I see and know everything."

"How many of you are on duty, and how many stay in the factory premises?"

"Four of us live in the premises, and we take turns for each day's routine. Two men at each gate, the front and the back gate. Another two join us from town who don't live on the premises. So we always have a set of two off duty, and in the night we all work together. Six of us work together all night."

"Is it the same extra two that join you in the day that come in the night?"

"No, a different set."

"Are you armed?"

"Yes, we have two rifles. We keep them with us in our quarters," Usman answered every question promptly. All of a sudden, he was no more in a hurry to go back to work. Miide was silent for a while before he spoke again.

"What time of the day do you think is best for the operation?"

"In the night, I think it will be best in the night. You can come in from the side of the fence that is directly behind our block, and I can distract the rest of my colleagues for you to gain entrance into the factory."

"Where is the account office?"

"It's in the warehouse, at the back of the factory. There is a shutter gate in the back. That is where the bullion van goes into."

"Who is in charge at the account office?"

"One Mr. Okorodudu," Usman answered, looking into the inquisitive eyes of Miide.

"And if we come in the night," Miide asked, "how are we supposed to gain entrance into the warehouse and break into the vault without making any noise?" Miide was not particularly asking; he was thinking out loud.

"That is why you're here," Usman said as Miide glanced at him and looked away.

"Can we meet here tomorrow again?" Miide asked.

"Ah, tomorrow Wednesday will be very busy. I am on duty." He paused. "What about Thursday? I should be able to make it on Thursday."

"Good, meet me here on Thursday then," Miide concluded, but he was interrupted.

"Ah, not here. I don't drink, so I don't like it in the restaurants," Usman complained.

"I don't drink too, but it's safe here in the afternoon, but for now we can meet in the canteen if that is where you want. Meanwhile, I want you to watch the flow of your customers tomorrow and on Thursday for me. How many of them come on Wednesday and Thursday, I want to know, and if they make appointments before they come, or do you have a list of their names at the gate?"

"Yes, we do. We usually check up their names before we let them in."

"Then I will need the list of requirements to be one of your dealers. All these I want you to get for me by Thursday. Two last questions: How did you know about the vault and the money? Have you ever seen any money there before?"

"Yes, I have." He was silent. "There was this weekend the bullion van did not come. I think it was bad. So our office had to take the money to the bank in one of our pickup vans, and I happened to be walking by the back door that day, so the accountant called me in to assist him in carrying the sacks to the vehicle. They were very big ones, and he had brought them all to the door of the vault, so I just picked them up. Somehow some of them had bad zippers, so I could see the contents."

"What denominations was it?" Miide asked in concealed eagerness.

"It was mixed, but there were a lot of bundles of fifties," he said. Miide looked at him and nodded gently.

"My last question, for now: how are you hoping to get out of the case after all this? I hope you are aware you security guys will be the first suspects?"

"Don't worry about me. Of course I will be suspected at first, but I have some kind of immunity. I'm connected to the GMD, and by the way, I think I'm old enough to be your father. Don't call me guy. You are too rude for my liking."

"Talking about being rude," Miide said as he rose, "how you paid that girl her money at the canteen is a good example. Good day." He walked out and was joined by another young man who was about the same age as him. Usman watched them for a while before jumping to his feet and rushing out.

Miide rubbed his stomach out of hunger and then yawned. He was almost home now, and then he saw Kachi at a distance with a group of people, so he ducked and peeped to see what was happening. He looked intensely at Kachi and noticed that she was smiling and kind of enjoying what she was doing. He also saw that there were more children around her than the few grown-ups, so he came out of his hiding place and proceeded toward her. As he moved closer, his eyes widened in surprise at what Kachi was doing. She was giving some children clothes, some of which were hers that did not fit anymore and some she bought to make it go round.

"Kachi, what are you doing?" he inquired when he eventually got to her. Kachi, who was caught by surprise at Miide's sudden appearance at home at that time of the day, became frightened.

"I'm just trying to give these children some of my old clothes. I will come and explain when I get home," she answered, and Miide nodded slowly and started walking away. He then froze when he noticed some of them were holding what seemed to him the same denomination of money, five naira notes. His jaw dropped in shock, and he shook his head slowly as he made his way home.

Livid when he entered the room, he lay back on the bed, with both hands under his head waiting for Kachi. He had forgotten about hunger. After Kachi finished with the children she was distributing things to, she went toward the house and waited a little outside, deliberately taking her time. She wanted to be sure Miide's annoyance had abated. After about thirty minutes, she went to their door that Miide, as usual, left opened. She peeped through. Seeing that he was asleep, or at least his eyes were closed, she let a smile slide over her lips at the realization of her expectation. She knew full well that Miide would sleep after every slight provocation. She tiptoed to his bedside, squatted, and picked her sandals from under the bed and gently stretched her hand across Miide's face. She took her Bible from the other side of the bed. She pulled her headscarf loosely from the standing hanger and drew a nylon bag from the window. She put her Bible into it and was going out when she heard his voice.

"Where do you think you're going?" Miide asked with his eyes still shut. As Kachi froze with a wide gaze at nothing in particular, Miide repeated, "I said where do you think you're going?"

"I'm going to church," she answered, sounding as defensive as she looked. Miide opened his eyes and sat up on the edge of the bed.

"You are not going to church today," Miide declared.

"Aaagh! Why, what have I done?"

"You are just not going," Miide repeated, looking at Kachi who was completely dumbfounded.

"Come here." Miide motioned to her with his forefinger. "I say come here," he ordered, raising his voice slightly, so Kachi moved close to him but still maintained her distance out of the premonition she had always had. She was afraid Miide would lose his temper one day, and this could prompt him to beat her mercilessly. However, he had promised her, after his temper had subsided on many occasions, that he would never do so; and he had hitherto kept his word. "Listen, I'm stopping you from going to that church of yours because if I don't, you are more dangerous to me than the risk I take outside there. You know why? It is because if you continue your stupid benevolence, you will get us both killed one day. Very soon people are going to start wondering and questioning what I do, and even though we live in the smallest room in the whole of this area, I think we're most likely the richest. And you know what they'll do when they suspect me? They would inform the police. I can't stand to be arrested, that is why you could be in danger. I'm convinced that if I can get this church out of your head, I'll have less problems with you. So stay home and stop being naive." When he finished, he lay back on the bed, ignoring Kachi who was still wondering if she had heard him correctly.

At first it was like whispering. After a few minutes, it turned to some kind of murmuring. Meanwhile, Miide had turned to face the wall, scheming out his plans for his operation at the factory. Suddenly Kachi burst into a wail.

"Uuuuuuuuuu, ahhhhhhh, aaaa!" Miide shrieked out of shock and turned to her to see what it was.

"What is it?" he asked soberly, but Kachi wailed more. "Wait, wait, what is the problem? Is it church?" But Kachi did not reply but wailed even louder. "Oh my god, I'm trying to think. Shut up, I say shut up!" he shouted, but Kachi cried even more. "Okay, okay, go go go, get out of here, go!" He picked up her Bible and put it in her hands, made her put on her sandals, and pushed her out. "In case you don't meet me when you come back, just make sure you take the money to the bank in the morning. Come on, get out of here!" He slammed the door after her and held his head with his two hands. "Ah, the only problem I think I have is this girl," he said, trying to feel his head for any aches.

Just as the door slammed shut behind her, Kachi dried her face, grinning and leisurely finding her way to the church. Miide got back in bed and continued his deliberations.

Mike returned to where he was now used to calling the canteen road, the neighborhood where he was so convinced Kachi lived. At 9:00 a.m., the first routine of the day was to drive around and search for Kachi. Mike was in the second week of the search. Despondent, Pius sat in the front passenger's seat of the Mercedes-Benz X-Class, absolutely unhappy and hateful, but deriving some relief as they began to breathe in some air of civilization, entering into Victoria Island.

The phone in his hand buzzed. He pulled the antenna and affixed it to his right ear.

"Hello." He waited for some reply. "Oh, please hold on a bit, ma." He turned and gave the phone to Mike. "Your sister, sir."

"Oh." Mike sighed and anxiously grabbed the phone. "Hi, sis, where have you been? I've been trying to get through to you." He listened. "Honestly, I've been trying to get you, believe me." He listened again. "No, sis, I've not abandoned you, and I'm not seeing any girl yet. What makes you think any girl could make me forget you? Wait, wait, and honestly take it easy. Really, I don't know what happened to your phone. Every time I tell my secretary to call you, she says she could not get through." He listened again. "All right, so that you can believe me, here is Pius, talk to him. Pius, when was the last time we tried to get through to her?" he asked audibly enough for Catherine to hear him handing the phone over to Pius, but Pius looked into his eyes and whispered, "Two weeks ago."

"What?" he exclaimed, keeping his voice low. Pius nodded to affirm his statement, and Mike withdrew the phone and said "You see, Cathy, I'm sorry, but honestly I've been trying to get you, okay? I'm sorry."

He listened more calmly now, and then he exclaimed, "What, what, do you mean come over? You should come around, Cathy." He listened again. "What do you mean never? Cathy, do you realize this is home?" He listened. "Our home I mean. Besides, you know I'm taking care of business here. I know I'm going to come around, but not now. That would be when I'm going to Asia for a meeting in about six months, then I'll stop over in the U.S. I hope you don't have any problem there?"

"It's only that they have a new director of finance," she answered briskly.

"What do you mean?" Mike asked.

"He delayed my allowance for last month unnecessarily, so I had him fired."

"Oh my god, Cathy, why? That is just like killing an ant with a gun. All right, I'll call you next week. Bye." He punched the button and rested his head. He took a deep breath and spoke to Pius.

"Where are we going?"

"To the bank, sir. The MD reported in last week about the land boundary the new branch is having with the neighbors, and you said you would check on it today," Pius explained.

"Is it really up to two weeks since we tried my sister last?" Mike asked after some silence.

"Yes, sir, actually, a little more than that," he answered and was tempted to add, "We've been more busy with your mystery girl." They had a quiet drive the rest of the way to the bank branch. Their banking arm was a subsidiary of Moses International Corporation. Pius and Mike alighted from the car and headed to the entrance of the bank.

"Good morning, gentlemen, can I help you?" announced a voice from their far right as they entered. They turned to see a very radiant-looking receptionist fumbling with the tail of her braided hair. She was dressed in a miniskirt suit, the same color as the window blinds in the bank; it was sky blue. Pius noted this as he walked toward her. Mike followed closely behind him. Pius stood in front of the receptionist and scanned her over before she spoke up again, showing off her dentition extravagantly.

"Good morning, sirs, this is Fortunes Merchant Bank." She was letting anybody who cared in there know that.

"May I help you?" she added as she gave Pius a cautious look, pulling her skirt to cover her exposed thigh out of embarrassment. She turned a little to face Mike, who looked to her as more of a gentleman, and exposed a smile from the corner of her mouth. Her makeup-coated face betrayed her wrinkles.

"No, you can't," Pius said. "Where is your manager's office?" "Inform him your chairman is here," he wanted to say, when Mike suddenly nudged him and smiled to the receptionist, who despite her efforts to conceal her thigh had not been very successful.

"Sorry, ma'am, we'll like to see the branch manager."

"For what purpose, sir, is it official?" the receptionist asked.

"Ah yes," Mike answered, with a smile.

"Okay, you can go up the stairs, sir, then go down the corridor. The last door on your left is his secretary's office."

"Thank you very much," Mike said and turned to go up the staircase as Pius, who all the while had been looking at the receptionist with utter contempt, turned to follow him without uttering another word to the lady.

He suddenly turned back and said to the receptionist, "With your makeup, you could be mistaken for just another piece of furniture." Pius then ran ahead to lead the way for Mike before he mounted the stairs.

As Mike climbed the stairs, he slowed down to examine the services on the floor of the banking hall. He was looking from the cashiers to the customers and the inflow of customers in the new branch. He didn't think there was enough orderliness, but he excused them. *They'll improve. It's a new branch.* He was about racing up the last few steps, when he thought he saw something. He paused and looked back down into the little crowd in the banking hall. He squinted. Just then his eyes caught something; it was a figure, somebody. He stared harder, thrusting out his neck. He descended a staircase and stared even more. He eventually came down the stairs and walked into the lines of people waiting. He walked toward the lady who was next in front of a cashier. He touched his forehead for a minute, trying to remember something, and then called her.

"Kachi." She turned with a shriek to see the caller; confused, she gazed.

"Sir, I don't think I know you" was what was on her mind, and it was written all over her face too. "I, I, don't . . .," she was beginning to say, and with that, Mike's mouth broke into a very wide smile like he had just confirmed something.

"Oh, I think I know you now, sir, you were the one who came to the canteen the other time." Mike's smile broadened as he nodded.

"Excuse me," the cashier called her and pushed her passbook out from the window. She took it and thanked her, and she started walking toward the door side by side with Mike.

"I've been to that canteen many times to ask of you, and they always told me you have left the place, but I never believed them."

"Yes, I'm no more working there. Something happened, yes." She remembered and turned to look into his face. "I think it was the last time you came. My boss got annoyed with me and sent me away. It's a long story anyway."

"That's true." He put his forefinger to his chin. "I remember she got really upset with you about something. I could not really figure out what it was, but if it had to do with me, I'm deeply sorry for whatever inconvenience I might have caused you," he said, putting his hand to his chest.

"No, sir, don't worry. I'm no more there, and as I have said, it's some sort of long story, but I'll get another job," she assured him as they exited the bank for the parking lot.

"Job, I can help with that," Mike suggested.

"Sir, don't worry. It's not easy to get a job in this Lagos, so don't let me bother you with my own problem. I can manage," she declined with a warm smile that made Mike's jaws weak.

"Okay, where are you going now? I'll take you there. My car is here."

"Ah, don't worry, sir, I'll take the bus."

"Excuse me," Mike alarmed, "my name is Mike, and I'm a very young man. Please stop the sir thing, and call me Mike."

"All right, sir," she said and waved him bye as she exited the gate.

"Wait, wait, I'm taking you, wait!" Mike shouted as he ran to his car and told his driver to go after her. "If you lose her, you lose your job," he told him.

Meanwhile, Pius was already knocking on the bank manager's secretary's door when he noticed that Mike wasn't behind him. He went back downstairs wondering what he was doing in the banking hall. He wasn't at the stairs. Pius got down and looked around the banking hall, still unable to find Mike. He walked over to the receptionist who was now having a telephone conversation; he waited in front of her, looking into her eyes as he was being depleted of patience. For another minute, the receptionist did not end the conversation, so he pressed the knob on the phone and cut off the call.

"Where is the other man that we came in together just now?"

"Why should I know? Didn't you two just go up the stairs together?"

"I could not find him behind me when I got upstairs. Did you see him come back downstairs?"

"No, I didn't."

"You sure?"

"I said I didn't see him, aha. He's not a kid, is he? He couldn't have gotten lost here. Look for him around. He could be somewhere in the banking hall or outside in the parking lot. Look for him and stop disturbing me." Pius nodded and went around looking for Mike as she had suggested. Meanwhile, a call came in for the branch manager in his office from another branch of the bank, asking if he had received the chairman.

"No, ma, I haven't seen him here. Is he supposed to be here? I mean, I didn't know he was coming here, ma," the manager explained, bewildered and shocked.

"Manager, you don't need to know. All you have to do is receive him, or does your chairman need your approval before he visits his bank?" the voice on the other end asked.

"No, ma, he doesn't. I will look on now and get back to you immediately after he gets here, ma."

"Please do. Some other urgencies here require his attention. This is the executive director administration, Moses International Corporation speaking, bye."

"Bye, ma," the manager managed to say and dropped the phone. He picked up his intercom and punched two buttons.

"We are supposed to receive the chairman here today. Did you know that?" he yelled into the phone.

"No, sir, you didn't tell me," answered the secretary.

"I know I didn't tell you. I just want to know if you have seen anybody like that today."

"No, sir."

"Okay, I want you to call the reception and find out, alert them, then call me the head of operations immediately. You also should come into my office now, now, now!" he yelled and dropped the phone, looking around and unsure of what to do next.

The receptionist was speaking to the secretary on the phone when Pius returned.

"Of course not, I will know when I see somebody like that—" Pius cut off the line again.

"Are you mad?" she inquired in anger.

"No, but if it will interest you, the man I'm looking for is your chairman." The receptionist froze and could barely say her next words.

"Excuse me?" she said, her eyes bulging.

"You heard me well," Pius said, standing straight with his hands in his pocket. The receptionist put the phone piece back to her ears and punched the buttons.

"Madam, I think I have somebody from Moses International Corporation here." She dropped the phone, apparently after the other end went dead. "Do you mean to say, sir, that you're from MIC?" Without a word, Pius unbuttoned his jacket, flashing the MIC emblem on his tie; she took a deep breath. A minute later, the manager descended accompanied by two heads of department; the receptionist rose and pointed to Pius. The manager ignored her, stretching out his hand to shake Pius's. Pius obliged. Pius also flashed him his tie only long enough for him to see.

"Mr. . . . ?" And before the manager could give him his name, Pius asked the manager egoistically, "How many cases of kidnap have you had here so far?"

"None, sir," the manager answered timidly.

"Then I think you just got your first record then," he said, taking the manager by the arm and walking him aside for a talk. "And do you know who is missing here?" he said quietly for him alone to hear. "The chairman . . ., and I think"—he folded his hands at his back and walked back to where the rest were—"this is beyond you here for now. You will do well to call the MIC for me to be picked up or you get me there."

"My official car will take you right away, sir," the manager declared.

"Good," Pius replied, his hand still at his back, absorbing every look that was on him, of respect and honor that was usually bestowed on anyone who carried the identification of the prestigious MIC at any of their subsidiaries.

However, as Mike followed Kachi with the car, he met her at the bus stop; and he beckoned her to get inside his car.

"Please come in. All I want to do is take you home, I mean your home."

"No, sir, I say don't worry. Besides, I don't want you to know where I live. My brother is a very stubborn person and hot tempered too. He must never see you with me let alone at our place. I just don't want trouble for you." Mike alighted from the car and stood by her.

"Ah, a, a, you see now, it's too late. Even if you don't let me take you, I will follow you home because I have to see you again," he said, looking at the ground, shy with her. "But if you let me take you, I promise not to get to your house. I'll drop you at the beginning of your street, then you just point your house to me, please, please." Now they looked into each other's eyes, and as if they communicated and agreed, she consented to go with him. Mike opened the door for her like his first lady, and she settled herself in with Mike, and they proceeded.

"So what where you doing in the bank? Do you have an account there too, sir?" she asked very quietly.

She asked with such innocence that made Mike absorb her voice into his heart before he thought of the question. He shut his eyes briefly before answering.

"Firstly, you call me Mike. We are friends, right? And yes, I have an account there," he said and looked the other away, through the window. He hated lying. They drove all the way as Kachi led the driver on. Mike didn't look her way, but he was so oblivious of every other thing around him but her presence.

He felt close to her, but at the same time, he felt like there was a huge mountain between them. He listened to her heartbeat. He heard it louder than his; he heard her nostrils pull in air, and when she exhaled, he felt like taking in the same air she let out. He looked at himself and wondered if he still carried his own body, if his flesh was still there in the car. He could only feel his heart, his soul came out to him, he was in the land of oblivion, and he could only see two things, two souls trying to merge.

"I think you should stop here." These were Kachi's words that snapped Mike back to consciousness, after about twenty minutes' drive of descriptions that were unknown to Mike.

"What?"

"I want you to pack here," she said in a voice that made Mike want to drift off again.

"Are we close to your house?" he asked.

"Yes, we live down this street."

"This street? My god, I've always gone the other way. Okay, pull over," he said to the driver. He got down from the car and held the door for Kachi with such elegance she felt it.

"Thank you very much, sir."

"Mike, Mike," Mike cut in, but she could not bring herself to call him by his first name.

"So which one of the houses do you live in?" he asked, being particularly slow in speech. He had been careful so she could hear him. She turned to face the street.

"You see that last house on the left?"

"The bungalow you mean?"

"Yes, the unpainted one, the house behind it is where I live with my brother."

"All right, can I just walk you home?"

"No please, you said you won't. My brother could be home."

"Okay, let me just walk you down the street then. I promise I won't get to your house. I want to see you get home safe."

"I'll be fine, don't worry, sir," but Mike did not let her finish her statement.

"I promise I won't get to your house, please," he said, looking into her eyes, and just as if they communicated better with their eyes, she nodded and cast her gaze to the ground. Then she looked up and looked him over. He realized he would call attention to them in the slum neighborhood if he walked her down dressed like he was.

"Oh, this?" he said, putting both hands to his jacket. He pulled it off and ripped off his tie, throwing both in the car. He loosed his shirt at the neck and tucked it out. It all made little or no difference.

"Are we ready now?" he snapped, and with a smile, Kachi slowly nodded. "Wait here," he said to the driver, shutting the door as they walked on. As casually as he now looked, Kachi still looked around nervously, as a few eyes in the neighborhood were glued on Mike.

"Don't worry, I can see them too. I won't dress like this when coming next," he said, looking straight.

"You won't be coming, will you?" she turned and asked him briskly.

"Not unnecessarily, I promise." They walked the long street without talking much.

"That is where I live"—she pointed—"the one behind. Will you go now? I don't want my brother to meet you here."

"Yes, I will go now, but how would I see you again?"

"I don't know. Do you want to see me again? Why?"

"Yes, every day, I want to see you tomorrow. Let's just say for now, I'll like to be your friend. Let me see, eeeeemmm, can we meet at the bank? The way I see it, it looks like that's the only place we can meet for now."

"My brother will not send me to the bank tomorrow."

"Why don't you just come there without letting him know?" Mike argued, stealing looks into her eyes once in a while.

"There is no way he won't know." She cast her eyes to the ground again, and when she looked up, they were looking into each other's eyes. "Okay, I'll try."

"Thank you. Should we say twelve o'clock?"

"No, maybe two o'clock. He would leave home after his lunch, that is if he comes home at lunch, so I'll leave immediately after he leaves, and if he doesn't come home for lunch, will you be free from work at two?" He smiled.

"Anytime, I'll be there from twelve," he assured her and stretched out his hand to take hers. Thinking he wanted to give her a handshake, she also stretched out her hand toward him. He took it, turned it over, and kissed the back of her hand. She withdrew her hand swiftly, looking around nervously to see if people saw them.

"I'm sorry, I forgot we are out here. I'm so sorry. I'll see you tomorrow." But she did not reply to him. She grabbed the nylon bag that contained her passbook with both hands and ran toward the house. When she got to the side of the house, she stopped and turned. Their eyes locked again, and she waved.

"Bye-bye," her lips read. In high spirits, Mike returned to the car, taking slow, long steps. With his hands in his pockets and with a simple smile on his face, he opened the door, looked up to the sky, and took a deep breath. The sun penetrated his eyes. He shut his eyes and entered the car.

"Take me home," he said, resting his head, his eyes still closed. There was a buzzing noise, and he shrieked before he realized it was the cellular phone. He remembered it was supposed to be Pius's phone, but he had received his sister's call on it, and he had been sitting on the phone all the while. He picked it up.

"Yes?"

"Sir, where are you, sir?" It was Pius.

"I'll see you in the morning," he said and disconnected.

On getting to his Ikoyi mansion where he lived alone with his stewards, cooks, and maids, he headed for his room at once, replying to each of his workers' greetings gently without looking their way. He settled in bed after a futile effort of trying to watch the television, and after a series of tossing and turning in bed, he fell asleep, but his heart was wide awake.

Having been in bed for long and not able to get any sleep, Kachi was upset, but she was not clear on what exactly she was upset about. Now she lay on her back and held up her right hand. She put it to her nose, the spot Mike kissed, and smelled it. She smelled it again and held it to her nose. She kissed it and slept.

CHAPTER ELEVEN

"Next bus stop, next bus stop, bus stop! Pay up, everybody, pay up. If you are coming down at the next bus stop, pay up now o!" shouted the conductor of the bus, to collect his fare. "Oga, wey your money. Madam, your money?"

"Auntie, your money? Collect your change. Oga na, where you enter? Na fifty naira be your money o, no be forty naira. Collect your ten naira change, madam." He continued negotiating as he collected his fare from the passengers and gave some change back to those it was due. At the same time, he argued with some to pay him their complete bus fares. "Oga nla," meaning fat boss, "wey your money?" He was talking to Ben.

"Who are you calling oga nla? Are you crazy? You must be a very stupid boy, you this useless boy." Ben flared up. The hard big buttocks of the woman standing in front of him pressed hard at him, which was making him very uncomfortable. He was on board a luxurious city bus.

"Sha give me my money. All this your big grammar no concern me. Wey my money?" the conductor asked in pidgin again.

"I can't reach for it now. I'll pay you when I get down," Ben explained.

"Why you no wan give me my money now?" the conductor inquired.

"I said I can't reach it now," Ben shouted. "It's in my inner pocket, and if you are not blind, you can see am hard pressed, front, back, and on both sides," he managed to say, holding the cross bar at the roof with both hands, and the conductor burst into laughter.

"Ah ah aaaah ahh," he roared, "you are so fat you can't put your hand in your pocket." He roared again as some passengers joined him in the noise. When his roaring laughter subsided, he asked for his fare from the man standing next to Ben.

"Your money, baba?" The fairly elderly man reached for his breast pocket and brought out two notes.

"For I and this gentleman," he said, pointing to Ben.

"Oh me!" Ben exclaimed. "You don't have to, sir, I have my money. Honestly, I just can't reach for it now, and I have my reasons for keeping it there. Please don't bother. I will pay for myself when I get down."

"I know," the elderly man said gently. "If I wasn't sure, I wouldn't be paying. Just let this insolent child stop making noise." He raised his chin at the conductor.

"Thank you, thank you very much, sir." Ben stared at the conductor with contempt. "Insolent indeed," he added. "I'm very grateful," he said again and shook the man with one free hand.

"You're welcome," the man said, then the bus came to a halt at the bus stop, and the passengers alighted.

"Are you getting off here too?" Ben asked his benefactor.

"Oh yes, I'm going to that factory road."

"Okay then, I can return your money." Loosening his belt and his zipper a little, he put his hand inside his trousers to take money from another trouser pocket he wore underneath.

"No, not at all. I said you shouldn't bother. Please take it as a favor from me," the man said with a smile.

"At least let me show this foolish boy that I have more money than he's made today," he said, bringing out some money to show the conductor who waited for the rest of the passengers to come down. The conductor was now getting back into the bus as the driver moved, shouting as the bus sped off.

"Oga nla!" he shouted mockingly at Ben, and Ben showered curses on him.

"Leave him and let him go. He's not worth the stress," the man admonished Ben, turned, and left.

"Okay, sir, thank you very much, and God bless you," Ben said. The man waved at Ben, and they went their separate ways.

Thirty minutes later, Ben walked into a canteen to eat; there were just a few people in there, so it was quite easy for him to quickly notice a familiar face that was seated at a side table. His face lightened up as he walked to the table.

"Ah ah, it's you again, sir," he exclaimed, and the man who had paid for his bus fare earlier on looked up at Ben. For a moment, he looked confused, then he forced out a smile after his recognition of Ben.

"Oh yes, it's me. We meet again."

"Do you eat here often?" Ben asked and pulled a chair from the table to join him, took his seat, and adjusted in the chair.

"Not really, I'm actually waiting for someone. I have an appointment here to meet with somebody, but I do eat here once in a while, and you?"

"Me? Heh, it's my first time here. I'm only in this part of town for a job opportunity that I was told to check back for in a firm on Benbow Street. But that is just by the way," he said, waving his hand as if to dismiss the issue. "I think now is the best time and place to repay you for your kindness. By the way, my name is Ben, Ben Kingsley again."

"Usman, WO2 Usman, retired. People fondly call me Officer. You can call me that too." He gave a broad smile as they shook hands.

"It's a pity you still see it that way. You don't have to repay me for anything."

"Yes, I know, but people like you are not easy to come by. So you were in the military? That's interesting to know, and I can see the government has made retirement blissful for you," he said, looking Usman all over.

"Says who? I stand here today only by the grace of God Almighty. The government didn't make anything blissful instead. I can almost say we were repaid evil for the good we did the nation. Being out there in the jungles of Liberia where most of us were butchered and killed, some had one or both of their limbs amputated by ferocious rebels. Yet we get home to wail and cry before we can get the pension that is due us, after we had incurred enough debt to consume the entire pension as soon as it came. Look, I don't want to talk about it," he said, waving it off. "I suffered, my brother," he continued, "I suffered with my family. It wasn't funny at all."

"I'm so sorry," Ben sympathized. "I feel for you, and I understand what you are talking about—"

"I don't think you can ever understand, my brother," Usman cut in. "We starved. My family went without food for long periods, and my children fell sick, and I could not even pay for their hospital bills. Heh heh, imagine, after all I did for this country, and yet some leaders keep depleting the nation's treasury. How much will it cost to pay pensioners, for god's sake, how much?" A waitress came to their table and stood to take their orders.

"That is it!" Ben exclaimed, pointing to him. "That is it, the leadership. They have crippled the economy of this country by looting the treasury. Look at me, look at me, I've graduated for eight years, eight good years, sir, and ever since then I've not found a job. I've not worked for a day, and I have a second-class upper degree in mathematics from the University of Nigeria. I have walked almost every area in Lagos, written over five hundred applications, yet people who are not as qualified as I am get the jobs I could not get. Why? Because they have connections, and these same people they know up there are the people stealing the nation's money. They employ this new guy they know or fix them up somewhere, primarily for their own use, thereby breeding another set of federal thiefs."

"You've been a graduate for eight years," Usman said, surprised.

"Look, let's forget about this country's issue and eat," Ben said with another wave of his hand. He looked around for a waiter to take their order since the girl that came earlier left. "Hey, you come here!" he shouted to the same girl. "So what did you say you would take, Officer?"

"Hm, hm." Usman smiled. "I told you I didn't really want to eat. It's a young boy that I'm waiting for." He checked his watch and frowned. "He is a very disrespectful young boy. He should have been here by now."

"Who's this guy anyway? Please forget him and let's eat," Ben said, and they both looked up at the same time into the eyes of the girl already waiting with a scowl on her face.

"I want four wraps of pounded yam, let me start with that, and give me two pieces of meat," Ben said, and he and the girl looked at Usman for his order.

"Give me *fufu* instead, two wraps, and two pieces of meat."

"Is that all?" the girl asked, turning to leave as both men ignored her.

"But I think, I think I should pay this bill since you still haven't secured a job. I think I should pay," Usman said.

"And what work do you do now, sir, if I may ask?" Ben asked as he picked the jug of water on the table and poured water on his right hand into a wash-hand basin, in readiness for the food.

"Ehe, it's just by sheer providence that I got a security job at the factory, and even though it's a guaranteed job, I don't think that is what I want to settle for, for the rest of my life, after all my sacrifice for this country. I'm not getting any younger, and I think I deserve my own share of the national cake. So I'm beginning to make plans not to die poor and also to make sure my children don't suffer," Usman confessed and lifted his hands off the table as their orders arrived. The waitress put their plates of food on the table and left.

"I would love such plans for myself now o. I need it before I die of hunger. If not for a neighbor of mine, the good Samaritan the Lord has sent to me, I would have died of hunger. She has not been doing it for nothing though, yet the truth is she's a lifesaver. She's the one that gives me money and most times foodstuff to keep my body and soul together. Most times she gives me five hundred naira, and at times it could be one thousand. She just gave me another five hundred naira yesterday. I take my time to spend the money, and moreover, since my last experience with a thief, I've devised a secure way of keeping my money in Lagos."

"Yeah, you wanted to tell me something about the reason you keep your money that far away?" Usman inquired as he looked at the wall clock and hissed. "What kind of useless boy is this," he murmured and swallowed a ball of fufu.

"You won't believe I was picked. My pocket was picked and my wallet taken. I saw the boy that did it."

"Did you get him?"

"No, I couldn't," Ben said as he took another mold of pounded yam. "I ran after him, but he outran me. He was a young boy, tall and slim, and very athletic. I suffered for the money. Afterwards, I was stranded and couldn't go out for anything. Thank god for the lady I told you takes care of me, I would've starved. So since that time, I've been on my guard."

"That is terrible," Usman exclaimed, quietly holding a morsel of fufu halfway to his mouth.

"You can say that again." They both got busy with their food.

Miide entered, looking straight at their table, walking toward them like he was already aware of Usman's location in the canteen.

"Good afternoon," he said, looking at Usman. Both men looked up at him.

"You're late," Usman exclaimed while Ben replied his greeting with a full mouth and faced his food again.

"Can we talk now?" he asked and started walking back toward the door. Usman rose after him, dipped his hand into the washing bowl, and quickly rinsed it.

"That is the young man I've been waiting for," he explained to Ben, and just as if Miide heard them, he paused at the door and looked back at them. Ben gave Miide a second look, sighing, "Mhmm," with his full mouth. He looked at him again at the door and for a moment thought he caught a hint of recognition but immediately got engrossed in his food again. As Usman joined Miide at the back of the canteen, Miide voiced out, "Never ever mention me to anybody. Never introduce me. Never talk about me." He looked into Usman's eyes lividly. Usman almost started defending himself but thought for a moment and decided not.

"Ahmm, okay, that's all right."

"So how far?" Miide asked almost immediately.

"How far with what?"

"I mean, what have you been able to gather as information?"

"You should have said that. I'm not a small boy like you, so I don't want you speaking to me in slangs," he complained as Miide carefully looked around. "I spoke with one of our staff about the requirements for being a dealer. He said the requirements were not much but that you have to register with the company, then make sure you come for the product every week for the next three months and for the—"

"What do you register with, or how I mean?" Miide cut in.

"You have to pay a deposit, but really it's not extra money. It's just the money for your goods, but you pay it up front two weeks before you come to pick the goods."

"Two weeks?" Miide exclaimed. "Shit."

"What is wrong with that?"

Miide thought for a moment. "Can you remember right now any of your dealers' names?" It was Usman's moment of thought.

"Yes, I can remember one Madam Rosian. She always tips us at the gate."

"Where is she?"

"Em, em, I think she's from that Isolo side?" Usman said doubtedly, scratching his chin and looking at the ground.

"I need you to be sure."

"She's from Isolo," he exclaimed. "I can remember now. I'm sure it's Isolo. She's definitely from Isolo." Miide looked at him a little longer and kept quiet.

"What is the inflow of your customers these days?" Miide continued. Meanwhile, Ben was almost through with his food when he finally recognized Miide. He remembered him. Looking at him from behind now gave him a very familiar view since he had run after him for a long time when he stole his wallet.

"Oh my god!" he exclaimed and rose from his table in a hurry, dipping his hands into the wash-hand bowl and spilling water on the table at the same time. He needed to have another look at Miide, so he rushed out to see him. He walked slowly and stood beside Usman, looking into Miide's eyes, as Usman answered, "Fifteen customers on Wednesday and ten so far today before I left, since I'm not on duty this afternoon, and they all came with their trucks."

"It's you!" Ben shouted, pointing to Miide. "It's you, you are the thief that stole from me. I remember you now. It was you!" He raised his voice, grabbing Miide by the hand and trying to hit him with his fist as Miide kept his cool, confidently waiting for him to come to his senses.

"What?" Usman murmured in surprise and grabbed Ben by the arms, holding him back. "Wait, what are you talking about? This can't be the person you're talking about. Wait, wait," he defended as he struggled with Ben, pulling him back from Miide who still hadn't flinched.

"Thief, thief, thief, I will kill you today!" Ben shouted. He was trying to free himself from Usman's grip. Usman saw that Ben was making a scene, so he forcefully pulled him to a standstill and, holding him by the collar, drew Ben close to his face and spoke to him quietly but seriously.

"I said take it easy. What's your problem? Stop shouting and be calm."

"Are you together?" Ben asked, but Usman ignored him and took him farther apart for a moment until he had calmed him down. Usman came back to Miide who still stood arms akimbo with a semblance of calmness.

"I'm very sorry for that. He's okay now. Can we finish now, because I want to go and resume my work for the evening shift," Usman apologized to Miide who was looking the other way as if he was being watched.

"I want you to meet me here in two weeks' time, I mean exactly upper Monday. Late evening at 8:00 p.m. Be careful and vigilant and make sure you're not followed. Now, before then, anytime you see me, don't get familiar. I mean don't do as if you know me, anywhere you see me, anywhere. I hope you understand that, Officer?"

"Yes, I do."

"Good night, and don't forget Monday, 8:00 p.m.," he added as he walked away. "And when you're coming"—he paused—"you can bring that big fool with you." He threw Ben a glance.

"Is it true you stole from him?" Usman quickly asked, but Miide's gaze rested on him with such contempt. He shook his head and ignored him. As Ben joined Usman, the waitress walked up to them and demanded her money. Usman paid without hesitation, and Ben watched absentmindedly.

"I can't believe you're letting that thief get off like that. I think you owe me an explanation for what you're doing with that boy. How are you related to him and . . ., whatever, whatever!" he shouted confusingly, throwing up his hands. Usman looked at him straight in the eyes, motionlessly for a while, and when he saw that he was calm and listening, he spoke up.

"I thought you said you would like to make plans for your fast-approaching future so you don't die too poor, and also for your children, so they don't curse you when you're gone."

"What has that got to do with this? Of course, I said so," he answered reluctantly. Usman looked at his wristwatch, acting as if he was in a hurry.

"I can't wait any longer. I have to resume at work now. When and where can we meet again so we can talk and I will tell you what you need to know?"

"Anytime I guess. Just give me the time," Ben said, making a face with his mouth. "Oh, I've forgotten I have to decide the time since you're jobless," Usman said mockingly.

"And what is the meaning of that, sir?"

Usman laughed. "Just let us meet here at ten o'clock tomorrow morning, and I'll let you know that there is no plan when there is no money, eh, eh, eh." He laughed a little more. "Mr. Kingsley, good day, heh, eh. Is it okay if I call you Ben? Okay then, good day, Ben," he said without waiting for his reply, and Ben stood, watching him with indignation as he walked away.

As Usman was about handing over the following morning, a pickup van drove into the gateway blasting its horn. The incoming security man taking over from Usman went there to attend to the early customers. He looked at his wristwatch, and it was 7:40 a.m. There were two men in the van, and seeing that it was not a customer's vehicle, he motioned to the driver to turn off the vehicle's engine and for one of them to come to the gate. So the passenger got down and came to him at the gate.

"Good morning," the security man greeted.

"Good morning," the reply came, and from the sound of the voice, Usman raised his head from the table in the security post, as he recognized the familiar voice.

"What can I do for you?" the security man asked.

"We're here to register for dealership," Miide replied.

"Oh, but it's quite early. The man that will attend to you is not yet around. The staff have not come in yet." Usman sat still with his face in an old newspaper reading nothing. "If you'll wait for him, he shouldn't be long anymore. I think latest by eight, ten o'clock, he should be in," the officer continued.

"We'll wait then," Miide answered promptly.

"You can bring in your vehicle then and pack here," the security man said and started opening the gate as Miide went back to join the driver in the van. They drove in and packed in the premises, waiting in the van. The other security man joined Usman again as they finalized their handing over. He finished, and he left for his quarters.

At five minutes past 8:00 a.m., the deputy manager at the factory came in; and after the introduction, he invited Miide who claimed to be representing his boss under the guise of Mr. Seye into his office.

"Have your seat, Mr. Seye." The deputy manager motioned to the chair in front of his desk, "I hope you have been hinted on our basic requirements, which of course are not hard to meet at all in as much as we need more dealers than we need the end users. We intend to make it quite easy for you to make our dealership," the man confessed with a smile.

"And why do you need more dealers than end users, if I may ask?" Miide fraternized with the manager.

"Not exactly, Mr. Seye, if we don't have end users, who would the dealers or our retailers sell the products to? But since our dealers pay up front, we always make our money. The end users are also important notwithstanding."

"Are you trying to say you're less concerned if the retailers get to make their own sales or not?" Miide scrutinized.

"Not at all, Mr. Seye, I can boldly tell you we produce quality. I mean, we have the best in town, and I think you're a proof of that. Hence, you're here. By the way, who recommended us to you? You're meant to have a referee anyway. It's part of our requirements."

"Yes, Mrs. Rosian, recommended you to my boss."

"Oh yes, Mrs. Rosian," the manager said, blurly trying to remember the name. "Yeah, I know that name well. She's one of our biggest dealers. I will just give you this form to fill, then you can take it along with you to the accountant and pay your deposit with this form to him. I hope you have your deposit with you?" the manager asked, looking serious all of a sudden.

"Yes, I do."

"Good," he said with a broad smile. "How much?" he quickly added.

"Not much, sir, just twenty thousand naira."

With a look of dismay after a moment, the manager said, "Okay, you can go and pay. Your referee is a person of great importance to us." He tried to smile.

"One more thing, sir."

"Yes."

"The reason we're becoming your dealer is because we have an order for your product, and we will like to meet up with it, and the order is needed next weekend."

"Oh no, we can't do that. It's against our policy. Mrs. Rosian or what's her name should know that," the manager queried, almost flaring up.

"Of course, she did say so, sir, and she also told us if we will be willing to pay more, you might be able to assist us."

"Mmh?" The manager sighed and then calmed down.

"Yes."

"As I've earlier said, your referee is very valuable to us, and we don't want to lose her, so, so"—he kept quiet for a moment, obviously trying to get the best figure—"so it will only cost you an additional twenty-five thousand naira." He looked mischievously at Miide.

"That will not be any problem, sir."

"Really?" he asked in amazement, eyes wide.

"Not at all. We won't disappoint you."

"Okay, just make sure you come straight to my office when you come, then I will direct you to the accountant."

"Okay, sir, so I will go and pay to the accountant now," Miide said and rose.

"It's good doing business with you, Mr. Seye." He stretched out his hand across the table and shook Miide's hand.

"It's my pleasure," Miide replied.

"And when you're coming, come early because at the latest by two o'clock we will be getting ready to close registration for the day."

"All right, sir," Miide said, knowing that this means that they will be moving the money to the bank after the close of registration.

"Don't forget, come to straight to my office," he reminded as Miide exited his office.

Twenty minutes later, Miide left the factory and got into the van, and the vehicle left the premises. At some point, far from the vicinity, Miide paid the rented van driver his fare and got down.

"Don't forget nine o'clock on Friday. Please don't disappoint me," Miide admonished him.

"I won't forget. I'll even make it before nine," the driver assured him.

"Okay then, bye." Miide waved and walked along the road. *I need to get to base now. I must make arrangements for the guys I will use for this operation. But before then, I should get something to eat and buy Kachi's sanitary pads. I think her menstrual period starts today. If I'm not mistaken, today should be the eighteenth,* he thought and later rearranged his priorities; he first stopped over at the base. The base was a dilapidated building that was on the verge of collapsing. It was where the former kingpin of the various groups converged with the gangs.

They actually purchased the property from no one, but they managed to procure the land papers from the government. The former kingpin did a poor renovation job on the building, fit enough for their kind. The military government sentenced him to death for multiple murders during a bank robbery operation. His protégés had gotten hold of their fortress and called it "the base," and since then, no one had dared to trespass. Miide discussed briefly with two of the guys there who with great enthusiasm agreed to his plans. They planned to meet on Thursday. Afterward, Miide dropped in at a store and bought Kachi's things.

"What . . . and you collected it?" Ben exclaimed, sitting opposite Usman as he hinted him on how he met Miide.

"Yes!"

"That makes you an accomplice or whatever. According to the law, you are a criminal . . .," he almost shouted again.

"Good you know the law and you're still hungry. I don't, and I have money to eat," Usman pointed. "I'm talking fifty thousand naira here, you idiot. When was the last time you saw that kind of money? Heh, eh, how much did you say he robbed you of the day he picked your pocket? Two hundred naira, or was it three hundred?" Usman asked in annoyance and brought out a folded wad of naira notes from his pocket. He counted out two thousand naira and slammed it on the table before Ben. "That is your money. He took it from you and gave it to me. Now I'm giving it back to you. So it's your money, yet it's stolen. Won't you take it back? You'll be a fool not to because he stole from you."

"Of course, I will. He stole from me," Ben said and picked up the money. He folded it and put it in his pocket. Usman, who obviously waited for him to do just that, then accused him.

"Good, you see, you're a thief yourself. Is that the amount he collected from you?"

"Stole from me, you mean?" Ben corrected.

"Whatever!" Seeing that Ben could not answer, he asked, "Are those the exact notes he collected from you? And thirdly, am I the one who stole from you? Why did you collect stolen money from me?" He added, "You see, I'm not trying to criticize you, but tell me, you know the nature of the rich men, the wealthy people we have in this country, don't you?" Ben nodded slightly. "Which one of them, Ben, which one of them will not collect this money from Miide like I did that day?" Ben's chin rested on his chest as he assimilated his words.

"They will!" he said loudly. "Even the richest of them with all the money they have will still take it given the same circumstance," he affirmed, knocking hard on the table.

"That is what I'm saying. Look at it this way again. We do all the work in this country. I fought for the nation, and it is people like us that are the same masses that pay the taxes, yet we are being robbed of decent livelihoods by the same aristocracy. They steal the millions and billions and restructure the law and the constitution so they can be above it while all of the masses are dealt with by the same law since they are below it," Usman lamented, picked up his bottle of soft drink, and gulped the content. Ben, mesmerized by his speech, followed after his gesture. On setting his bottle back on the table, Ben responded, "That is understandable, but what is this thing between you two, I mean, since you had to meet here yesterday? I hope you're not planning to perpetrate a repetition of that unscrupulous act with that guy?" he asked, and Usman looked at him with disdain.

"Look here, my friend, it doesn't matter. As long as my life is not in danger and I'm not risking anything to make money, that settles it. Besides, I've been in worse danger and risk. I think your story so far is pathetic enough, and I think you need help. I thought you said you're planning for a better future?" He stressed with more disdain, "This is a good chance for you, and I can assure you, you have nothing to be afraid of."

"Who?" Ben asked in surprise. "Oh, are you trying to get me involved in this? I'm sorry if I gave you that kind of impression. You're talking to the wrong person! What . . . wait, wait, I don't even get the picture yet. What are you trying to say?"

"No wonder you have not gotten a job since you left school. I'm very sure when those companies saw your CV, they were impressed, but on seeing you, they could see foolishness written all over your face, apparently the same reason the boy himself called you a big fool . . .," Usman scolded.

"He called me a fool?" Ben inquired.

"Of course, and I think so too. Otherwise, you will not be jumping to conclusions like that. Anyway, all I need you for is to escort me here next Monday, I mean upper Monday, and you can go home with as much as twenty thousand." Usman emptied the bottle, rose from his seat, and walked out. Ben was speechless. "You know the factory, don't you? You can check me there anytime," Usman said as he exited.

Kachi walked slowly, reluctantly as she approached the bank, not knowing if she really wanted to go and what to do when she got there, since she didn't have any transactions to carry out. She walked across the gate, looking into the parking lot to see if she would see any trace of her date. Not wanting to raise the suspicions of the security men, she went about the next two buildings before she turned and started coming back. Then she made up her mind to go into the bank to see if Mike was there since he said he would be there long before she came to the bank. She noticed a man who had crossed the road alongside her when she approached the bank a while ago now oscillating between the two ends of the gate. He was dressed in a black suit and had both his hands in his pockets. Once in a while, he murmured grumpily. As she approached him, the mobile phone in his pocket rang. Shocked, he dipped his hand into his jacket pocket. He looked at it angrily, punched it, and fixed it to his ear. "Hello, yes . . . He's not available right now, and he doesn't want to be disturbed."

Kachi heard him say as she passed by him and turned into the driveway, heading for the door to the banking hall. "Hi," a voice called from behind her. She heard it but didn't think it was for her. "Kachi." She now heard and looked back and saw Mike slam the car door shut. She stopped and turned, relieved as she tried to return Mike's smile with a slight grin.

"I thought you weren't coming anymore," he said as he tried to give her a hug. She shrieked, and he backed off, but so as not to let the effect linger long, he avoided saying sorry and quickly spoke up. "I actually got here at twelve o'clock."

"I am sorry, but I had to wait long enough to be sure my brother wouldn't be coming home for lunch," she explained so innocently Mike almost regretted making his last statement sound like a complaint, when he actually meant to impress her.

"Oh, it's nothing. In fact, you came at the right time. It's lunchtime, and I thought we could go out to eat together," Mike proposed as he walked her toward his car. He didn't get a reply, so he looked back at her and noticed she was looking toward the gate. "That man has been standing there since . . .," she was saying as Pius himself looked back to see the two of them staring at him. He stared harder to be sure of what he was seeing; he straightened himself, buttoned up his jacket, and started walking toward them.

"Oh, that's my PA. I'm sorry, you have not met him," Mike explained.

"Your what?"

"My PA, I mean he works for me," he said and opened the door for her to enter the car.

"Where are we going?"

"I thought you would grant me the pleasure of eating lunch with you."

"I'm sorry, but I can't stay long."

"I know, and I promise not to keep you for long," Mike almost swore as their eyes locked again, and Pius looked on, infuriated. Kachi nodded slowly and proceeded into the car, and Mike followed her. Pius got into the front seat, and the ever-waiting driver started the engine and moved out of the bank premises.

"Lunch," Mike said to no one in particular, and Pius reluctantly motioned to the driver to make the next turn. "Pius."

"Yes, sir," Pius answered in a concealed grunt.

"Where were you looking when she passed by you?"

"I didn't know who I was looking out for, sir," Pius said, irritated.

"Pius was actually waiting for you when you saw him at the gate," Mike explained to Kachi with a smile. The rest of the way there was silence, more than appropriate. Mike looked Kachi's way a number of times, but Kachi maintained her straight glare at nothing in particular. After about fifteen minutes of driving, the driver pulled over at a restaurant, and Pius got down to open the door for Mike who was already out and holding the door for Kachi to step out. Decked in a navy-blue suit and a sky-blue shirt without a tie, Mike looked elegant as his shirt exposed a V-shaped white vest underneath Mike gave his elbow to Kachi to hold, assuming that she understood his gesture, but even though she didn't take it, he kept close to her; he could see the timidity in her. Pius was already holding the door open for them. Mike led the way to a particular table, where he most of the time sat. He drew out the chair for Kachi to sit, but she had already gone around the table to the other side.

"No, come and sit in here."

"I-I will sit here," she said quietly, not wanting to be heard; she kept peeping at the few people scattered around the large expanse of the restaurant.

"No, please, I drew the chair for you. That's the way it's done," Mike explained quietly, and Kachi moved around the table to settle in the chair he was holding for her, then Mike took his seat, opposite her.

"Good day, sir," a voice exclaimed by their table, and Kachi was startled because she didn't see the waiter coming.

"How are you," Mike replied with a smile, and the waiter who was decked in a white shirt and blue trousers with a blue tie held out two menu lists for them. "I hope you have good cuisine for me this afternoon," Mike said and collected one of the lists. The waiter was about to give the other one to Kachi when Mike stopped him.

"No, don't worry," he said without looking up from the list he was holding, "I shall choose for my guest." The waiter withdrew his hand and took a closer look of Kachi, and he wouldn't take his eyes off her. He was caught off guard when Mike beat his arm with the menu list to startle him.

"Yes, sir."

"You know what, I've decided to eat simple and light today, so fried rice and fish for both of us and any white nonalcoholic wine to go with it," Mike ordered. The waiter collected the menu and gave Kachi a last look before leaving.

"Right away, sir," the waiter said. Kachi kept her eyes straight on Mike and avoided the waiter's stare as even more people stared at her. The waiter was stopped briefly by another man heading toward Mike; they had a little chitchat, before the man approached the table.

"Good afternoon, sir." The gray-haired man with a nicely cut mustache bent slightly to greet Mike.

"Good afternoon, Austin. How are you?"

"It's good to have you here again, sir."

"The pleasure is mine."

"Enjoy your meal, sir."

"Well, am trying to, if you'll allow me," Mike pointed jokingly, and they both laughed. The restaurant manager looked at Kachi and greeted her too, briefly.

"Good afternoon, ma'am," he said with a weak smile. Kachi only bent over nervously; she responded inaudibly.

"You will enjoy the food here. I'm sure you will, and immediately after, I will drop you home." Mike tried to start up a conversation to get her attention off the stares.

"Where is your friend?" she asked apprehensively.

"Who?"

"Your friend, the one that came with us."

"Oh, Pius?" She nodded, and he smiled and looked down on the table.

"Kachi, I told you Pius works for me. He's just my PA, not my friend. So, em, em, he can't stay here while I eat. He's with the driver in the car," he explained modestly.

"What work do you do?" she asked.

"Hm, hm, hm," Mike sighed, as he cast his gaze on the center of the table between them and picked his nails. "Okay, let me put it in a way you'll understand it. I work in my dad's company . . . yes, in my dad's company."

"Your daddy has a company?"

"Yes," he said with a shrug and looked away, while Kachi nervously glanced at the remaining occupants in the restaurant, her hands in her laps. Mike looked into her eyes again, wondering what was on her mind or what other questions she might want to ask; but before she could say anything, he asked, "Why did you ask?"

"I've been seeing you with these big cars since I've known you."

"Ahmmm, yeah, my dad has lots of automobiles." He nodded affirmatively. "Lots of cars."

"And he lets you use them all just like that, with a driver and that man?"

"Hmmm," Mike sighed and looked about on the table confused, not knowing how to answer the question. "Yeah, he lets me have them. I'm permitted to use them I mean." The waiter arrived with the meal on a large tray; he set the plates of food and a bottle of wine on the table and left. "It's fried rice and fish," Mike told her, studying the expression on her face. "You'll like it, I can assure you." Kachi looked into his eyes, as if she was finding it hard to believe or she needed some kind of encouragement before she started eating it. Mike picked up the fork and held it out deliberately so she could see what he took and how he was holding it, but he didn't look her way. He took the spoon and served himself some stew and fish. "May I?" he asked her, and she nodded.

While he did, she picked up her fork too and held it with both hands at the handle on the edge of the table. She looked at him as he gently served her until he was through; he lifted his head and caught her staring at him. He picked up the bottle of wine, and Austin moved in from where he was standing by to serve it. Mike quickly motioned for him to stop. He filled both glasses himself and then repositioned the bottle, before he commenced eating. She ate slowly and delicately, and Mike peeped at her randomly as he ate, looking into her eyes. After a while, Kachi left her fork on the plate, and Mike looked at her inquiringly.

"I'm okay," she said quietly.

"Are you sure?"

"Yes."

"You don't like it, right?"

"Of course I do. I'm just okay. I'm full," she explained, but Mike looked at her doubtfully, wondering what was on her mind. "I want some water," she added, and Mike looked at her glass of wine, knowing she had not touched it.

"Don't you want the wine?" he asked her, and she shook her head. He looked aside at the man waiting on them, and he beckoned to him; he walked briskly to his side.

"Can we have some water here?"

"Right away, sir," the waiter said as he walked away, showing up some minutes later with a plain jug of water and a glass cup on a tray. He put it in front of Kachi and asked if he could pour it; Mike nodded, his eyes not leaving Kachi's. The waiter did and left them again. Kachi drank the water and put the glass back on the table.

"I'm sorry I noticed you didn't drink while you were eating. That's probably the reason why you could not eat much." Kachi did not respond. She only stared at him. "But I would still like you to have a taste of the wine. It's just fruit. There is no alcohol in it. You'll like it. Please try it." Mike kept his gaze on her for a while longer than normal. She lowered her gaze unto the glass, stared at it for a while as if examining it. She then slowly picked up the glass. As she raised it to her lips, she returned her gaze to Mike and kept staring at him as if she needed him to sip the content. Before she could stop, Mike, as if reading her mind, gestured to her to have more; and she seemed to heed him by opening her lips a little wider to accommodate more of the liquid. She settled the glass on the table and looked into the smiling face of Mike; she could not bear it, so she looked away shyly.

"Did you like it?" he asked, and she nodded affirmatively. "Good, am glad you did." Mike again motioned to the waiter to come and clear the table. They both watched him as he did. When he left, Mike, in a sober voice, spoke.

"Yes, I will like to ask you for something," Mike said, resting his elbows on the table and both hands in a fist at his chin. Kachi listened almost apprehensively. "I, I will like you to be my friend. I mean I want us to be close friends, very close . . ." He paused and spread his hands before his face, and he looked into them and eventually put them to his face; he removed his hands and spoke on. "What I'm trying to say is, I will like to see more of you, but I'm not sure if you feel the same way." Kachi was silent for some moment to make sure he was through before she spoke.

"But I thought I told you my brother would not allow it?" she said regrettably. "He's, he's . . ." She slightly hit the back of her hand on the edge of the table.

"We can always see like this. He doesn't have to know. He can't just keep you in there. You have your life to live." He paused again, seeing that questioning look on Kachi's face. Again, he wondered what she was thinking.

"Are you a Christian?" she asked.

"What?"

"I asked you if you're a Christian."

"Eh, eh," he chuckled lightly. "I don't get what that has to do with us being together, but of course, I am. I'm a Moses, oh sorry, I don't think I ever told you my full name, Michael Oludare Moses," he declared with such pride and affirmation that made Kachi swallow hard and want to cease asking him questions.

"Is that it?" She was quiet.

"Do you go to church?"

He chuckled again. "Yeah, I used to when I was in the United States and my parents were alive, but I've been quite busy ever since." He shrugged.

"What did you say about your parents?"

"Guush, sorry, just forget about it. Forget I mentioned it at all," he said and waved it off, looking aside at nothing in particular.

"Are they no more?" she asked sympathetically, but Mike, still looking away, didn't answer. "Mh? Mh?" She sighed, and Mike nodded slowly. "I'm so sorry, I'm very sorry," she said, meaning it.

"I know you are." Mike looked her way cheerfully. "Can we change the subject now? Thank you." He smiled and drank from his wine. When he put the glass down, he pointed to her glass too, and she obliged.

"What time is it?" she demanded. Immediately, she put the glass down.

"It's quarter to four," Mike said.

"Then I have to go," Kachi said. "I have to go. My brother will be worried about me now."

"What?" Mike asked with a shrug. "You are not a little girl anymore, and besides, you can't be lost. You could have gone anywhere of your choice."

"No, it's not like that. I don't really go out except to church. I don't go seeing any friend, and he knows it," she explained pitifully, holding the edge of the table with both hands in readiness to rise.

"And talking about your brother, you have not told me what he does?"

"He doesn't want me talking about him," Kachi said defensively.

"Oh no, I don't mean any harm. Honestly, I just thought I could be of help, that's all. I'm sorry to have upset you if I have." Kachi remained quiet with guilt written all over her.

"I'm sorry, I didn't mean to—," she was saying when Mike interrupted her.

"No, it's okay. You can never offend me. You have not, and you can never, since no one can offend another without the other's consent. I refuse to consent to any wrong you can ever commit against me." He put his right hand to his chest as if he was swearing an oath.

"All right, I don't, I won't."

"Can we go now?"

"Yes of course." He rose and joined her at her side.

"We have not paid," she pointed at once.

"Oh, I have."

"No, we haven't. I didn't see you pay."

"Yeah, I've paid before today. I've paid for a long time to come, which reminds me of how we'll see again. I don't think we have any problem with how, but when?"

"I don't know," she said regrettably.

"Well, I'll choose a date then. Shall we say tomorrow?"

"No, not tomorrow."

"Day after?"

"No, it's too early."

"Then please let me see you on Monday, please." She was quite shy looking in and out of his eyes, and when their eyes locked again, she nodded.

"Okay, Monday. Where?" Mike looked back at the waiter.

"Austin."

"Sir," he answered and moved briskly up to stand by him with both hands at his back.

"Austin," Mike continued after a moment he had arrived, "my lady's name is Kachi. Anytime she's here, whether I'm here or not, give her my treatment and let it be on my bill, anytime."

"Yes, sir," he consented enthusiastically, smiling more than necessary. "Moreover," Mike continued, "she would be meeting with me here on Monday. Make her feel at home if she gets here before me. And she will meet with me more frequently here as from now."

"All right, sir, understood, sir."

"That will be all," he finished and looked back at Kachi. "Should we say the same time?"

"I don't know," she murmured, amused at the way Mike spoke to everybody else besides her. And when Mike's look lingered, she consented, "Yes, same time."

They proceeded to the door, and just before they exited it, Mike produced a card from his pocket and gave it to her.

"Take this," he said. "If you ever need to get in touch with me at any time, just call any of those two numbers on it. You are sure to reach me immediately. Don't lose it and don't be careless with it. Only a few people have it. Don't forget. If you ever need anything, help of any kind in any emergency, just call, okay?" It was more of a request than an instruction, and she nodded. Mike pushed the door open, and she walked out first.

On seeing the two come out, Pius and the driver jerked back to life from their dormancy. Mike and Kachi got into the car, and they were on their way.

"Let me have it, Pius?" Mike demanded from the back.

"Sir . . . ?"

"I said let me have it."

"What, sir? Oh, sorry, sir," he slurred and then opened the glove compartment, producing a slightly bulky envelope, and gave it to Mike. Mike held it for a couple of minutes and gave it to Kachi quietly.

"You might have need of this," he said.

"What's inside?" she asked him.

"Wait till you get home," he told her, as she gave the envelope a second look. She kept it on her lap and stared out the window. Then she looked his way and murmured something.

"What?" Mike asked, not hearing what she had said.

"We're still going to talk about your parents," she said. "I will like to know."

"Of course, we will," he said and smiled. "I'll tell you about my family. As a matter of fact, there is a lot we still haven't discussed about you too, you know. We'll also talk about your family." When he said this, Kachi looked expressionlessly into his eyes and then looked away. She was quiet the rest of the way to her house.

"It's okay here," Kachi said quietly to Mike as they approached her house.

"What? Why here? At least let me take you to the point I dropped you off the last time."

"No, no, it's okay here. Please tell him to stop now," she pleaded. "Pull over," Mike ordered, and the driver slowed down, stopping the car beside the road. Mike stepped down from the car, and so did Pius, who had been totally silent throughout the whole drive. Kachi also got down from the car as Mike held the door open for her. She looked around to be sure she did not raise too many eyebrows for bringing such glamour into their neighborhood. When she was certain she had not attracted too much attention, she turned to Mike to say farewell, and then she suddenly froze.

"Are you okay?" Mike inquired. When he didn't get any response, he noticed she wasn't actually looking at him, so he turned to see what it was that absorbed all her attention. It was Miide looking at them. Not understanding what he was seeing, Miide was also confused looking at Kachi for an explanation. Kachi left Mike's side and walked slowly but cautiously toward Miide, stopping a few feet away from him. Miide walked past her toward their home, stretching out his long legs before him as if he was in a match pass. His tall frame made him look flexible, though he was as rigid as his attitude was, and he was carrying a paper bag. Kachi finally caught up with him. Miide stopped suddenly and looked back at Mike.

"You leave now, and I don't ever want to see you here again, do you hear me?"

"Who do you think—," Pius started saying when Mike cut in, "Piuuus."

"Yes, sir."

"You heard what the gentleman said, didn't you?" Pius's response took a few seconds.

"Yes, sir, I heard," he said at last, still looking ferociously at Miide who was waiting for them to leave.

"Get into the car and let's go." They got in, and Miide watched as they turned the car and sped off. He walked on, and Kachi followed him. They got home, and Miide dropped his paper bag on the floor, then he lay on the bed. Kachi put down the envelope she was holding on the cupboard, took her bag from the hanger, and put the envelope inside it. Then she picked up the paper bag Miide dropped on the floor and looked at the contents.

"Miide, I'm not on my menstrual period yet. Why did you buy me sanitary pads?" She brought out the bag of sanitary pads from the paper bag. She looked his way, but Miide did not flinch. He rested his head on his two hands, looking straight up at the ceiling, his legs crossed. "I thought I even told you not to buy me pads anymore. I'm no more a kid, and I can buy it myself now," she grumbled. She walked over to the base of the bed and put the bag down there. She came back to the cupboard, opened it, and carried a pot out of it. With both hands, she carried it delicately going to the kitchen when Miide spoke up.

"Was that not the same guy I saw with you the day I came to the canteen and I was calling you from afar?" Kachi froze and slowly turned her head to look at him from the corner of her eyes. She waited for some moment before she answered.

"Yes."

"And I hope he's not the same guy that got you sacked, because I can remember one of the girls at the canteen that day said that your madam saw you with a man after she had sent you on an errand. That was why she got mad with you."

"No, it wasn't that. I had come back from the errand before he came, and she saw me with him, and I have never before—," she was trying to explain when Miide asked again, raising his voice lightly, "Was it him or not?" And Kachi kept quiet again before answering.

"It was him."

"Who is he?"

"Just my friend." Miide chuckled.

"What were you doing in his car?" he asked, and Kachi looked down at the pot she was holding, then she looked at the door and then looked the other way and then at the pot again. Then Miide, who up till now had not looked her way, turned to her and repeated himself, "I asked what you were doing in his car?"

"I went to see him, and he brought me home," she managed to say and looked away at the door.

"What did you say?" He sat up on the bed and glared at her intensely, his jaws wide apart. "Listen to me carefully and listen good: you will not see that man again, understood?" he pointed to her and rose from the bed, coming straight toward her. "You will not let me see you with him anymore. Whatever makes you think that guy means any of the lies he has told you already, I don't understand. That kind of person does not have anything to offer you. All he's attracted to is your beauty, and once he's ravaged you in bed, he'll be done with you. You'll never see him again. If he tries that, he will have me to deal with anyway. I'll simply kill him. But I will not even give him the chance to mess you up. Forget about this guy! Hope you are listening to me? Forget about him! He can never be serious about you. Can't you see? That kind of guy is not meant for you!" he shouted and stormed out of the room. Kachi was still on the same spot when he opened the door again, and just letting his head in, he said, "And today is the eighteenth of the month. You should by now be feeling close to menstruating. Maybe you have quickly gone deep in the delusion of love to notice it, big girl." He then slammed the door behind him. Kachi, after a moment of trying to clear her head, still with the pot in her hands, walked close to the wall to see the calendar. She confirmed it was the eighteenth of the month; she returned the pot to the cupboard and left for the toilet, where she drew up her dress and lowered her pants halfway, and before she could look into it, she knew she was beginning to feel wet.

Kachi then suddenly blurted out, "Oh no, you see, that is why I don't want him monitoring my life anymore. He knows more about me than myself." She lamented, "For god's sake, I'm old enough to take care of myself."

CHAPTER TWELVE

The pickup van slowed down as it got into the driveway that led to the factory gate at about midday. There were two other vehicles already at the gate waiting to be passed in, a goods bus and a minitruck; both were there to convey their goods. The first two vehicles got passed, and the security man raised his hand for the van to stop as it drew near.

"What is your name?" he asked, looking into the book he was holding with the other hand.

"Mr. Seye is my name," Miide answered from the passenger's seat, beside the driver. Another huge guy sat in the back of the van of Gavilon Enterprise. The man at the gate looked through the list in his hand thoroughly, a minute longer than necessary, and it seemed like forever to Miide. He eventually nodded and waved them in, still looking into the book as if he wasn't sure of what he saw.

The driver parked behind the minitruck in what looked like a queue that went all the way to the back of the warehouse. Miide and his men remained in the van. The trucks and vans of different sizes drove out one after the other with their load of goods mounted high in the open back of their vans. Miide's van drew closer to the account section at the warehouse and on its turn reversed into the rear of the warehouse. When he got down from the van, he noticed two men standing at the entrance; they were the men helping with the loading of the goods. Miide waved at them and faced the man in the back of the truck who was dressed in a red polo T-shirt with very dirty black jeans and rugged brown boots. The man sat on the bare floor of the van and handed one of the two bags with him to Miide, who on collecting it headed for the front entrance to the warehouse and to the deputy manager's office. There were a few people walking around in the hall, but when he knocked on the door, he heard a single voice, and he opened and entered.

"Aha, Mr. Seye, how are you?" the manager exclaimed and rose to shake him.

"I'm fine," Miide answered, taking his hand.

"You're welcome. So how's business?" he asked, now taking his seat and motioning to Miide to settle into the chair opposite him.

Miide opened up the bag in his hands and produced a gun. He pointed it at him, and Mr. Okorodudu suddenly froze, breathlessly staring at the gun. Miide walked around the table and gave him a slap across the face. He fell back on his chair and started gasping for breath. Another slap across the face and he sank deeper into the chair.

"Please, please," he moaned, looking around the room as if looking for Miide.

"Shhhhhhh," Miide sighed to him, putting his forefinger to his lips, "if you don't shut up now, I'll shoot you right in the head." But Okorodudu continued looking aimlessly around the office room, saying, "Please, please, I'm sorry." Miide gave him a blow in the jaw and exclaimed quietly, "I said shut up, or are you crazy?"

Okorodudu became silent, and Miide added another slap to his head. "Look up and listen to me now. Look up!" Okorodudu came to his senses and looked up slowly with intense apprehension; his red eyes that were devoid of tears could still not look into Miide's eyes, so he just kept gazing at nothing. Miide sat at the edge of his desk, bending over him. "I've brought your money. Do you want it now?" Okorodudu did not reply, and he asked him again, "I said do you want that money you asked me to bring now?" He gave him another heavy blow in his nose in addition to his now-swollen jaw. Okorodudu's nose bled immediately, but he didn't know it. Just the impact of the blow lingered.

"Yeeaah," Okorodudu sighed, and Miide put his finger to his mouth again for him to be silent. He heeded, still reposed in the chair, moaning.

"Do you still want the money?" Miide asked again; and Okorodudu, still rubbing his face with his left hand and anticipating further assault from Miide and thinking how to stop it, answered him between clenched teeth, "No."

"Now tell me, that's the way. You make people pay more when they come for your products, right? How many people have you collected money from that way? I know they are uncountable, and I know you're one of the people that cursed that dead head of state and criticized him for corruption. Are you not corrupt yourself? Are you not?" He kicked him in the groin, and as he fell off the chair, he hit him hard on the head with the base of the gun. Okorodudu fell rolling on the floor, one hand between his legs and the other rubbing his head.

Meanwhile, the men at the supplies section said to the driver and the other man in Miide's van to pay up before they were supplied the goods, but they explained that Miide had gone in to see the manager, and they would wait for him. The men who loaded the truck with the goods stood still, looking at the driver and the man in the red polo shirt, wondering if they were ready to buy any goods. One of them went in and called the cashier who came to find out the situation of things.

"All right, gentlemen, please drive out of this garage so we can attend to this last truck behind you, then we'll load your van too when the man you're waiting for comes."

"Can't you supply the truck like that, take the goods there?" the man in red replied rudely.

"What do you mean? That is too far a distance for these men to take the goods to. It is better you take your vehicle out of this garage so the next truck can come in," the cashier ordered.

"All right, we're not ready to leave the garage. If these guys can't take the goods there, then let the truck wait for its turn. At least we got here before them," he affirmed and kept mute afterward. The cashier and the truck loaders stood there confused.

"Now get up," Miide said to Okorodudu and helped him up with his free hand.

"Get up, I say, get up." Okorodudu managed to rise to his feet, his hand still at his groin and the other gently patting his bruised head. With a bleeding nose and a swollen jaw, he tried to open his swollen red eyes slightly, enough for him to see where he was. He then straightened up. "We're going out now, and listen to me. Please don't give me an excuse to kill you, because that is all I need, and I will kill you and the rest of your people. Forget about the security men at the gate. They can't help you. I know all about them already. They have only one single-barrel gun there now, two in the night, and I'm sure by now my men outside would have killed them. So don't try to be funny. Straighten up and don't raise any suspicions when we get outside there, okay?" Miide pushed him to the door and stopped him again. "I'm taking you to the cashier, and we're going to take out all the money bags in the vault." On hearing this, Okorodudu shrieked and looked into Miide's eyes, shocked. "Yes, I am robbing this damned factory with or without you alive. I don't know why you care all of a sudden now. I thought you were a very heartless person. You don't care if your customers get to sell the goods you give them as long as they pay your company and you get your salary at the end of the month. Come on now, keep a straight face, and reply to anybody who talks to you. To do anything funny at this moment is to put your life and those of the other people outside there in jeopardy, do you hear me? Where is your handkerchief?" Okorodudu produced one from the inner pocket of his jacket. "Clean your bloody nose with it," he instructed, pointing the gun in his face.

"Please don't kill me," he pleaded as they walked out of the office into the factory hall, taking a secluded corridor down to the cashier's office. Okorodudu knocked on the cashier's door for a number of times before he called out for him, and so he answered from the back where he'd been trying to get Miide's van out of the garage to no avail.

He walked up to the manager and was about providing an explanation for this when Okorodudu cut him short.

"Open your door."

"Sir?"

"I say open your door," he repeated, and Miide was standing beside him, gently looking around to make sure it was all clear before he apprehended the cashier who was moving closer, each step to observe if everything was all right with their manager as it seemed he was acting very strangely. "Open your door . . .," Okorodudu ordered firmly, and the cashier brought out the keys from his pockets and inserted it into the door, still looking to and from Miide and Okorodudu, as he turned the key. He looked back one more time, and he was facing Miide's gun. His eyes opened wider, and Miide pushed them both into the door, and it gave way into the office. The cashier quickly raised up his hands in surrender. Miide looked at him in surprise and chuckled.

"You are a very stupid man. You think this is a movie, ehn, ehn?" Miide asked him.

"No, sir."

"Then why are your hands up? You've been watching too many movies. Put your hands down, my friend. Now, come here." He waved the gun at the cashier whose hands were now behind him.

"Yes, sir," he said as he approached him in fear.

"Come on, stop that. If you hadn't seen me with a gun, would you address me as sir? I hate hypocrites, or do you want me to kill you?"

"Ah no, sir, oh no no no, please, I'm sorry. I won't say it again," he exclaimed.

"Shut up." Miide put his finger to his lips. "Now listen . . .," Miide continued when they heard a knock on the door.

"Sshhh," Miide sighed, pointing the gun to the door; and after another knock, he nodded to the cashier to answer it.

"Yes, who is there?"

"Oga na me" was the response from the other end.

"It's one of the loaders," the cashier quietly informed Miide, who smiled and signaled to him to open the door as he stepped back a little. The cashier opened the door and let him in; and when he had walked in, Miide slowly pushed the door close, revealing himself, gun in hand, pointed to the loader. The man, on seeing Miide, with a shout, fell to the ground and was mute as though dead.

"All right, get up and come here. You, move back there," Miide told the cashier to join Okorodudu who was seated gently in a chair, his two hands still in their respective positions on his body. The loader rose and came slowly to Miide, covering his face at a distance to prevent any attack from the gun, his eyes closed. "Come here and don't waste my time," Miide said and pulled him by the hand. "I want you to stand at this door and call your friend, I mean your colleague, okay. Tell him to come, that your boss is calling him." Miide then opened the door, and the man put his head through the door and called his partner. When the man wearing a red polo in Miide's van heard the call for the second loader, he got the signal from Miide and picked the second bag with him as he got down from the van. He went to the front and put the bag in through the window. He opened it and gave the driver a gun from the bag and carried it again across his left shoulder. He followed the loader in quietly.

When the loader got into the cashier's office, he shrieked silently when he saw Miide with the gun but did not shout. "Good . . . you're still more sensible than these idiots who call themselves men, when they are chickens." When Miide's partner in the red polo shirt saw where the loader entered, he whistled. Miide replied to him and opened the door for him. The people with Miide in the office did not hear the man in red whistle; they only heard Miide respond. "Now don't waste my time. I want to leave here as soon as possible, and I will. It's only left for you to decide if you still want to be alive or dead by then. Cashier?"

"Yes, sir, no no, I mean yes."

"Which door is this?" Miide asked, pointing the gun to a door at the other end of the office.

"It's the door that leads to the garage from here."

"What is it meant for?"

"It's for the bullion van, when we're loading it." Miide looked on, and he continued. "It is shielded from the factory hall and the rest of the warehouse so people don't get to see when we're carrying money," the cashier explained.

"Good, firstly, I give you exactly sixty seconds to get that vault opened, else somebody else would open it after you're long dead." The cashier took him by his words and rushed to his desk, opened a drawer, picked up a bunch of keys, and inserted one of them into the keyhole on the other side of the vault. He opened it, breathing heavily, and then he looked back at Miide.

"Well, you're five seconds late. Jasper, kill him," Miide ordered, and the loaders and Okorodudu fell to the floor and covered their heads with their hands in fear. The cashier himself squatted, closed his eyes, and covered his head with his hand.

"Yeeeeh please. Please!" he shouted. Miide raised his hand quietly for Jasper to stop, not saying a word, but they were all still on the floor not knowing it. After a long moment of silence, they raised their heads slowly, one after the other, and saw that the man had lowered his gun; but when the cashier wouldn't look up, Miide called him, "Cashier, come over here. You guys are fools. You would have given yourselves some hope now. If only you would let me shoot one of you, then the rest of the people in the factory would hear the gunshot and come to rescue you, but you're sure too foolish to think that fast. But let me give you another chance. Do you want to risk it and sacrifice somebody to get help? Who goes then?" He raised his gun again, and they all lay flat on the floor. "Ah ah, you cowards. Get up, you fools!" Miide noticed both the cashier and Okorodudu had been spying at the clock on the wall. "I can see the cashier and Mr. Okorodudu are so time conscious for the billion van today. I must say, don't be in a hurry. I know it comes in at two, and I will be long gone by then. Everybody on this street sees a bullion van drive in here every Friday afternoon. Cashier, I give you another one minute to open this gate now." The cashier rose, walked briskly to the table, and removed the first bunch of keys from the drawer. He picked a key from it and opened it. "I should have given you thirty seconds for that," Miide joked. He walked over to the iron gate, closed it, and stood by it. "I want you all to rise, go into that vault, and bring out those bags. Do that fast . . ." They all filed into the vault, walking as fast as they could mostly because of the dread that had come upon them since Jasper had come into the office. He had not said a word since he came in, and he looked more deadly than the grave. "Jasper, take them to the vehicle as they bring the bags." Miide counted them as Jasper took them through the door, two bags at a time.

When they were through, he had counted twenty-two bags in all. "Jasper, is that last truck still there?" Jasper nodded in affirmation. "I want you to load some of their products on top of the bags so as to cover them, then let the driver take the van out of the garage so that the next truck can come in. Tell the man in the next truck that the cashier said he should come in to pay." Jasper did exactly that, and the man from the truck walked in five minutes later with a polyethylene bag. He had walked in and closed the door behind him before he noticed the gun in Miide's hand. He opened his mouth wide in apprehension, and the bag dropped from his hand. "Thank you," Miide said. "But I can't just believe there is anybody as stupid as this in the world. Anyway, that does it," he said, waving the gun at him to join the others, and he picked up the bag. "I want you all in there." He pointed at the vault. "Now, move."

"Oh, please, we're going to suffocate in there," pleaded the cashier.

"Do you want me to do it faster then?" He pointed the gun at him. "Somebody would rescue you before you die, or you give me your phone number here, so when I get out, I'll call your office to inform them. But I can't leave you here. I'm not as stupid as you are. Come on, get into the vault now." They all got in, and he locked them in. He put his gun in the bag of money he was holding, picked up his shuttle bag, and joined the rest in the van. "Let's go." As they drove away, he looked at the other truck driver still waiting for his partner. At the gate, he smiled to the security men and gave them a hundred-naira tip.

"Please, I should tell you the cashier is in the vault. Did you hear me? The cashier is in the vault. Bye," he said as they drove off. Two streets away, they passed by the bullion van going into the factory.

Koja felt a poke on his arm, and it became increasingly intense. He gradually became more conscious of the physical world that he had only been away from in spirit and soul but still present in the body. He opened his eyes, and he quickly narrowed it again from the brightness of the fluorescent light. He saw the figure that had been poking him but could not make anything out of it, so he put his hand just above his eyes to shield it from the ray of light so he could see well.

"Oh, Pastor . . .," he said and sat up on the bench he had been sleeping on. Rubbing his eyes with the back of both hands like a child, he gazed at the wall for the clock. It was twenty-five minutes past 1:00 a.m.; he had only slept for two hours. "I'm very sorry, sir," he said and forced out a smile, "I didn't know it was you. Good morning, sir." He bent his back to touch the ground, greeting the Yoruba way.

"Good morning, Koja, how are you? Firstly, am very sorry for interrupting your sleep at this early hour, knowing full well you just came in from work a couple of hours ago." The old man in his late sixties, wearing a shirt and trousers and barefooted, sat beside him; and Koja shifted to give him more space. "Are you fully awake now, my son?" he asked, and Koja sighed in response, touching his eyes with his middle finger. "There is just something we have to talk about before morning so as to take action on it by then," the pastor continued and rubbed his knees with both hands. "My son, the church council met yesterday, mhm, as usual, you know, every Sunday." He nodded and paused for a moment before he continued. "And we discussed a lot of issues, mhmm, quite a number of issues, and one of such issues we discussed is yours, and heem, when I say yours, I mean your stay here. My son, you have been here for a while now. I don't know for how long exactly, but I'm sure you have spent a number of weeks here, and as you can remember when you came, I took you in and later informed the church council of your circumstances, and they eventually consented to your stay here, temporarily. I mean till you can lay your hands on some job that would be worthwhile and that would enable you to get a place for yourself. After the meeting yesterday, the church council thought I should convey the outcome to you since it was I who took you in at first. My son, this definitely is not pleasant news for you, and I'm not happy about it either, but you know, I don't run the church. The council does. I just preach. My son, you have to leave. The church can no longer accommodate you. I'm sorry, but I want you to do that this morning before daylight so people in the premises won't ask questions. I will handle the situation when you're gone. My Lord God Almighty would go with you as you go," he said, briefly holding Koja's hand as the old clock bell rang once at 1:30 a.m. The old man rose and left briskly as if he was avoiding any ensuing arguments or pleadings that he knew might follow, but Koja sat still dazed, not particularly surprised. He looked up and saw the pastor almost at the door.

"Pastor . . .," he called out, and the pastor stopped and turned his head halfway to the side, obviously not wanting to look back completely at him.

"Thank you, sir," Koja said, and the pastor waved his hand over his head and left. Koja remained in the same position for another ten minutes with his face in his hands, and then he lay back on the bench and slept again, waking up twenty minutes later.

Each time the bell rang, he opened his eyes, so when it was five o'clock in the morning, he rose and picked up his extra shirt from the chair where he had hung it and wore it on the one he had on. He slid into his rubber slippers and began his day as usual. He had started carrying loads and bags for people to get enough money to feed himself. He had been doing this at the market for the past two weeks, a week after he walked into the church in the night for a sleepover. The pastor himself had suggested the idea to him, and he immediately and enthusiastically accepted, and since then he'd been making some money. So feeding wasn't a problem ever since. He did this job till 6:00 p.m., and then he moved to a second job he had just found in a factory where he did the same thing, but that was indoors, where he helped to load goods into vehicles. He left the church and exited the gate unto the road, looking along the road. Some people were out for the day already, but he felt that there were still too many people at that early hour of the day. He buttoned up his shirt and tried as much as possible not to think of his latest accommodation problem. He started up the road. *It's a new day,* he thought, and he intended to treat it as such. *This is a very good advantage. The trucks that bring in foodstuff from the north should just be arriving now. I better go fast. I learned those guys who carry for them make more money.* He concluded his thoughts and increased the pace at which he was walking.

Charles had adopted a number of ways to survive, one of which was the habit of returning late to the station to ensure the divisional police officer would have closed for the day and most of the night-shift men would have gone on night patrol, and there would be just a few policemen left when he came back. His second means was to "corporately beg" for assistance on the road so that he could keep feeding himself. He had also tried to get a job, but all the offers he got were rather too demeaning for him. He got two offers to wash dishes at a canteen and another to wash a public toilet, but both disgusted him. He had just gotten another offer at a modern restaurant on account of his personality to wash dishes and had been promised a promotion to be a waiter if he was well behaved. As he returned to the station that night, he was hopeful and was glad he was beginning to get his bearing. He entered the police station, and as expected, he met only one policeman at the desk. *One is probably in an office somewhere and another one probably went for a stroll or on errand,* he thought.

"Good evening, Officer," he greeted the man on duty and headed for his bench.

"Evening, Mr. Charles," the officer replied without looking his way. Charles gently put on the bench the nylon bag containing the junk food he had bought for dinner, sat down, and took off his shoes. He relaxed his back on the wall and took a deep breath before he picked up the nylon bag again to start eating when the officer spoke. "Mm, Mr. Charles, I hope the DPO's message has been conveyed to you?" he asked Charles, still not looking his way.

"Not at all," he replied with apprehension and turned his head in the direction of the officer who was still busy with the files in front of him.

"I thought my colleagues would have told yo. That is very wrong of them o. They probably forgot. Anyway, he told us to inform you that you have a week as from the last Tuesday to round off whatever arrangement you're making for your housing and leave here. I hope you're hearing me? Eh, eh, so he said by the coming Tuesday, he wants you out of here. I hope you are hearing me?" he asked again and continued without waiting for Charles's response, as if he knew he would not answer him. "So that is the new development, abi, we never try?" he asked and continued again with whatever he was looking at in the book with him. Charles put the nylon of food back on the bench and cast his mind back on the grave mistake he made, blowing the cover he had enjoyed by the policemen at the station who had kept him there without the knowledge of the divisional police officer. He had returned to the police station quite early, about 8:00 p.m. after the DPO had gone home for the day. He was very tired that evening, so he lay on the bench immediately and slept off. About an hour and a half later, the DPO came in on an alert check and found him in the station hall. He immediately inquired about him from one of the officers and was quickly given the circumstance that warranted his being in there at the station. His length of stay had not been divulged. This of course wasn't a free gesture from the police officer but had been keeping him there in return for the meals Charles had funded a number of times before he ran out of money. The policemen on duty that night had assured the DPO that he would be out the following Tuesday.

He straightened up and yawned, stretching his body; he shrugged to himself, made a sad face, and picked up his food again. He was eating his fried yam and stew.

"Officer, join me," he said. Not looking up his way, the officer peeped at him and reluctantly replied, "Thank you."

Usman and Ben strolled sluggishly to the factory after a long day's outing that they had spent sightseeing. They had also done some market shopping with the intention of doing some cooking and having another delicacy to cap it for the day. On getting to the gate, they noticed that it was tightly shut; and when they looked through it, they saw an armed policeman in the security post and a few others all around the compound of the factory with the bullion van, another police van, and a police wagon. None of Usman's colleagues were in sight except the policemen and some others in plain clothes. It was a quiet but tense environment.

"What is happening here?" Ben asked, both of them looking ignorantly through the iron bars of the gate.

"I don't know yet, but whatever it is, I think you should leave now." He looked in Ben's direction and repeated himself, "Leave, now."

"Okay, I'll be on my way." He looked at Usman strangely and started backing out.

"When are we seeing again?" Ben asked as he walked away from the gate.

"I don't know," Usman answered, not looking back. "Because I don't know when this is going to end, but am sure it would take some time," he said quietly to himself, and all of a sudden, he looked back at Ben who was pushing away his weight slowly, still waiting for a reply from Usman. Usman said, "Look here, don't come and check me o, do you hear me? Don't come near this place saying you're looking for me." He pointed to him with a frown.

"Then how are we supposed to see each other? We have a date for Monday, remember?"

"I know. Check me there, but if you don't you see me, check back the next day. You can keep checking back till you see me, but please don't come here."

One of the policemen was coming to the gate then, so Usman waved Ben off.

"I've heard. Bye. I'll see you then," Ben said, and Usman waved him off more subtly.

"Are you Usman?" the policeman asked.

"Yes," Usman answered, holding on to the gate to support him as he immediately felt weak at the knees by the question the policeman had asked him. He noticed the policeman's rank by the badges on his shoulder.

"Come in," the policeman said and approached the gate, thrusting his hand into his pocket to get the key, and removed the chain. The gate came loose.

Usman headed straight to the warehouse office, nodding his head to the policemen around as he walked on, but they all responded with glares that made him want to stumble. He got into the office hall to see the faces he knew, his colleagues, the manager, the deputy manager with a battered face, the cashier, and the rest of two office staff with the loaders all seated around in company of two other policemen, one in plain clothes and the other in uniform. The officer in uniform was at a desk writing on a piece of paper; and another man, very different from all the others, was dressed in a finely cut blue suit.

Head office, probably, Usman thought as he looked at him. Even though he had not seen anybody from the head office before, he had heard so much about them and was able to recognize them on sight.

"Usman is here now" came a voice from behind him, and shivers ran through him. The policeman who had opened the gate for him joined them. "Manager, who else is not here?" he asked and stood arms akimbo as he became the center of attraction.

"Just a few more people, the two extra loaders, but they are not on duty today, and three other security men, but every one of them won't be around until tomorrow," answered the manager.

"Very well then, let's go to the station. Officer?" he called to the other man in uniform.

"Yes, sir," he answered.

"Move everybody into the van, and make it snappy. I have things to do in the office," he ordered.

"Yes, sir. Okay now, let's move, everybody!" The junior officer got the staff of the factory out and into the waiting van and another vehicle, a Peugeot 504 station wagon. The police chief and the representative of the head office on legal matters got into another car. They were all conveyed to the police station, and the factory gate was locked.

At the police station, the representative of the head office dropped off the chief of police.

"Thank you very much, and like I said, you don't have to worry. I can assure you, we will get the perpetrators of this theft, because there is no way such an operation could be carried out without the help of somebody on the inside. So whoever it is among them will surely lead us to the whole thing," the chief assured the representative and shut the door of the car.

"Before you go, Officer, I want you to put to mind what I told you the other time about the man, Usman. He is with us via our general manager who is currently abroad. I don't know how exactly he is related to him, but I think he's a relation of his. I don't want to put my job on the line here, so I want you to treat him gently and very soon, today, release him. Besides, I don't think he would know anything about the whole robbery considering his relationship with our GM."

"Oh no!" the policeman said and shook his head. "We don't judge such issues that way, sir, believe me! We cannot exempt anybody yet. This is a delicate and serious issue, and we have to treat it as such."

"I know, Officer, but what I'm trying to tell you is that I don't think my GM will like the idea of one of his relations in police custody at all. He would prefer the case scrapped, and so would any one of us."

"All right, I'll see what we can do, but we must still do our job. There is nothing to worry about anyway. If the man is innocent, his vindication will be sooner than you expect. See you later, sir. We have to get to work, bye." He waved and walked into the station, and the executive car zoomed off.

After a series of individual interrogations, the police chief asked them individually whom they suspected could be a part of the robbery. Everyone who was brought to the station except Usman said they suspected one of the two extra loaders who were to resume duty later that night. The cashier and two other staff mentioned Koja's name and pointed out how he lived suspiciously. They stressed that he kept to himself a lot, and when asked if there had been any report of him for doing wrong, they said no. The chief confronted the manager on this issue. He did not oppose it but added that he only saw Koja as a harmless loner.

"Do you have any record of his background?" the police officer asked.

"No, we don't" was the reply.

"What do you mean no? When you employ people there, don't you require their CV, or at least some sort of resume?"

"We and other factories don't require CVs from such people. He's not a permanent staff. He's not even on our list of temporal staff. When we employ loaders, they are there today and tomorrow they are gone, so most times we pay them on a daily basis. It's only of recent we just decided on weekly payments because of the short notice they give us when they leave. It usually leaves us helpless concerning who would help with loading the vans," the manager explained; and after a long, hard look, the officer made some notes on his pad again.

"You can wait in the lounge. I'll see you in a minute," he said to the manager. He put both hands against his desk, took a deep breath, and closed his eyes. He opened it again and picked up the statements written by each of the staff of the factory about the robbery as best known by each of them. He sorted through it and singled out Usman's statement; he read through it again, starting from when he arrived at the gate and saw policemen, to when he was ordered into the waiting vehicle with the rest.

"But why could he alone not have any suspect? Why didn't he think anybody in the company could have a hand in it?" the chief murmured to himself, tapping the piece of paper with his finger. "His statement shows no concern for the woe that had just befallen his working place. His words were devoid of sympathy, of genuine sobriety," he concluded his thoughts, stared at the paper a minute longer, and rose to join his team in the lounge. He sat again and pressed a button. A second later, one of his men came in and saluted him.

"Corporal, I'm afraid we have to let go of the manager and his deputy, but they have to keep reporting here every morning, and I also feel really reluctant to let the Officer Usman go, I mean the security man that came in last," he said and looked again at Usman's statement another moment.

"Why, sir? If we're detaining the other security men, we should detain him too. It would be only unfair to do otherwise," the corporal said, but the chief kept staring at Usman's statement and sighed with a smile of mischief.

"The management doesn't want him detained because he's connected to their boss. The irony of the matter is that it is this guy that the management of the company has given so much immunity that I feel so strangely about."

"What about the other man they all complained about?" cut in the corporal.

"That one?" He gave a brief chuckle. "Don't be surprised when he gets here and you find out that guy is nothing but what they all say he is, a harmless loner. Do as I've said, Corporal, and tomorrow we can put the rest of them on bail, but they all must continue reporting here every morning, then later we can decide on the best time for surveillance."

"Yes, sir," he exclaimed. He turned to depart when the chief called him back, "Corporal."

"Sir."

"I think since nobody seems to know where the suspect lives, somebody has to go and wait for him at the factory. If we don't see him, we can't say. He might not get our message since there is nobody to convey it to him. So you make sure you send somebody to do that tomorrow."

"All right, sir."

Koja emptied his sachet of water into his mouth after eating what was supposed to be his lunch. It was 6:00 p.m., and he was fatigued after a long day's work. He stood arms akimbo, contemplating on going or not going to the factory for his second job. After a while, he decided, "I think that was okay for today." He waved off the idea and picked up his shirt. "I'll make it there tomorrow and then explain to the manager." He started walking down the road, looking around for no particular attraction, trying to distract himself from the thoughts in his mind.

After wandering around for a while, he could not but surrender to the turbulence of his heart. He stopped and looked at the sky as the day slowly faded away. "Where am I going to sleep tonight, for god's sake?" he grumbled. "And I have to be careful where I sleep because of the police that patrols in the night." He turned and stumbled on the solution to this. As he got closer to the market, he saw the rest of the market carriers' union and remembered that some of them actually slept in the market.

"That reminds me, some of these guys that do the early morning loading usually hang around somewhere here. They don't go home, that is if they have any home to go to. I think they sleep around here." He stopped walking and scratched his chain with his left hand. "I think some of them sleep in the back of the parked trucks and some in the basement of the uncompleted parking lot building among all other places. The uncompleted building will do," he said thoughtfully and proceeded to the market.

"When I get to the factory tomorrow, I'll talk to one of those guys to help me with accommodation." Koja passed the night at the market.

Despite all the noise made by the trucks that came into the market early the next morning and the carriers unloading them, Koja was too deep in sleep that he was not disturbed or woken; even the hardness of the floor laid with torn cartons was not discomforting enough to take away from him the sleep that was instilled on him by the tiredness of the previous day.

At 7:00 a.m., the dawning of the day eventually roused Koja to life He lazily pushed against the floor, lifting himself up to sit, with his back against the wall. He gave out a wide-mouthed yawn; he looked around at the few cartons that were left after the rest of the occupants of the basement had packed theirs. He was the only person left, but he sat still just to clear his head and put his mind to work.

After about five minutes, he rose and walked out of the building into the Saturday morning sunlight. He quickly shaded his eyes from the sun rays. he noticed there were a few cars parked in the parking lot already, and he approached the first water seller he saw. "Give me a sachet of pure water," he said as the little girl put down the bucket she was carrying and brought out a sachet of water for him. He wanted to collect it, but the girl held it back, producing her other hand in request for her money. Koja looked at her for a moment, brought out a dirty five naira note, and gave it to her. He tore the sachet at the edge and took a mouthful and rinsed his mouth, with his finger brushing his teeth. He spat again and then rinsed his face, pouring more water in his hand to rinse his face. When he was satisfied, he threw away the empty sachet and started walking away to start work.

The mattress, he thought, *I may be going back there tonight.* So he turned and went back to the basement. He packed the torn cartons he had slept on and put it in another corner from the rest where he could easily recognize it. He left the building. As Koja got out, a car was just parking in the lot, a jeep. The occupants were a woman in the backseat and a driver behind the wheels. They were just alighting from the car. Koja quickly looked around for any carrier, but there was none, and his face brightened up. *This is a beautiful day,* he thought and moved quickly to the side of the jeep as the driver was bringing out the sacks and baskets for their shopping.

"Good morning, ma, would you be needing a carrier for your shopping?" The woman gave him a glance but did not respond, and Koja stood there waiting, and when the woman was ready to enter the market and he was still there, she spoke to him.

"Pick up those bags and let's go," and then she walked ahead.

"Thank you, ma," Koja exclaimed enthusiastically, picking up the bags, and followed after her.

As the woman rounded off her shopping, Koja walked ahead in front of her with a large bowl of sacks containing various foodstuffs on his head and pulled another one along with his free hand, the woman following with a smaller bag. She added to the bowl Koja was carrying, and when she felt her handbag had become too heavy for her, she put it in the bowl without telling Koja. Along the way, she stopped to buy something else and wanted to pay. When she looked into the bowl, her handbag had disappeared.

"Where is my bag?" she asked Koja who did not even know when she put the bag in the bowl he was carrying.

"Which bag, ma?" he answered through clenched teeth from the weight of the load on his head.

"The bag I put on your head. I put it in the bowl on your head." She was beginning to raise her voice now. "I hope you don't want to get yourself into trouble, young man. If you don't produce my bag right now, you will be in trouble."

"I still don't understand what you're talking about, ma. I didn't see you put any bag on my head. You didn't tell me you put any other thing there apart from the foodstuff and the last thing you added just now. I don't even know what it was because I didn't look back when you're putting it there," he defended innocently.

"You will know, you will know, by the time I'm through dealing with you, you will know what I'm talking about, he eh. You, you, you this thief!" she yelled and gave him a slap. *Prar . . . prar*! Two slaps. She beat him on his chest and back while he still carried the load on his head. She shouted on him, and people started gathering around them. She continued slapping him all over, and he could not defend himself. Some of the other carriers approached them and pacified her, stopping her from beating Koja whose lips had already started bleeding

But all pleadings fell on deaf ears as she pushed Koja toward the parking lot. Her driver from the parking lot sighted them and ran to join his madam.

"Joe?" the woman shouted, calling the driver.

"Yes, madam," he answered.

"This thief has conspired with his cohorts, and they have stolen my bag. Run now and get me the police," she ordered her driver, and he left. When they had gotten to where the vehicle was, Koja's colleagues assisted him to put down the bowl on his head, and the woman shouted even more, wanting to stop him from putting it down. So when she saw that he had put it down, she held tightly to his shirt so that he would not run away, but Koja was stroking his lip instead. When the other carriers saw the kind of vehicle that brought the woman and knowing that she had sent for the police, they left.

About twenty minutes later, the driver came back with a policeman, and the woman who had been a little quiet for some time started shouting again on seeing them.

"Police, please, come o. This thief has stolen my bag o, and I have money in it," she exclaimed when the police and the driver approached them.

"Good afternoon, madam, and please take it easy," the policeman pleaded, trying to take the woman's hands off Koja.

"Look here, policeman, he mustn't run away o, do you hear me?" she shouted and let go off him. The policeman took hold of Koja and was trying to get some explanation from the woman.

"I'm not saying anything here," the woman refused. "Take this man to your station. I want him locked up. That is a thief. Let's go." She pointed to the car as the policeman pushed Koja along. They all got into the car as the driver finished packing the bags of their shopping into the boot. They went down to the police station.

Back at the marketplace, at the far end under the bridge, three young men stood before Miide as he counted the money. He looked up at them.

"Three thousand five, is that all that was in it?" he asked them.

"Yes," they answered in an unrehearsed unison.

"Are you sure?" he asked again.

"Honestly, Chief, that was what was in the bag. I can't mess around with you, you know. See, look at it, and you can even check us if you like since we've not been anywhere else." He handed out the bag to Miide who looked at it and ignored it.

"He eh, what were you saying about the whole escapade? I thought you said something about somebody being in trouble. I want to know how that is supposed to be any of my problems?" Miide inquired of them.

"Chief, no be like that o. What am saying is that, after we don take the bag, you know say na one carrier the owner of this bag put am on top, so he was the one the woman accused for it, and she has taken him to the police station. And the way I see am, that woman wicked. You no say after I don take the bag give okapi. I wait small to see the outcome of the thing. Am sure she would go and lock him up." Miide relaxed where he was, gazing into the distant market for a while. The other guys had to speak up to awaken him from his thoughts.

"Chief." Miide snapped back to his immediate surrounding. "That na why I talk say make I tell you, because I know say you no go like that kind thing."

"Do you know him?"

"No, Chief, but if I see am, I go recognize am," one of the three guys answered.

"Find out for me by Monday. If he's not yet back, we'll go and bail him. It's only dangerous now. Let's wait and see if his colleagues will do anything to help him," he suggested and waved them away, pocketing the money. "And you, get rid of that bag. You are on your own," he admonished the guy carrying the bag as the boys walked away.

"Yes, Chief."

"I'll see you boys later."

"Sit down there," the policeman ordered Koja and pushed him violently to a bench behind the concrete desk in the police station. "In fact, stand up, stand against that wall!" he yelled again as Koja rested, sitting on the bench. He pushed him against the wall. He gave him a slap so he could stand well. Then the woman and her driver just walked in at the time of the slap, so she nodded her approval.

"Madam, please sit down here." He gestured to her. They were both given sheets of paper to write their statements of what had happened; five minutes later, Koja was through, and the policeman marveled.

"See, see," the woman shouted, "he's so used to it. You can see it's not his first time of writing this. He knows his usual lies and has quickly put it down." She finished hers too and gave it to the officer.

"This will be all for now, madam, you just go home and check back tomorrow."

"Are you sure of what you are talking about? Don't release this thief o, Officer. In fact, I want to charge him to court," she lamented.

"Don't worry, madam, we will handle all that. I am going to lock him up immediately. You just go home now."

"No, lock him in first. I want to see him in," she affirmed and stood arms akimbo. The policeman called on his colleague to lock Koja up.

"Take off your slippers, your belt, and everything in your pocket," he ordered Koja and started frisking him. When he had done all he ordered, he locked him in the cell.

"What time should I be here tomorrow?" the woman asked.

"About this same time is okay, madam. We'll be expecting you oo."

"Good night," she said suddenly and walked out, not looking back. Koja was alone in his cell. He sat on the bare floor at the corner with his back against the wall, and he buried his head in his hands. He was still in that position for a while, and then shivers started running all over him. He gave very silent groanings and was still again; he slowly fell on his side and lay down.

The corporal read through Koja's statement and was fascinated by both his handwriting and his use of English, and his story was so brief and explicit.

"A market carrier? Where and how did he learn to write like this?" he murmured to himself. He checked his wristwatch. "I'll put him on interrogation in about a couple of hours," he concluded

The sergeant walked into the station, and both corporals on duty jumped to their feet and saluted him. He gestured to them to follow him and walked into his office.

"Yes, have we heard anything from the factory?" he asked as he settled into his chair.

"No, sir, but the corporal is still there."

"Huh, could he be our man? Could he be at large already?" he asked, talking to himself. "What about the managers? Has any one of them . . . ?" He trailed off.

"No, sir, but I believe they will still turn up. I don't think we actually gave them any particular time to come today, sir."

"You didn't, you didn't? I ask you, who took down their statement yesterday?"

"I did, sir."

"Then why didn't you tell them to report here this morning?"

"I forgot, sir, am sorry."

"You forgot? You forgot? I'm trying to run an investigation here, Corporal. Over three million naira has just been stolen as confirmed by their bank, and they have confirmed that they have never taken less than that amount from the factory every week, and you are saying you forgot?"

"I'm very sorry, sir."

"I hope the rest of them are still in the cell and you did not forget to lock up the cell overnight."

"Yes, sir . . . no, sir . . . I mean yes, sir, they are still in the cell." He panicked, and the sergeant stared at him with a scowl. "Any other development?"

"Yes, sir, a man was brought in for stealing. The woman he stole from brought him in, but I arrested him."

"Have you taken his statement and interrogated him?" The sergeant immediately looked up to reprimand him again when he quickly answered, "I just locked him in, sir, it's not been long that we got in. I was just thinking about the process when you came in, sir." He looked pleadingly. The sergeant looked at him, his gaze getting more intense by the moment.

"Get that done now," he said, "and get somebody to relieve our man at the factory while we hope to find our suspect."

"Yes, sir!" he yelled and saluted, marching out of the office.

While the corporal was interrogating Koja behind closed doors somewhere in the station, a knock came on the sergeant's door, and the factory manager came in.

"Good afternoon, Sergeant," he greeted. He approached the desk and offered him his hand. Reluctantly the sergeant took it, and they shook hands.

"It amazes me still, Manager, how you people treat this case with such levity, just as if nothing happened and the stolen money was nothing . . .," he let out at once.

"I'm sorry, but I don't understand what you're talking about," the manager confessed innocently as he took his seat opposite the sergeant.

"You don't understand? We instructed you, every one of you, to report here this morning. It wasn't a plea. We meant it, and now look, you're the first person, and see what time you came in? Look, you have to know I'm not even doing things the right way. If I were to do it the right way, every one of you should still be in that cell, but I don't understand your head office's intervention in this case, coupled with the shocker that you don't know the residence of a staff of yours."

"Sergeant, I told you," the manager cut in and was trying to explain, but the sergeant shut him up.

"Notwithstanding, Manager . . ., sorry what is your name?" he objected with his finger and asked suddenly.

"Chief Ete," the manager answered.

"Better, because in this entire issue, Manager . . . by the way, I am Mr. Olopade. As I was saying, notwithstanding at all, somebody, I repeat, somebody, perhaps one of his colleagues, should know where this guy lives."

"He may not even have a house. Most of them don't. They usually come in from the market. That is where they do their major load-carrying job." The sergeant gave him a long stare of disapproval and rose from his seat.

"You will come into the interrogation room where you will be asked a few questions," he informed the manager before going to the door that he opened for the manager. "Then you'll report here at eight every morning." The manager followed him, and they both exited the office. The sergeant led the way to the interrogation room and continued talking as he went ahead. "You will have to bear with us like that. The case may not take long to figure out, though, the way I see things, because I think we suspect the right person. I'm beginning to think he's at large." He looked back at the manager as he grabbed the door handle and opened the interrogation room.

"Koja?" the manager asked as he entered. Then he kept staring at Koja in the interrogation room.

Usman walked in and out of the canteen twice. He had seen Ben at a corner, but Miide was nowhere in sight. He stayed out awhile, looking along the road in the dark. He looked in the direction of the kiosk where they had met the last time and along the road again, and he decided to join Ben inside to wait for Miide.

Has this boy duped me? was the thought that crossed his mind as he sat beside Ben who had not seen him yet.

"Old soldier," Ben exclaimed.

"Don't say that again! Who told you I am old?" Usman protested.

"Ah ah ah, do I need to be told?" Ben was trying to be funny.

"I may be older in age, but I'm still more active and agile than you are," he defended with not a very serious scowl.

"Ah ahhhaa, hugunn un," Ben cleared his throat. "Anyway, how are you?"

"Fine," Usman answered, looking toward the door.

"How's the situation of things at your office now?" he asked, raising a glass of drink to his mouth.

"Fine."

"Fine? Then what was happening that day?"

"Nothing."

"Nothing? Okay o, let this girl give you a drink then."

"I don't want. Maybe later." Just then he sighted Miide at the entrance. Miide signaled to him to follow.

"Let's go . . ." He nudged Ben and rose.

"What?" Ben shrieked and was looking at Usman who was already at the door; he took a last gulp speedily and stormed after him. Miide had crossed the road too fast to catch up. He understood what he was doing. Ben was closing up on Usman; but far behind them both was Jasper, Miide's partner, walking slowly, following them to see if there were any irregularities or if they were being followed. Miide would look back to Jasper at intervals for a sign. If it was negative, he would disappear; and if not, he was to proceed as intended. There was no negative signal.

Miide entered a bar and walked to a table where two young men waited by a bulky traveling bag that was placed under the table. He waved at the two of them, and they left the table.

Miide reclined in a chair and was joined a few minutes later by Usman and Ben. Jasper waited at the door. They both sat across him waiting for him to speak first, but he took his time, feeding on their increasing confusion and impatience.

"How is your case at the police station?" he asked.

"I really don't know, but the way I see things, I suspect my connection is working for me already," Usman replied.

"I don't know how you mean, but I'll suggest you be very careful. Whatever happens, you're been watched."

Miide took his time again, looking at the two of them randomly; Ben was still trying to figure out what they were talking about. Miide kicked the bag under the table.

"That's your money," Miide said nonchalantly, still looking at Usman. After a moment of silence, Usman peeped under the table then leaned on his elbow against the table to be closer to Miide and spoke quietly.

"How much is this? I mean how much is everything, and how much is mine?"

"All was four point two million naira, and we took one million each," Miide explained briefly.

"Who are the 'we' you're talking about?"

"You don't think I did that job alone, do you?" Miide said quietly, and Ben's eyes widened. He swallowed hard and became uneasy and restless. "I had two other guys with me."

"And how am I sure all was what you called it?"

"Do you seem to have any choice than to believe me?" There was silence again for a moment, then Usman picked up the bag strap and drew it closer to himself. "I don't take from who doesn't have. I give to them. Mrrr. . . . ?" Miide said, referring to Ben, and when Ben did not give his name, he continued, "I really bothered you that day, didn't I? Well, I regretted it later, and since I discovered you were with the old soldier here the other time—" Usman cut in.

"What did you say? Who is old soldier? You better don't repeat that again," Usman warned, but Miide only chuckled and continued.

"Yes, since I saw you with him that night, I thought . . ." He trailed off, bringing out a slightly heavy nylon bag, and pointed it to him. "That is ten thousand naira."

"You must be joking. What makes you think I want to be any part of this? To hell with you and your money. Usman, I can't believe this. You were a patriotic citizen of this country. Look at what you have become. I should get you people arrested." He stood there looking at the two men randomly and fuming, then he stormed out of the bar.

"What are you going to do about your friend?" Miide inquired.

"Let me have the money." He collected the nylon bag from Miide and stuffed it in his pocket. "He needs money. He will come back for it." Usman thought for a moment. "I can't take it to my room at the quarters. It's dangerous. Can you take care of this for me till tomorrow?"

"That won't be any problem," Miide offered after a brief consideration.

"But I will need you to meet me here with it early tomorrow morning."

"Better still." Miide tipped, "I think I need your assistance too, or of your friend perhaps. What's his name now?"

"Ben."

"Ben, good, I need to go and bail somebody at the police station, and I need somebody with a personality to help me do it or at least go with me. I know they will attend to him better. Can you talk him into doing that?"

"I'll try, but when would that be? I don't think I will be around tomorrow."

"Tuesday will be fine. I hope the person is still there by then," Miide consented. Usman dropped the bag strap, quickly opened it, and took two wads of money and thrust them into his back pocket.

"We'll see tomorrow then."

"I can see you're learning fast. You're learning to trust me," Miide jokingly said, but Usman ignored him, and they dispersed.

Ben entered his compound from the back to avoid his landlord, who still ridiculed him whenever he saw him, even though he had almost finished paying his debt. When he opened the rear door that led to the corridor, he was nose to nose with his landlord and froze.

"Aaah haa," the old man laughed, "were you trying to avoid me, entering from the back? Ahhhhh." He laughed again.

"Good afternoon, Landlord," Ben said and walked past him as the man continued to laugh.

"Don't worry, I won't ask for my money now because I know you have a lot of things to spend money on, most especially the news that just came in for you from your mother." Ben, who was about to open his room door, stood still and looked back at the landlord. "Hm, hm, yes, your people from the house you lived last before you packed in here came. They sent a young lady. I presume I've seen her here before, right?"

"Yes, she brought me a message here sometime ago. What did she say about my mother?"

"Eh, ehm." The landlord looked sober now. "Em, she didn't bring a very good news. Your mother's sickness is back again, and the people taking care of her need your financial assistance. Besides, she demanded to see you herself. And I think this time it's really bad. When old people send such messages, hmmmm, who knows? So I'll advise you honor this call," he admonished him, went to him, patted his shoulders, and left him to have some privacy. Ben rested his back against his door, devastated. He folded his arms to his chest, his chin to his chest. He lost his bearing and could not think straight for the moment. He opened his door and entered and for another ten minutes or thereabouts could not remember what it was that had just happened to him or who he just spoke with. He lay on his bed and slept. When he woke up, he was back in his right mind, and the first thing he remembered was his first contact of the day, how he had found Usman conspiring with an armed robber, and then he drifted into his current trouble. He meditated on it into the night and at a point sat up on his bed and asked himself audibly, "It's like this, what's my problem, and what's the solution?" After some minutes of silence, he concluded, "My problem is money. I think my problem is money, how to get to the village and what to take to the village." He lay on his bed again and drifted off a bit. Just then he remembered; he sat up again and thought for a moment. He lay down again and thought for a while longer. At last he murmured something like "I'm sorry, Mama," and slept off.

In the morning, Usman got his bag from Miide, moved to the motor park, and boarded a bus to Kogi where his family was; and they were glad to see him. He took his wife to the bank where they lodged the money together and gave her access to it in his absence. When his wife asked him of the source of such a huge amount of money, "I got into this lucrative business. Just keep praying for me" was his response. By 11:00 p.m. the same day, he was back in Lagos, and nobody could tell that he traveled.

"So like I said, Mrrr. . . . ? The DPO was discussing with the representative of the factory's head office on legal matters on his visit to know the latest development in the investigation."

"Mr. Adewala, Adewala, Esquire," he responded and listened to the DPO.

"Okay, our investigation is definitely still in progress, but concerning these men in our custody, we have interrogated them seriously, and so far we deduced they are innocent. Most especially Mr. Koja, whom we apprehended last. Emm ah, we are thinking of putting them on bail tomorrow, but of course they will keep reporting here as long as the investigation lasts. I must also tell you the truth. The staffs of your factory have not been forthcoming. They have not been cooperative at all. We told them to report here every morning at eight o'clock, and they come here anytime they want. Most times they don't even come. And that is the only way we can get tips that will lead us to the loophole in the robbery plan, by the discrepancies we see in their repeated statements. So please get them to be more cooperative. We will really appreciate it, or else we'll have to use force."

"I'll see to the attitude of the factory staff, but as you have promised, make sure you get to the root of this robbery and bring out the perpetrators."

"That is our job, and I've told you we will do it, but I really have to confess, even you are not helping matters at all. The security man Usman, whom you did not allow us to detain, is a major hindrance to this investigation," the DPO lamented, and Adewala absorbed it. He was mute for a moment before he replied, "I did not say you shouldn't interrogate him. All I said was that you should not lock him up here. I can't give my boss that kind of report, or has he not been coming here?"

"He's been coming, but we could not exert pressure on him like the rest."

"It doesn't matter anyway. I mean, if the rest could be proven innocent, he's definitely innocent too. Just let us keep it that way. I'll check back here next week. I hope to hear something more positive by then." The DPO rose. They shook hands, and the company's staff left.

On Tuesday morning, both Ben and Miide sat behind a taxi headed for the police station. Ben was decked in his old jacket with a tie to match and a white shirt underneath; he had a folder bag to complete his gentleman appearance. Ben had not replied to him since their meeting with Usman the previous night, but Ben had to succumb to their enticement because of his extenuating circumstance. They had put forward a very attractive bait. Miide spoke.

"There is something else I've not told you," he said quietly but confidently. "You will have to go in there alone, at the station. It is not safe for me to go in with you." He didn't look Ben's way, but inevitably Ben looked his way.

"What exactly are you saying?" he asked.

"I'm not going in with you. You're going alone," he declared.

"Are you mad? How on earth am I supposed to recognize the person I'm going to bail? I'm going into a police station, for god's sake," Ben charged.

"I've told you his name. His name is Koja, that is all you have to know. I don't know him myself," he confessed, still looking out of his side window.

"Ah a, then how is he to you, or am I just sticking out my neck for a nothing palaver?"

"What is the problem now? Does it take this much to bail somebody that has already been declared bailable? Or you're just being cowardly," Miide lamented.

"You this reckless boy, do you have any respect at all? Do you know am way older than you are?" Ben argued.

"Older, older?" Surprised, Miide now looked his way. "You want respect? You don't get that free. You know what attracts respect? Power and money, and you know what, you don't have any of them. Look here, I have money." He touched his pocket. "At least a lot more than you do, and look here." He took hold of something hard at his waist, underneath his clothes, a gun. "This is power, so you," he ordered, pointing at him, "should respect me. Age is nothing." Then they were quiet again for the rest of the trip.

At the front of the police station, Ben got down from the taxi and slowly headed for the entrance; he looked back at the taxi and saw it moving away slowly.

"Good morning, Officer," he said as he walked in to the officer who was bent over the concrete desk, looking into a large book.

"Good morning," he replied and looked up. "What can I do for you?" he asked with a smile after a good assessment of Ben.

"I have come to see somebody in your custody here and of course embrace any chances of bail for him," he explained gently with a smile.

"Mhmmm, what's his name?" He started turning the pages of the large book.

"Koja."

"Koja? Ha mn. He has a very serious case here, in fact two." Then he stared a little longer into the large book. "But he's lucky. He has been granted bail this morning. But we have not seen any of his people since then, not even his colleagues at work. He must be a bad person himself."

"Oh no, he's not. He's only unfortunate," Ben defended.

"Na, you say that one o, oga, na you say that one, so how are you to him?"

"I'm a brother to one of his colleagues, but he could not be here."

"Leave the rest, na story. You'll pay us five thousand for his bail, and you know, you go put our own too. That one go be two thousand naira because you see, his case is a very serious case, and we should not be letting him go at all. He should be here till the investigation is over, but you see, one has to temper justice with mercy, that is why."

"It's okay, Officer, you just said the rest is story, so don't worry. I am here for you. I'll do all you want me to do. Can you bring him out now?"

"No problem. Just sign here and fill in your particulars here." He pushed the large book his way and pointed his finger to where he had to sign. Then he went in to bring Koja who on seeing Ben could not express his confusion because he had been severely brutalized. Ben did not know what next to say to him, and to avoid making the officer suspicious, he focused on counting the money and paid the officer.

The officer in turn counted the money and when he was through said, "Listen, he has to report here every morning, okay?" He looked at Koja's stern face as he wore his shirt and slippers. "Because the case is not yet over. As a matter of fact, it's just beginning."

"I have heard, Officer, but could you please allow him to take the rest of the week off, because as you can see, there is no way he won't be seeing a doctor, as he obviously needs one urgently." The officer gave Koja a long reluctant look and then gave in.

"It's okay, but please he must be in next week. You can go." He waved them off. Ben took hold of Koja by the elbow. As they walked out, they were brushed in by another man going into the station; and immediately after they got out, they started hearing noises from inside, especially the officer's voice.

"Get out of here! Today is your deadline! This place is not your home!" he shouted at the man who was trying to explain some things quietly, but he wouldn't listen to it. He threw out a polyethylene bag that obviously belonged to the man and started pushing him out. "You are a useless man, so work and get accommodation for yourself. Get out of here, and don't let the DPO meet you here." He pushed him out to the main road as Ben and Koja watched in pity. Just then the taxi with Miide still in the back stopped beside them to pick them up, and they all watched as the policeman rained curses on the man.

"Get in," Miide ordered Ben and Koja, and so Ben got into the front seat, and Koja joined Miide in the back, but Ben could not take his eyes off the man in his predicament.

"I think this guy needs help. I don't know, but I think a place to stay is part of it." While Ben was saying this and looking at the man, Miide was looking at Ben, studying him.

"Hello, hello, excuse me," Miide called to the man, and he slowly approached the taxi, still looking back at the station. "What's the problem?" Miide asked when he was close enough.

"I dun understand, I really dun understand, man, thought these people were supposed to be a friend of the people, protecting the people?" Charles was lamenting. When Miide heard him speak, with such accent, he took a better look at him; and as he continued in what Miide saw as blabbing, he interrupted him, "Do you need a place to stay?"

Charles shut up for a moment and answered, "Yes, I need accommodation for the meantime. I just got a job, and I'll soon—"

Miide shut him up again. "Come in."

"Thanks, guys," he said and joined Miide in the back as the driver sped off.

"I think we all need good food first before anything else, at least for Koja here."

Koja started lamenting out of frustration. "Ah ah, life, life, am tired of this life! What have I done, God? If there is any god up there, he has to tell me what I have done." He straightened up, looked at Miide, and said. "I don't know which one of you bailed me and why, but if you really want to help me, let me go from here. I need to end my life the way I want, and I want to do it now. Please let me go."

"No, you won't. You don't need to go and kill yourself. That is what life has to give," Ben consoled him.

"And you have to get what you want," Miide added quickly. Koja looked into Miide's face longer than necessary. "Any problem?" Miide asked.

"Nothing, nothing much. It's just something about your face. You kind of look familiar, but I'm sure am just mistaken. Don't bother."

"Oh yeah, you were the guy in the cell!" Charles exclaimed. "It's your voice I've been hearing when they are torturing you in the night."

"In the night?" Ben repeated quietly in horror.

"Yeah, in the night, that was when they tortured him. You just got there about two or three days ago, right?" Koja nodded slightly. "Hm, I knew it, I know that voice."

"What's your own name?" Miide asked him.

"Charles, that's my name," he said as if amused by the question, looking at Miide questioningly.

They all had rice and chicken at a restaurant, which Miide paid for. Charles had begun to wonder who he really was, but Koja seldom touched his food, and Ben had his fill.

"Now," Miide said, "Koja, do you have a place?" He shook his head. "All right, you will come with me, and Charles goes with Ben."

"How do you mean? I don't think I have room for that, and besides, when did you become my landlord to decide who comes into my home or not?" Ben complained.

"I thought you had a plan, when you suggested we give him the help he needs."

"I didn't say that. I only said he needed help."

"If money is your problem, I'll fix it, don't worry."

"But am not going to be in town as from tomorrow."

"Better still, he'll keep your home till you come. Are you all right now?" he asked Ben, and he nodded.

"Fine, we have to go now because this man here"—he was talking about Koja—"needs a doctor, but first I have to go with you so that I can know your place now." He brought out a folded nylon bag from his pocket and gave it to Ben. "My regards to your mom when you go tomorrow, and I wish her quick recovery," he said and threw Ben a quick glance. He asked him again, "Why did you look at me like that?"

"I'm only surprised. That's the first time you sound like somebody from this planet to me." They chuckled over it.

"I'll see the old soldier tomorrow at the canteen, and I think we have to change that meeting place. It's too close to his office," Miide said, and they left.

Kachi looked at the wall clock again five minutes later, bringing her gaze on her wristwatch as before. It was the first time Mike was keeping late; she usually met him there waiting for her already. She didn't know what could be keeping him, and she wasn't finding it convenient sitting around the restaurant alone amid intimidatingly attired people. She had unconsciously grown use to covering her new wristwatch with the other hand, being shy of its conspicuous value, so she put both hands in her lap and still covered her left wrist with her right hand. She wore it only when she was coming to see Mike. The main reason Mike took her shopping on one of their meetings like that was to save her from the constant stares of other guests at the restaurant whenever they came around. She was dressed in a flower-patterned brown dress with a pair of beautiful fancy slippers and covering her head with a scarf. The waiter, Austin, approached her every now and then, asking her if she was doing fine; and seeing that she was yet to touch her drink, he asked her again and again if she would like anything else. She had been waiting forty minutes after she got there fifteen minutes late herself, then the door flung open, and Mike stormed in and marched toward her.

"I'm so sorry," he apologized, gave her a hug around the shoulder, and took his seat opposite her. "I didn't mean to be late. There was this delegation from the Japanese government, and I had to be there to receive them plus some other issues like my factory that was robbed and so on. The meeting took a while, am so sorry. I promise it won't happen again." Then he watched her eyes, looking into them with intensity. She looked back at him and gave a weak smile.

"That's okay. I wasn't cross, but now I can't stay any longer, you know," she confessed.

"How do you mean? I thought you're coming to know my place today."

"No."

"But we agreed on that a couple of days ago."

"No, we didn't, Mike. I only said I will, but not yet. We shouldn't be thinking of that now."

"I don't see why not. I am just inviting you over for a meal or at least know my place," he lamented and noticed her quiet stare at him. He then took a deep breath in surrender. He shied away from her eyes, and when he looked back into them, it was with a smile. "You're so beautiful in this dress . I feel so proud being with you, I mean being seen with you." She smiled back, tight lipped. "Tell me what it's been like with that brother of yours. I'm sure he got mad when he saw the clothes?"

"No, he's not seen them yet. I hid them. Besides, he's been very busy of late."

"Doing what?" he asked, but when she replied with only an empty stare, he let it to go. "That has only been my fear anyway. I don't want him going ferocious on you," he added with great concern, but Kachi broke into a simple smile.

"I told you never to worry about that. Miide has never harmed me, and he will never do it," she confided, and Mike was almost beginning to get jealous.

"Very well then, what have you taken?" He rubbed his hands together and licked his lips.

"Nothing, just this." She nodded to the drink in front of her.

"What do you mean? Were you not attended to?" Mike frowned and started looking around for Austin.

"No no, Mike, it was me, really, it was me. I couldn't take anything when I didn't see you, and he really persuaded me, really."

"He did?"

"Yes."

"Then let's order now." She made a face and looked at her wristwatch. "No, you can't go now. We have to eat." He waved the waiter.

"Mike, please," she pleaded. On second thought, he gave in, and they rose, leaving. She caught some people staring at Mike. Just then a voice spoke up from a close table.

"Excuse me, gentleman." Mike stopped and gave him audience. "A Moses, I presume?"

"Of course, the third. Do I know you, sir?"

The old man smiled and chuckled. "Like father, like son." He stretched his hand to Mike for a brief handshake. "S. G. Lukman, Chairman, Kachet Merchant Bank. I was in Harvard with your dad. He was a great man, and even though I could not make it to the burial, I registered my condolences at your office in LA. Please accept my belated condolences."

"Oh, thank you. That is okay now. It's been a while, and I will like to keep it in the past. I really appreciate your gesture, sir, thank you very much." He shook him a second time and moved on.

"I will pay you a visit at your Lagos office very soon. I presume that is where you are now," the man inquired.

"Most definitely, sir," he assured him with a back glance, as they exited the door, and Kachi asked, "Who is he?"

"You heard him. I don't know any better than you do. But he's wrong anyway. A lot of people believe I am more like my granddad, and I know so."

"What was your granddad like?" Kachi asked him.

"Soft yet as strong hearted as steel," he said, and Kachi spied at his eyes, as she had come to always do anytime he spoke of his lineage. He supported her as she climbed into the jeep that had the door held by Pius.

"And see the way you addressed him, like he's your age."

"My lady"—Mike looked into her eyes like a child—"in his world, my world, age doesn't matter. What matters is what he just did, getting to meet his kind in wealth and power." She let her eyes linger in his gaze till he looked away.

"Tell me about this Japanese visitor of yours."

"Don't mind them. They are just a bunch of old boring fellas. All they know and think about is making more money, when they can't even finish spending what they already have. They want me to make some contributions, charity and investment, that's all."

"Is it their president that sent them?"

"Yes."

"To you."

"Something like that." He smiled and looked away.

As they drove into the street, Kachi looked into Mike's eyes again, and he looked a little lost as to what she was trying to say, then it clicked.

"Oh, Pius, it's okay here. Stop the car," he ordered.

"Okay, sir," Pius murmured from the front. Mike got down, went over to Kachi's side, and opened the door for her.

"Is twelve o'clock okay tomorrow?" he asked her, and looking into his eyes, she let a moment pass before she nodded slowly. She waved to him with her right hand, but Mike held her left hand and squeezed it slightly, reluctantly releasing it as she walked away. He lingered for a while looking at her, then he got into his car and left.

"Where have you been?" Miide demanded as Kachi entered the room.

"I went out," she answered and went to where the hangers were to rearrange the clothes, not knowing exactly what she wanted to do.

"Of course, I didn't meet you at home. Where have you been?"

"I went looking for a job," she said, not looking back to avoid his eyes.

"That is a lie, and I've been watching you of recent. I know you've been seeing that guy I saw you with that day, and I told you I don't want to see you with him anymore. I am repeating myself now, forget about him!" he warned seriously and lay on the bed. Seeing that his anger had subsided, Kachi quickly started removing her new dress before he noticed it. Just then Miide noticed and wanted to start saying something about it, but he remained mute as he noticed something else he had always seen but never noticed. Kachi unzipped her dress from behind and exposed her back. The dress dropped from her shoulder down to her knees. She stepped out of it. She now stood in her pink panties and bra alone as she folded the dress. Miide's stares grew more intense. He had bought her this pink underwear himself. Kachi bent over to hide the dress in the bag, with her back still turned toward Miide, and he swallowed gently as she straightened up and slowly removed her bra. He quickly looked away and looked back again as she put on another dress. She came and got on her side of the bed.

"I'm sorry," she said as she lay still on the bed. Miide lay on his side, facing the other way.

"It's okay," he replied and wondered. He had always thought of her as his little sister, looked at her nakedness unnoticeably, and seen little until today. *What then has happened?* he thought. The little girl was no more.

Usman sat on the edge of the bed, with his back against the wall at an angle of the room, and Miide was by his side so they could hear each other's murmuring. Their eyes were on Charles and Koja who were playing cards on the other side of the room, recounting their ordeals from days gone by, Charles doing most of the talking as Koja listened to what life was like in the United States. Their voices were audible enough for both Usman and Miide to hear, especially Miide who, as he discussed with Usman, was thinking about the three men he was about to bring into what he thought would be his fold. He had been studying the three of them and knew he would have no problem with Charles, Ben was halfway done, but he could not but be concerned over what Koja's reaction will be after the address he was about to make. Ben walked in with two plates of food in his hands.

"Charles, help me with the rest of the plates from the kitchen," he announced, putting the two plates down, and deliberately made one closer to Usman to avoid having to serve Miide directly. He sat down separately and was watching the two parties as he waited for Charles to go inside the kitchen. But Charles was so engrossed in the card game he was playing and the chat. He rose again and went to the kitchen himself to bring in two other plates of food. He gave one to Koja and retained the other one.

"Charles, your food is in the kitchen. I believe when it is yours and yours alone, you will go and pick it." Then Ben looked Miide's way. "That will be yours." He nodded to one of the plates he brought earlier. Ben rose again, opened the cover of a bucket of water at the corner of the room, took the bowl by it, and fetched some water into it; he left it at the center of the room.

"You can all rinse your hands there," Ben said. He settled down and started eating his own food: hot water–soaked cassava grains, eba, vegetable soup, a lot of good meat, and fish. It was a delicacy prescribed and paid for by Miide. Usman also drew his plate closer, stretched his hand into the water bowl, and washed. He started eating. Miide's stare never left the card players.

"I'll advise you guys to eat now because we have some discussions afterwards." He sounded serious, and almost immediately, Koja dumped the cards and proceeded to his food, and Charles went for his.

"That is what I have been coping with since he got here," Ben said, looking at Miide. "He's as lazy and indolent. Imagine, how many times have I told him since I got in here to go help me with the rest of the plates from the kitchen? Mscheeewww," he hissed, and all went quiet as Charles brought his food and joined them. Miide watched as they ate like he was paid to do it.

"Won't you eat?" asked Ben who only got a slight nod from Miide.

It was Usman who finished first. He rinsed his hands, wiped his mouth with his hands, and pushed his empty plate away. The rest, as they finished, rinsed their hands as well; and Ben picked up the plates, leaving Charles alone who was yet to finish.

When they were all through, they sat, their backs against the wall. Charles picked up the cards again to face Koja, but Miide objected, "Charles, this is not the time for that. We want to talk." Charles obliged. "Firstly," Miide started, "Koja, you will not report at the police station anymore. That will be all for the case, and since they don't know anything about you and your whereabout, that does it. It's not safe, forget it. Now, gentlemen"—he gently pushed his plate of food to the side and stretched his legs, acrossing them—"your stories being what they are, are pathetic enough only for the bearers. You—" He pointed to them, his fingers slowly moving from one face to another, excluding Usman who was just listening, being on Miide's side already, and letting him take charge, delivering their intentions. "Ben, nobody gives a damn how long you've been without a job since graduation. Charles, nobody cares how you lost your family and got deported leaving everything you've worked for, for eight years behind. And, Koja, I hope by now you know nobody cares how long you spent in jail for confessing. What I am saying is nobody cares if you live or die. It all depends on you.

"You have eaten good food now. It was my deliberate intention for us not to eat out so that you may have the feel of luxury at home, and it has served its purpose. It didn't come cheap. It came through the way of the gun." He produced a gun from under his shirt and put it in the center of the room. Ben cringed, Koja almost flinched, while Charles showed a little surprise, opening his mouth slightly, and immediately regained his composure with a smile. Usman looked quickly into Miide's eyes, apparently not expecting him to be so outright; he looked at the gun and then at the men before them for their reactions. "There can be only two sides," Miide continued, "the rich and the poor. On one side is life, on the other is no life. Unfortunately, you happen to fall on the latter side." He paused and let it sink before he continued. "Fortunately again, there is a way out, the only way, the hard way. Listen, those who make it in life do things differently, for to get noticed, a lot must be done strangely. This is what I do, and I lay before you all an automatic invitation to each of you, which I undoubtedly believe you will honor, unless otherwise your souls repel this kind of delicacy." He gently drew his plate of food back to his feet and picked up the gun. He rose and returned it to his waist. Usman rose to join him.

"Lastly," Miide said, "nobody sees your future like you do, and if to you it is so dim, how dark then is it to the world?" He headed for the door followed by Usman. He stopped at the door again, looked back, and pointed to the plate of food. "Eat that. You might not be eating another one for a long time," he said and left. A few minutes after Miide and Usman had left, Ben picked the plate of food and started eating it, Charles was still smiling to himself, and Koja remained sober.

Going on the road, Usman asked Miide, "Do you think they will consent?"

"When you control a man's thinking," Miide answered, "you don't have to worry about his actions."

"Okay, now I have the addresses of the other factories . . .," Usman spoke on.

Lowborn men are but a breath, the highborn are but a lie; if weighed on a balance, they are nothing; together they are only a breath.

Do not trust in extortion or take pride in stolen goods; though your riches increase, do not set your heart on them.

—Psalm 62:9 and 10 (NIV)

Quotes:

Page 93: "Never give up on a dream just because it will take time to accomplish; the time will pass—anyway."—Earl Nightingale

Page 159: "When you control a man's thinking, you don't have to worry about his actions."—Carter Woodson

CPSIA information can be obtained
at www.ICGtesting.com
Printed in the USA
LVHW090506130619
621093LV00001B/20/P

9 781514 493694